DISMANTLED
APONLEA

THE KELLY JOHNSON TRILOGY
BOOK ONE

Raeven Brown
&
Maria Mckessey

Edited by: Kevin Anderson & Associates
Photo by: Kati Rosado Photography
Book Cover Model: Amayrani Suarez
Published by CProductions

Thank you Karen
for not letting this dream die.

PROLOGUE

Destiny's whistle can often be misconstrued for the wind. Identifying one's calling as an adolescent is rare but not beyond reach. It is almost always missed, but once and again there will be exceptions. The idea of two exceptions living next door to each other is inconceivable, but these are the stories to tell.

Aponlea is a land, a myth, a nation held on to by the oral tradition of its remaining descendants. Your invitation into such traditions is an honor only recently allowed. Nondescendants were once not to know these sacred customs. Now, you're welcome to read on. May it be that you are as a result inspired by a greater path, as you see these exceptions were. This is the beginning of Aponlea's culmination.

The Spark

"You won't understand because your life is perfect. You live in a bubble. You're separated from reality. You're fragile, you're naïve. You're stupid."

"Is that why you do this? Because you think I've got it easy?"

"Name one thing, Kelly. Tell me why I'm wrong. You have the ideal American family. White picket-fence, big house, family outings and trips, bright colors, sunshine, and rainbows — it's disgusting."

"Give me a break, Dane. You're a Morris. Perfection is in your blood. Who are you to tell me . . ."

"Shows just how much you know about my family. Absolutely nothing. You have no idea. It's hidden for a reason. We all don't get to have happy beginnings or endings. Trade a day with me, princess. You'd see then. And you wouldn't last."

"Just because things appear to be good for me now doesn't mean it will always be that way . . ."

"Yes, yes it does! It's their job to make sure of that."

"Whose job?"

Kelly pretended — like the countless times in the past — that Dane's words had only bounced off of her. She would keep staring through his bottomless dark eyes until she could burn a hole through them. She'd show Dane a face as hard as stone if it was the last thing she'd do. Because who cares that he'd just humiliated her in front of a bunch of students in the middle of the hallway. Who cares that all her things were scattered across the floor. Kelly would never show Dane what he did to her inside. He would *never* see that.

Chapter One

Kelly Johnson could have been a living house ornament for the Johnson home, a human decoration perched on a balcony, the silhouette of her petite body outlined by the moonlight. Every night, she appeared still and immovable, staring dreamily into the distance, always in the direction of Morris Manor. Like a loyal companion, it was as if she were waiting patiently, faithfully, for someone.

Not a day went by without a night out here. There was rarely a weather condition that kept her from her balcony. Today it was no exception, though the air was dry and nippy. It was nothing a heavy blanket couldn't fix.

She closed her eyes, breathed in frost, and continued to stare out at what she could make of the Morris estate. Their property was just so large. They were neighbors, and their yards were separated by a tall stonewall; yet it was like a different world over there. Their property was basically a compound. The Morris's had an indoor pool and a maids house. Kelly was certain there was more beyond the wall that she couldn't see. There was something eerily beautiful about the Morris residence.

The Johnson house, her house, had a different air to it. It had character; it looked lived in. A scenery of Victorian architecture enduring years and years of wear from a large and busy family. It was bright and inviting, with a yellow front door that her father often touched up with new paint because of the scuffmarks and scratches caused by heavy traffic.

There were balconies, like the one she had, and tall windows that absorbed every bit of sunlight. The lawn was well kept and the yard was fenced in, but it was far from perfect.

The Morris's house was more like a mansion, a palace compared to all the other homes in the neighborhood. The yard lights along the stone wall minimally illuminated the mysterious structure, evoking a story that the day kept hidden.

Kelly heard a rare sports car speeding up from the entrance of the neighborhood, and Kelly's whole body reacted. When it finally came in sight, it was driving up the extensive driveway of the Morris property. It stopped along the path and Kelly waited. This was another reason she would stand out on her balcony at night.

Moore got out of the car, shutting the door behind him and standing briefly to take a whiff of the air. Kelly's eyes were glued on him and she cracked a smile. One day she would see the inside of that palace. One day she would talk to this prince.

Kelly deemed him too old for her, though he was only three years her senior. His hair looked as if he just ran his hand through it to keep it back and out of his face, though part of it had fallen back down. She waited for his dark eyes to meet hers, as they often did. He would look up to her balcony briefly. It felt like an eternity each time, like he was searching her soul. Her desire was met as he stood outside his car and looked up in her direction. He never smiled or waved, but she was sure he was looking right at her. She wondered if he thought she was childish to just stare at him, but she couldn't help it. Something about the way he looked at her; the intensity of his eyes when they made eye contact. And then it would end as he made his way up the rest of the driveway and through the front doors that Kelly was unable to see with the columns and trees in the way.

A gust of wind broke her out of her infatuation and brought with it an uneasy feeling in her stomach.

A memory played vividly behind her eyes as she remembered the last time she'd confronted Dane before he disappeared.

He'd gotten really sick and had been bedridden for weeks. Part of her was curious to visit him, but the other part hated herself for actually feeling concern for him. She had every reason to hate him, after all. It seemed his sole purpose in life was to verbally tear her down with every chance he got. She wasn't his only target, but she was his main one. There was a whole list of students he tormented, not only through his violence, but through his words. He was disturbingly manipulative, and he exposed a person's deepest insecurities.

She hadn't been able to shake their last exchange; it had been weighing heavy on her mind since then.

Her world had been shaken. There was something behind what she grew up knowing, and she didn't know how to get to the bottom of it, except through the person who had been silenced by illness. She hated the idea that her whole understanding of life could crumble at any moment, that she had been believing in some sort of false reality all her life, that there was something more that had been kept from her with purpose. What purpose?

"What're you doing out here? Seeing if you'll turn into an icicle?" A smile rose on Kelly's face as her brother's voice rang from the entrance of the balcony.

"It is pretty cold," Kelly responded, still facing its ledge. She wanted to continue to be in her thoughts but she knew she wouldn't find any answers solely on her thinking. Her eldest brother always relieved her when she was troubled.

"I need to talk to you, Kelly," Joey came up to her side. "Just in a warmer and more reasonable setting."

"Okay, okay," she said, mustering up genuine excitement. She knew it would flow naturally from the presence of her favorite sibling, but she was still transitioning from what she'd previously been thinking about. The two headed into her bedroom, closing

8

the cold out.

Joey came politely into her room, smiling warmly. Kelly sat on her bed and watched as he paced her floor.

He had a sheet of paper clenched tight in his hand that he shoved deep into the back of his jeans as he approached Kelly.

"So what brings you here?" she asked in a light voice, her face literally brightening in the presence of her eldest brother. Joey chuckled to himself, sitting in Kelly's blue dish chair. Kelly hopped over her bed so that she could sit across from him.

Joey clapped his large hands together, rubbed them. Just watching the way Joey acted most times, even the simplest of actions, would make Kelly instantly forget what had been biting at her. Joey always succeeded in entertaining her, even when he wasn't trying to. Joey's dark brown eyes sparkled before he opened his mouth and Kelly knew she was in for one of his rants.

"Kelly, I have been dying to talk to you all day. Of course I had to wait patiently while you were at school, tortured at best by dictator after dictator teaching one thought as law. The law that their education is the fundamental source of human existence as we know it" — he pointed at Kelly's nose — "But don't be brainwashed by their theories. Look at me, I went through it all before you and I'm no better off than the person who never attended a day of school and sits on the side of the road or the couch in the basement of his parents' house waiting for fortune to find him and give him what he believes he deserves." Joey loved to show he had wisdom, even at twenty-one. And Kelly would listen, even at times like this when he veered off subject.

"And that's a boost to the top with money flowing like honey for him to spend on his selfish existence, buying product after product to feed the empty void in his heart. But what he doesn't realize is that fortune won't even begin to look at him, and so he'll die on that couch or that street the same way I will, without the success promised by this so-called education." It seemed he hadn't even come up for air, yet he hadn't taken in a breath after he'd said all of that. Kelly didn't know how he did it, but no matter; it made her laugh every time. She knew this wasn't what he'd come to tell her, but eventually he would get to it. She got comfortable atop her bed, crossing her arms and smirking smugly.

"Um, Joey, you own a flourishing pizzeria, so I would say there is a difference between you and that uneducated guy," she commented. Joey looked up thoughtfully, conjuring a quick response.

"Right, but I have rich parents; that's the difference, not the education." Joey thought he'd stumped her, gotten her to take in what he said and accept it, but Kelly still had a smirk plastered on her beautiful young face.

"So, what you're telling me is that I should drop out and just let Dad buy me my own business?"

"Not at all. Stay in school, it's good for you," Joey said quickly, regretting what he'd just planted in his fifteen-year-old sister's mind. Pursing his lips, he tapped his long fingers on his lap and closed his eyes for a brief moment. "I don't know how I got to that. I was trying to say that first I had to wait for you to get out of school and second, I had to wait until I got home from work — I think I forgot to put out the new schedule . . . hmm . . . I could . . ."

"Joey! What is it that you've been waiting to tell me?" Kelly blurted, making Joey jump a little in her disc chair. She wondered why he was drifting off subject so much more than normal. She could see it in his eyes, even through Joey's thick bubbly nature, that he was a little nervous about bringing about what he wanted to say. Kelly's eyes grew softer, allowing Joey to know he had her full attention at a serious level. Joey exhaled lightly and gave in.

"Two words, my sister — well, technically one — or would it be two . . . or is it four if translated?" Joey was fumbling for words, making Kelly roll her eyes.

"Joey, please spit it out already. You're killin' me here!"

"Right," Joey began, biting his lip at first, then looking up at Kelly with knowing eyes. "It has everything to do with some joining of family seals."

Kelly's eyes widened, pupils shrinking. She wasn't prepared for this: was she excited or deflated, heartbroken or joyful? She didn't have a sure answer yet, but she knew one thing for sure. She was stunned. With her eyes flicking here and there as she stared at her fidgeting hands, she knew she had to act quick before Joey started to feel regretful. Playing excited would have to do for now. "You're going to marry Melanie!" she gasped gleefully, meeting Joey's eyes and hoping he couldn't see through the real but uncertain feelings churning inside her. Thankfully, Joey hadn't noticed anything. His eyes glittered as he scooted closer to Kelly, at the edge of his seat.

"Yes," he breathed. "I'm telling Mom and Dad this weekend. I don't know when the joining of the seals will be, but—how do you really feel about all this, Kelly? I don't want to go on with it if . . ."

"No, Joey, you know it isn't about me." Kelly interrupted. She smiled warmly at her brother. "I'm happy for you. I love Melanie. I just hope her parents approve of this." Joey nodded, looking away thoughtfully.

"I'm almost certain they will. A, because it's me." Yet again, he hadn't failed in making Kelly smile. "B, because being a descendant of John is one of the most coolest things ever, and C, because Mom is a descendant of Jacob, and if there's one thing Mom ever taught us it's that there is absolutely nothing a Jacobs likes more than a Jacobs. I'm telling you, Kelly, it's a win-win. Melanie is going to be my wife, and I . . ."

"You're not marrying her just because she's a Jacobs, are you? You know, to take Mom's attention off your lack of a college education? Because that . . ."

"Of course not," Joey made an exaggerated appalled face. "That's why I started dating her," he smiled. "But then I fell in love with her," he expressed sincerely.

"Aw," Kelly said, without the same sincerity. At least she had tried to sound enthusiastic for him. Her act wasn't working, so she got back to business. "Where are you taking our parents for the approval lunch?" Kelly asked.

"I don't know. I kind of need your help on that one. Right now I was thinking — Gilby's, maybe?" His answer was slow, and Kelly's involuntary interrupting thoughts had to wait.

"You're joking, right?"

Joey cringed sheepishly. "Not the best place, huh?"

"We practically live there... and it's more of a teen hangout," Kelly said, thinking. "It should be at a fancier place, with reservations and such, not a pizza parlor that you own," She shook her head slowly, scoffing. Joey laughed, tossed a stray pillow at her.

"Okay, okay, hmm, what was my plan B again? Right, I didn't have one," He bit his lip and scratched the back of his neck. "Maybe I really should have gone to college."

"Oh, Joey, don't be like that. . ."

"It's alright, Kelly, I wasn't being serious. Anyway, I only suggested Gilby's because it's one of my few achievements our parents are proud of." Kelly couldn't help but snicker at what he'd said.

"They'd be even more proud if they knew their eldest son had exceptional taste in choosing a restaurant for the big day." She squealed for effect, but didn't find any enthusiasm in doing so. It still made Joey smile.

"Yeah, but that's why I need your help, because I don't have exceptional taste in choosing a restaurant."

Kelly smiled, placing her hands on Joey's shoulders, patting them. "Don't worry, Joey, I got this. Hmm, how about the Lily House?"

"That's perfect, Kelly! That's why you're my go-to gal!" He pulled her into a bear hug and squeezed her tight. He let go of her only to sit back in her disc chair and rubbed his slightly stubbly chin. "Now, how to invite them —" he trailed off in a low voice, eyes steering toward Kelly. Kelly rolled her eyes incredulously.

"Ugh, Joey, really? They're our parents; just invite them, no biggie. I'd worry about the joining of the seals."

Joey turned grim.

Kelly pursed her full lips. "You should be worried about Melanie's parents handing over the seal without her consent. That's a big deal."

Joey stared off into the distance. "There's no turning back after that. She'll either be thrilled to commit to spending the rest of her life with me or be contentious with me, stuck 'till death do us part.'"

"Joey!" Kelly breathed, appalled at how he was looking at things. She knew this process was proper, and it didn't exactly seem fair on the female's part, but the man himself would have taken a lot of meditation and time to make such a decision as the joining of the seals. It wasn't anything to joke around with. "Everyone knows Melanie is madly in love with you. You guys have been together for years. It's about time you two got married," she told him softly. Joey half-smiled, chuckling at his nervousness.

"Yeah, you're right."

"And her parents will have no problem handing her over to you, Joey. What more can a woman ask for than a man like you?"

"Thanks, Kelly. I feel slightly better about all this." Kelly smiled at her brother's kind words.

"I'm glad. But you know her better than I do. Does she seem like she'd be waiting for a proposal from you?"

"That's a hard question. Well, for me, it is. I thought all of the girls I dated were madly in love with me," Joey responded with a smirk on his face. Now it was Kelly's turn to throw a pillow at him.

"Oh, I forgot how much you loved yourself," she said, smirking. Joey shrugged.

After some light laughter, Joey's eyes widened, like he had an idea.

"Kelly, can you do me a huge favor?" Kelly nodded and Joey went on. "Can you get together with Melanie sometime before this Saturday's lunch? That way I could find out some of her feelings, you know?"

Kelly nodded again, staring past him. He was really anxious about all of this. And Kelly knew she had to support him. She really liked Melanie, but she wasn't mentally prepared to have her take Joey away from her. Joey was her best friend; whatever would she do when he moved out to begin his own life as a newlywed man? None of her other siblings shared the same bond she and Joey had. She had to stop herself quickly; a web of problems was spinning itself together in her head, all at the wrong time. And Joey noticed this time. He nodded his head closer to her face, eyes questioning.

"Is something wrong with that? I mean, I could probably get Jessica to do it, but she kind of has a tendency to get too involved with things," Joey said quickly, hoping to take the pressure off of Kelly.

"Oh no, it's not that," Kelly began, turning to climb off of her bed. She fumbled for something to say, to cover up what she was thinking. She looked down at her thumbs. "I just haven't really had talks with her about those kinds of things. It's always been small talk with me and her."

Joey's sigh was strained and he ran a hand through his short brown hair. After a minute of silence, Joey stood up and walked over to Kelly. "Maybe this could be a great opportunity to get to know her more, on a deeper level. This would really help me, Kelly. I don't want to make this a mistake for her." Kelly blinked, nodded, then looked at her brother and gave him a tiny smile. Joey kissed the top of her head. "I love you so much, Kelly. You know that, right?"

"Of course I do, Joey, how could I not?" Her voice wavered a bit and she hoped Joey hadn't caught it. She wanted to cry, which startled her a bit because

14

she wasn't completely sure why. Yes, she had mixed emotions, but she was normally strong. It usually took a lot to make her cry.

Joey took this as his time to leave. He started to the door, stopped once he was halfway out, and took a whiff of the air. "Mmm, mom's making spaghetti."

"Joey," Kelly called before he was down the hall. He peeked back inside her room. "Thank you for trusting me. You know, for coming to me for help." Joey flashed a wide smile.

"Why wouldn't I come to you, Kel? You're my best friend." He jogged off downstairs without waiting for her reaction. He was so used to trusting in Kelly that he thought nothing of it.

Kelly's eyes began to water. She gently wiped them away before any tears could trickle down her cheeks. She readied herself to go downstairs for dinner.

Chapter Two

Kelly was in the dining room helping her older sister Jessica set the table while their mother put the finishing touches on dinner. In the living room, her father was reading a book to Lisa, who was sitting on his lap, leaning sleepily on his chest as she listened to his low voice. Mike and Jason were off in Mike's room. Mike was probably giving Jason another lecture on life and how important the decisions we make are. Jason was probably inwardly rolling his eyes and regretting asking him a simple question. Zach was sitting on the giant sofa in the living room, reading some scientific book or something like that. Kelly found those sort of things boring. She hated science, but Zach ate it up. He was constantly taking things apart and improving them. He was known as the family's go-to person when it came to fixing things.

Kelly placed the last glass on the table, staring absently at it while thinking. She bit her lip when an image of Joey and Melanie popped up in her head. Her heart sank and she swallowed the growing lump in her throat. She couldn't wait until dinner was over so she could lie in bed and just pick up where she left off in her head.

Jessica poked her side, causing Kelly to jump. She eyed her sister warily, as if Kelly looked suspicious of something. "Kelly, go call everyone to the table. I'm gonna help Mom serve dinner," she said, already back in the kitchen.

"Oh, okay," Kelly replied, slowly heading into the living room. Through the craziness of the household, her dad and Lisa looked easiest to deal with first. She placed a hand on her father's shoulder. He paused from his reading to look up at Kelly. "Mom says dinner's ready."

Mr. Johnson nodded, closing the book. "Alright, Lisa, let's go eat," he said, stretching his arms once he was sitting up. Lisa was fast asleep, drooping to the side. Kelly giggled, taking Lisa in her arms and patting her back to get her up. Mr. Johnson stood. "I'm that boring, huh?" he said to Lisa, poking her nose. Lisa just rubbed her eyes and hid her face in Kelly's shirt. Kelly put Lisa down.

"Time to eat, Lisa. Mommy wants you at the table now," Kelly said. Lisa didn't respond, but did what she was told, walking clumsily to the dining room with her father.

"Mike, Jason, dinner's ready, come out to the table!" Mr. Johnson called from the dining room. Kelly decided her deed was done and made sure the table was set and ready before standing behind her seat. In a matter of seconds, Mike and Jason were at the table, and Jessica had come in with the large salad bowl, placing it at its center. When Mrs. Johnson came to the table with a two large serving platters of spaghetti, Zach, the youngest son, was the only one not present in the spacious dining room. Jason noted his impatience, bouncing at the tips of his feet.

"Zach, put your book down already. It's time to eat!" Jason finally demanded.

"Jason, you could have said that more politely," Mrs. Johnson corrected, disappearing back into the kitchen briefly to retrieve two baskets of bread sticks she had baked. "Zach, honey!" she called as she set the basket next to the salad and spaghetti. Zach came in soon after without a reply. He stood behind his chair, tugging at the long sleeves of his shirt. Everyone picked up their plates and lifted them.

They recited a prayer in the Aponlean language, the language of their ancient ancestors, then sat down. Most of the Johnson kids had no idea what the words

17

they were chanting meant, but it was a tradition that had been passed down for centuries. It meant "we lift this food in thanks." They would say it every night before sitting at the table and eating. They also had an assigned seat at the long cherry-wood dining table. Mr. Johnson sat at the head; Mrs. Johnson sat to his right; Mike, the second-oldest son, sat to the left of Mr. Johnson; Jessica beside Mike and Zach beside her; on other side of the table, Lisa, the youngest, sat beside her mom; Kelly sat beside Lisa, and Jason sat next to her. Joey sat across from his father, at the other end of the table. He was the oldest son, and such was the tradition.

Though Kelly had never questioned the traditions, as they were the reality she grew up with, she had a strong feeling toward them. All of her friends were descendants also, a fact she never questioned. She wasn't allowed to discuss Aponlea with those who didn't share the ancestral patriarchs of the dead civilization.

"Remember," Mr. Johnson began his traditional reminder to his children. This one was started by Mr. Johnson's mother, and he continued it with his family as he felt it was important for his children to accept. "May we be like John and Peter and rise to the occasion, stand for good while others fall for darkness around us, and remain untouched by the greed of this world."

Kelly found herself mouthing the words as he said them. They might as well get a plaque saying it. "If we teach you anything in life, it's that." Most nights Kelly found those words a meaningless chant, since she had heard them so often, but tonight was different. She actually listened to the words and meditated on them. John and Peter, two of the twenty men whose lineage made up the descendants, were held in the highest regard. She had been told why before but had forgotten what made them so important that they would be singled out. She herself descended from John on her dad's side, and that gave her a stronger sense of connection this night.

She liked the idea of having a name that stood out from the others. She wanted to do something important enough to change the course of the future and be passed down from generation to generation. She felt with her dad saying those words that he wanted each of his children to make an impact on the world.

When Mr. Johnson had finished speaking, the dinner table harmonized with voices. It was an everyday occurrence; three or four different conversations were usually held over the long table. Tonight, on Mr. Johnson's side of the table, he and Mike were talking about business. Kelly ate in silence as her mind started on the meditation of his words and then switched to problematic thoughts revolving around Joey and what she would say to Melanie without giving anything away.

A new question plagued Kelly's mind; she had to get it out to her dad. Asking would be scratching the surface of what had been plaguing her for weeks now. Kelly looked over at Mike and her father, who were talking business. She had to find a break in their conversation.

"Mike, did you sign those papers last weekend?" Mike looked up from his food, alarmed.

"You mean from the February Project? They were on my desk, right?"

"No, I left them with Janice. She was supposed to give them to you."

"I had a major school project to finish. I haven't been in the office all day today, so it might be on my desk." Mike took on a lot of responsibility. He somehow managed to get his associate's degree while completing high school and working with his dad. Kelly didn't know how he did it or why. She wished he would relax more sometimes. At least he was finished with high school, but the demands of getting his bachelor's as well as taking an important position in the family business was a lot in itself. He tried too hard to make their father proud, even though he didn't need to. Even Kelly knew their dad was proud of all the children. He made that clear as often as he could.

Mr. Johnson raised an eyebrow, twirled his fork into a bundle of spaghetti. "I was going to let you supervise the project, but if you think it'll interfere with your studies, I don't want it to be a burden to you."

"Dad, since when have any of these things been burdensome to me? I can handle it," Mike responded eagerly. Mrs. Johnson cleared her throat softly.

"Mike, sweetie, your father has plenty other associates who could be of service to him — right, honey?" Mr. Johnson nodded, looking at Mike with sincerity. Kelly saw the concern in her mother's eyes. Mike was such a workaholic; he was adamant that he could handle it, even with his complexion showing he was still getting over the bug he had.

"That's right, son. I can always hand this over to Erik. It'll be no problem."

"Dad, it's alright, I can . . ."

"Mike, why don't you take a few days off of work?" Mrs. Johnson suggested, her crystalline blue eyes worried and glistening through the warm light of the hanging lamps in the dining room. Mike shook his head and opened his mouth to protest, but Mr. Johnson spoke up before he could utter a sound.

"Son, I think your mother's right," he announced firmly, giving Mike a look that stopped him from interrupting. "I don't want you to overwork yourself, especially since you've been sick the past week. Take time to focus more on your studies. And just rest. You know a position's always open for you."

Mike nodded slowly, sulking as he looked down at his plate. He began picking at his salad, "Yes, sir." This satisfied their father to an extent and he reached his hand out to ruffle Mike's soft, wavy brown hair. He had a habit of doing it. It was one of his quirky ways of showing affection, and Mike was known to be the one who frantically tried to restore his hair to appear more presentable. But he just left it after Mr. Johnson lifted his hand away from his head.

"Chin up, young hermano," Joey chimed from across the table. "You have plenty of time to conquer the world." Joey seemed to have been listening in on the conversation too, letting his ears tune in to whatever he found interesting. Kelly held back a snicker; Mike was so stubborn. But she was oblivious to her own stubbornness at times. It must have been hereditary.

Kelly couldn't get her question out yet, she didn't know quite how to word it. Her eyes drifted as she searched for the perfect phrasing. Her eyes caught whim of Jason in the process.

Jason stabbed a homemade meatball with his fork, holding it up to his eyes, observing. "What are the chances of me being able to fling this meatball so that it lands right in Jessica's hair?" he murmured, almost talking to himself but half-expecting someone to reply. At some point, he eyed Zach for an answer, hesitating when his younger brother looked him up and down and then returned quietly to his meal. Jason thought better of it, not wanting a detailed response to his question. Joey leaned over his shoulder.

"Without having mom's bomb go off? None," he whispered before he returned to dressing his salad. Jason glanced at his mother, then at the meatball before him.

"Be alert, Jess. Jason's planning something," Kelly warned with a blank expression. Jessica looked around her seat, under the table, around the room, anywhere her mischievous brother could possibly have detonated or set fire to, rigged or reprogrammed, super glued or whoopee-cushioned — the list went on. She glared at her younger brother. Mrs. Johnson stopped helping Lisa with her spaghetti to look up at Jason.

"Jason," was all she had to say. Her voice wasn't loud, nor did it echo, but it was authoritative. And it was enough to make Jason drop his fork and act obedient again, for the rest of the meal at least. Jessica gave Kelly a grateful smile.

"No prob, sis," Kelly said aloud, only to irritate Jason. A smug smile tugged at her lips as she began to fork another mouthful of spaghetti into her mouth.

"Don't think I won't get you back for that," Jason hissed at her under his breath. Kelly blinked, as if unfazed.

"Jessica and I made a pact after you pinned your prank on me at last summer's camping trip." Kelly whispered back, her eyes not leaving her plate. Jason scoffed.

"Good luck with that. You know Jessica is Mom's angel; she'll snitch on you one of these days." Kelly shot him a disgusted look. She hated his immaturity.

"Jason, she doesn't do that anymore. She hasn't been that way since she was twelve, and you know that."

"Has she changed much in five years?" He whirled his head toward Joey sharply. Joey sat up in his seat, wiping his mouth with the deep-red napkin on his lap.

"Of course she has. Jessica's perfect," he answered, amused. Jessica let out an exasperated sigh, delicate fingers pressing the bridge of her nose.

"Mom." She'd had enough of the negative attention on her. Mrs. Johnson noted her distress and gave Joey a knowing eye.

"Joey."

"It was a compliment," Joey retorted. Then he smirked. "I love Jessica. I'm lucky to have such a beautiful sister." Mrs. Johnson sighed, exchanging looks with her husband, getting a tired expression from him. An apologetic look from Joey sent her attention back to getting Lisa to finish what was left on her plate. Kelly knew Jessica hadn't taken Joey seriously to begin with, so she simply stuck her tongue at him halfheartedly and moved on.

Jason snickered to himself. "I guess that means I have a pact with Joey now." Kelly rolled her eyes.

"Uh, no, you don't, man. I'm sorry but, compared to the girls, we don't stand a chance," he stated, leaning back in his chair. Jason was surprised, even slightly heartbroken. Jessica giggled.

"Aw come on, Joey, you're gonna leave me hanging?" Jason whined, making his eyes big, creasing his eyebrows. He looked like a puppy, pulling off what only he and Kelly could do successfully. Physically, Jason was a male version of Kelly. They were twins, after all. Unfortunately for Jason, it didn't have the same effect on Joey as did Kelly's expression.

"Yep," Joey said, stretching his arms until he yawned.

"Joey's right, Jason," Zach stated. His voice always seemed to blend with the low hum of appliances throughout the house, but it was loud enough to make everyone but the parents — who were indulging in their own deep conversation — to turn their attention to their ten-year-old brother. He only spoke occasionally, and it was the first he'd said all through dinner that night. "You wouldn't even stand a chance against Lisa." Kelly and Jessica burst out laughing, almost in unison. Even Mike joined in the laughter; Lisa laughed because everyone else was laughing; Joey joined in and Zach remained silent. Kelly watched as Jason glared at him. He was the one most picked on these days, but he brought it upon himself. He had been quite bothersome these days. His jokes were often seen as mean and his tricks as annoying.

Perhaps her question wasn't right for tonight. The mood of the table didn't make Kelly feel comfortable asking it, nor did her stomach. She could feel a strange nervousness seize her otherwise determined self. She would get the opportunity, but now she wanted to enjoy her family. She felt a change coming, with Joey's news and an intuition she had brewing. Dane's words had to have been the beginning of the rattle that would wind up shaking her whole world.

◆━━━◆━━━◆

Vivian Morris's jeweled heels echoed through the stone corridors of the Morris home as she made her way to the main dining room. The train of the long black dress she decided to wear for the evening billowed behind her. Her rich, long, curly black hair was pulled back into a loose bun, held together only by an emerald-encrusted hairpin. She turned a corner, entering the dining room where a gourmet dinner decorated the bare black marble table. Her husband, Xavier Morris, was already seated at the head of the table when Vivian took her seat to the right of him, placing her delicate, bony hands atop his.

Dinner was at 7:30 every evening. Mr. Morris and his only daughter, Beauty, were rarely ever late, often the first ones at the table; Vivian wasn't far behind. Moore was expected to arrive in the next minute, followed by Dane, who always seemed to be last. And it was even more expected tonight, for it was the first time he'd be eating with the family since his three-week stay in the hospital.

Their dinners were formal, even when there were no parties. It was a normal, everyday custom, just as one would brush their teeth and wash their face in the morning, the Morris family dressed formally for dinner. Beauty never wore the same outfit twice. Tonight she wore a rich, forest-green cocktail dress that hung loosely at her knees, and a sheer gold shawl hugged her shoulders. Her black hair fell in voluminous waves down her back, and a black ribbon with a miniature charm of a white lily caressed her smooth tan skin, serving as a choker necklace.

Moore walked in wearing a white dress shirt untucked over black pants, sleeves cuffed evenly on each arm, the sleeves cleaving just enough to show his sculpted physique. The other set of feet close behind but not yet shown through the wide opening of the room, was Dane. He had settled for a simple blue button-up shirt, also untucked over black pants. His arrival sparked everyone's attention, causing them to look up briefly at him as he stiffly walked across the room. He passed Moore, who had paused when Dane came in. Moore caught him by the shoulder, gripping it hard. Dane tensed — bit back a sharp hiss from the fiery pain accumulating in his shoulder. His body had become very weak since his excursion; his once toned

24

body had become very frail. Moore's handsome face had an expression of stone, but one side of his lips twitched upward for a second.

"Welcome back to the dinner table, Dane," he uttered, letting go of his younger brother's shoulder. Moore had to have known Dane was still in pain, sore and recovering. Dane winced; Moore's grip made him lose balance and he stepped forward unsteadily. He continued to his seat, oddly feeling no need to glare angrily at Moore on his way, turning his face to the side to hide the pained grimace on his face.

Moore paid no mind, taking his place in the seat across from his father. Dane sat down slowly, carefully in his place next to Beauty, glancing at her from the corner of his eyes and missing the tight smile she gave him. With everyone at the table, they too began the ancient Aponlean chant, but their version was longer.

After being seated Dane scanned his surroundings. It was the first time he was at his dinner table from being taken ill. He was in a coma for one week and recovery for the other two. He was told by the staff there were no visitors. So the people welcoming him back, as warmly as they could, had not taken the time to check on him once. The discouraging thought was enough to cause uneasiness in his stomach, but his body had finally recovered its appetite, and that outweighed the other feeling. He ate his food as politely as he was taught, but quicker than usual. He had a hunger that needed to be satisfied.

"It's good to see you back, Dane," Beauty finally greeted as she watched him digging into his food. He met her words with no answer, as he couldn't help but feel cynicism in place of belief in the sincerity of any of his family's words. Her words were soft enough not to disturb the silence that often surrounded their meals.

Adelina, one of the family's two maids, served more food on Dane's plate as she saw he was almost finished. She didn't even have to ask if he wanted seconds. She was one of the only ones who cared

25

enough to get to know Dane and learned how to read him well. She had been helping him all afternoon get readjusted to the place he called home.

"Thanks," he said even softer than his sister's words. Adelina nodded in response.

The table felt colder than usual, unless Dane had forgotten the feeling it held. He figured his father and Beauty must've gotten into some sort of argument earlier, as they usually did. Mr. Morris was resentful of her being his first-born and not a son. Instead Moore was treated as the firstborn and Beauty left by the wayside. He would often find fault with any of her plans to the point of contradicting himself when she would try to do something he had told her to.

Dane hadn't missed the tension of his family's dynamics. In fact, he couldn't pinpoint anything that he had missed. And from the lack of welcome from either parent, he could tell he wasn't so missed himself. His father's first words upon his return were "I hope you learned whatever lesson Radehveh wanted to teach you and won't repeat your mistake."

Radehveh, his family's god, was what drove both his father and his brother. Every inch of their lives were in submission to what they believed he wanted of them. Dane's family was deeply religious and lived by the family's mantra, "Live up to the name of Morr and bring glory to Radehveh."

Live up to the name of Morr, a man unsympathetic enough to harm anyone who would come in the way of his vision. The life of others meant nothing to him when it came to establishing his own legacy and trying to earn acceptance of Radehveh. He had gotten his legacy, though it came short of his goal. His descendants worshipped him and his actions, and until a few weeks ago, Dane was one of his followers. Now he couldn't remember why he thought any of it was important anymore. His hospital stay had awakened a new outlook on life, a new beginning, where he'd relearn everything, to decide what really was important to him. Because visiting him didn't fit into the overall goal toward Aponlea's culmination, it wasn't important enough for his family's time. Now he had more of a sense of the importance of relationships and people. He also had the mystery of what he'd found at his bedside when he first awoke from his coma.

Chapter Three

Kelly looked ahead at the steady pace of her neighborhood passing as Mike picked up speed. It was the one day of the week he was able to take Kelly, Jason, and Jessica to school. The other days he had classes at the university. Kelly loved it when he was able to give them a ride, absolutely despising the school bus.

It was another chilly day, as expected; but no snow, to Kelly's dismay. Frost still hung from the rooftops of homes, though, and cars parked on driveways were encased in sheets of ice. Trees were bare of the beauty summer, spring, and autumn gave them, but Kelly still liked to look at winter's uniqueness. Everything matched in the winter, when snow visited the state of Connecticut frequently and powdered the land with pure white. The trees were abundant, and, naked as they were, Kelly still harbored an admiration when they sparkled with crystals of frozen ice.

Kelly was wearing her burgundy hooded sweater, the emblem of Charlitton Preparatory School embroidered in gold at the upper right. She left her house in a pleated khaki skirt under a white button-up blouse with a burgundy sweater vest, but her mother took one look at her and forced the hoodie on her.

The car came to a stop at a red light, and Kelly's smile faded. To the right of her was the black Lexus sedan. Dane was back. She could tell it was his. She had seen it countless times on the way to school, though not in the past three weeks.

She sucked her teeth, turning her head away from the site of it. Her lips curled up as if she was about to let out a hiss. "Guess who's back in school," she muttered to Jason, hugging her backpack in the backseat. Kelly played up her dismay in an effort to hide her curiosity about the conclusion of her last conversation with Dane. But she had built up a reputation for so long it was now habit. Kelly Johnson couldn't go soft just because of an ailment of her nemesis. This light was taking forever. Jason rolled his eyes and said nothing. She didn't have to say any more to him.

"Who?" Mike asked, before Jessica could.

"Dane Morris," Kelly said, shaking her head.

The thought of him having his own personal driver caused a flare annoyance in Kelly.

"Where has he been?" Mike asked.

"He was in the hospital for three weeks. A beautiful vacation."

"Just ignore him, Kelly," Jessica suggested. "He's not worth the effort."

"Seriously, don't get back into your old routine with him. I won't be bailing you out anymore," Jason said.

"If he would leave me alone . . . " Kelly said.

"Would you like me to ensure that?" Mike asked in a threatening tone.

"I'll be fine." Kelly wasn't one for being rescued. She liked to fight her own battles, and that's what she had been doing with Dane Morris. Their little pranks started in middle school but had lasted through her freshman year. They seemed more and more childish, but it was a matter of pride between the two of them. Each had to get the last trick in. It was still Kelly's turn.

"If he ever goes too far, you know you have

four brothers here for you." Mike stated.

"I know. It's mostly been just stupid fights." Kelly said. She didn't like the direction of the conversation. She felt so fake because she didn't really feel that much disdain for him anymore. In fact, she was quite fine with dropping the whole feud; it was what she had tried to do in their last encounter. Thoughts of last night's balcony view came to her mind; it would make for a good change of subject. "You and Moore are the same age, right, Mike?"

"Yeah," Mike said. "We graduated in the same class last year." Kelly wished she was just one year older. She could've gone to high school with Moore. Her fascination with him started when she was little. She remembered when she was five her mom took her and her siblings to the park to play. Mrs. Morris had taken Beauty, Dane, and Moore that same day.

Kelly was playing in the sandbox when Moore came up to her. He was eight then. He talked with her about a kingdom he was going to discover and rule over. He would be able to fly then and turn invisible. He told her about his imaginary friend named Emilio. It all seemed so silly now, but back then her younger self ate up every word.

He told her if she wanted to go too, he would take her. He seemed to have such a vast imagination and told her all sorts of plans he had. He was so animated then, much different from his silent character now. The stories he shared with her that day opened her mind to an eagerness for something out of this world.

At first, Kelly's mom hadn't noticed the exchange. But as soon as she found the two of them talking the Johnsons left the park immediately. They were not allowed to talk to their neighbors. They came from the dark bloodlines. Half of the ancestral patriarchs made up the dark bloodlines.

Their descendants were shunned by the other

half. Perez, the youngest of all the twenty men, was the only exception. For some reason his descendants weren't looked down upon as much.

That conversation with Moore those years ago made a huge impression on Kelly, and she grew up with a longing to know more of his stories, more about him. It was strange how she could hate one brother but have such a fascination with the other. They resembled each other in appearance, and if she didn't loathe Dane so much, she could admit he was handsome as well. She just couldn't think that knowing how he was.

"Did you guys ever talk?" Kelly said, breaking her thoughts.

"We had a couple of classes together, but not really," Mike stated. "I guess one time we had a project together. That was interesting. I didn't tell Mom or Dad about it, for obvious reasons. We talked strictly about the project for the most part. He didn't make a lot of friends and mostly kept to himself. He was definitely a perfectionist."

"He's so creepy," Jessica added. "I remember seeing him in the halls, and he just had such a dark look to his face. Everyone was terrified of him, and he didn't have to do anything to cause the fear. It was just the way about him."

"Did you talk to him?" Kelly asked.

"Why do you even care, Kelly?" Jason piped up.

"I am just curious."

"Well, you should learn to just let some things go." Jason was as vocally disgusted with their family as their mother.

"It's not like we've ever gotten much of an explanation as to why we have to avoid our neighbors," Kelly said.

"With how Dane is, that should give you an idea."

"I guess." Kelly figured she should drop the

conversation. It wasn't worth it. None of her siblings had any of the answers she longed to have answered.

Kelly got out of the car close to Jason, but he was practically ignoring her, cracking inside jokes with his buddies and hurrying off. Jessica went her own way. Kelly kept on across the red bricked path that wound through a clean-cut garden over rich green grass. Michelle, Kelly's closest friend, was sitting at the edge of the large fountain that marked the gathering hub for Charlitton Prep. Kelly jogged over to her and Michelle rose to hug her.

"Morning, Kelly! What's been up? I tried calling you all night last night but you never picked up," Michelle said. She slung her arm over Kelly's shoulder as they walked into the front building of their large high school.

"What time last night? I went to bed early, strangely enough."

"That explains it. And you're usually the one keeping me on the phone," Michelle said. They arrived at their lockers on the farthest wing on the left of the building, where Jason was yanking at the closed combination lock on his locker. They quietly made their way over and Michelle started a bit when Jason whacked the metal door with his backpack.

"What's wrong with him?" Michelle whispered through the side of her mouth, looking Kelly's brother up and down. It wasn't unusual to see Jason in a bad mood every once in a while, but this early in the morning? It sparked some interest to observant onlookers such as Michelle. Kelly shrugged.

"I don't know. He was fine earlier this morning. I think it has to do with Dane being back, though," Kelly said under her breath, passing her friend to approach Jason calmly, only slightly concerned. She got in front of his locker and twisted the lock a few times, knowing the combination. It opened with a click and she moved away to grin smugly at him.

"There ya' go, little brother," she joked. She almost reached over to pat his head but thought better of it and went four lockers down to her own locker. Michelle indulged herself with giggles but tried to cover them when Jason flashed an annoyed glance her way that had shown too intensely on his face. Michelle hurried off to her locker, where it stood decorated with colorful magnets and pictures right next to Kelly's.

"We're twins, Kelly. I'm not your little brother," Jason mumbled, fishing for the books he needed for his first class.

"Ask mom — she'll tell you otherwise," Kelly said. Jason shut his locker door, looking at Kelly with a face that was starting to strain with pent-up agitation.

"Please, Kelly," he said, half begging. Kelly didn't quite understand what he meant, looking at him passively and granting his request. He stalked off a moment later, headed to homeroom.

"O-kay," Michelle said slowly, closing her locker door. Kelly sighed, staring off in the direction he had left.

"He'll be fine later. Once he has some time to himself, he'll back to the witty pest of a brother I know so well," Kelly reassured, though she wished she felt surer than her words. On most days, Kelly could joke around with Jason without any arguments, but other days — like this one — his demeanor would change just like that, as if he would snap any minute. His outbursts were rare and they left her uneasy. They didn't always just blow over, either. Kelly learned from experience that days like this often ended badly. Maybe today it was different, though. Maybe Jason was in a bad mood for another reason, and not because of Dane. That could change a lot of things for the outcome of the day.

Kelly linked arms with her friend, tugging her forward. "Come on, let's get to homeroom," she said. Michelle nodded and playfully raced down the slowly dissipating crowd of students.

Charlitton Prep was very much like Princeton in that it was a large and beautiful campus but small in population. It stressed uniformity. Tardiness and absence were not tolerated. There was a thick enough handbook for the appropriate style of their uniforms alone, describing each element of clothing in a very detailed dress code. So Kelly never messed around with her attendance—it saved further lectures from her parents anyway. Her uniform, on the other hand, had been corrected a few times.

It had been five minutes before the bell. Most students were in homeroom by now; they had to be in their seats as soon as the bell rang. Kelly was leaning on her desk, chatting with Michelle.

"So," Kelly began. She looked up at Michelle with tired eyes. "The day we so dreaded has arrived at last."

"Yep," Michelle drawled, shaking her head.

Kelly breathed, running a hand through her short brown hair. "I saw his . . . own personal chauffeur driving beside us this morning."

"I guess this means our vacation's over."

"It was nice, wasn't it?" Kelly said, smiling morosely. The school was free of the violent fighting. And Kelly could take a breather from her rival. It was endless between them, the cruel pranks. Though Kelly never backed down, it was still nice to be free of it for a while. And at one point, when Dane was out of school for so long, she thought it was over. She should have known he'd be back eventually. Now that it was her turn to get him back, she didn't know what she'd do.

"Believe me, it was bliss," Michelle said, chuckling. "I didn't have to help you with any your crazy revenge schemes."

"Yeah, well, planning them was the hard part," Kelly answered, picking habitually at her nails.

"You know, you don't have to do these things anymore. It can be like a new start, it's a new year, remember! The last one of this century, and maybe ever with Y2K around the corner, so let's just make it count," Michelle said, trying to be optimistic. She smiled a little for effect. Everyone was saying exactly what Kelly had known to be true, which strangely made her want to ignore it even more. She liked it when she had an original idea but not when others acted as if it were their own.

"And let him get away with tormenting me further? He's not going to stop just because I did, Michelle." The bell rang right after she said that, startling them both. Students rushed to their seats.

"Uh, I'll try to answer that later," Michelle said quickly before sitting down herself. Kelly wished it were that easy to just stop what she was doing and try and make things right, just so Dane would leave her alone, but it didn't work that way. It just didn't.

<hr />

Fifth period. The class Kelly had been anxious over all day, the only class she and Dane had together. She started to the only empty desk, knowing already who was seated beside it. She headed straight toward her destination. As tightly as she was clutching her books to her chest, they still fell out of her arms when she tripped in her step. She caught herself, thankful for only a few bouts of light giggles throughout the classroom and not a cacophony of laughter and smart remarks.

"Blame the boots," one student commented, and

a few more students erupted with snickering. Kelly rolled her eyes, acting as if she hadn't heard him.

She began picking up her book and papers, not thinking much of the task as she stacked the papers atop the book in her arms when a hand picked up the remainder of the sheets and placed it on top of the others. She hadn't noticed who it was until she looked up. It was Dane, and the sight of him made her blink profusely as she watched him gather the stray sheets of notes that had also slipped out of one of her notebooks, and with such nonchalance that it caught her off guard — sort of frightened her.

When he handed them to her, she took them quickly, not meeting his dull, dark eyes.

"Thanks," she sputtered after contemplating the usually simple response. Yes, to anyone else it was simple: anyone but Dane. Dane hadn't said anything in return. He got back in his seat, looking ahead and waiting for the lecture for today's class to begin.

Kelly lowered slowly into her seat, eyeing Dane suspiciously at the corners of her eyes. Dane hadn't looked back at her once. What does he have up his sleeve? Kelly thought, not realizing she was still looking at him, studying his strangely distant expression. For a few minutes, as she occupied herself with flipping aimlessly through pages of her English book, she thought of possible reasons why he might have had the notion to pick up the books. It boggled her brain, so much that it hurt.

The thought had her heart pumping with anxiety and anticipation. Here he was, playing out his first scheme of attack on his first day of return, and Kelly wasn't even prepared for something to get him back with. Her breathing grew heavy, so she forced herself to breathe through her nostrils as anger coursed through her like an unexpected hot flash. How could he toy with her pride like that, and with such a straight face?

She needed answers now, she thought, leaning to the side toward Dane's desk. The sudden absence of light in the classroom stopped her from going on. The students quieted and Mrs. Farr began a film, running it on the TV she rolled out from the corner on its stand. She announced that she was leaving for a few minutes to make copies for something and slipped out of the classroom.

Now was Kelly's chance.

"Why did you help me pick up my stuff?" she said in a low voice. It was loud enough to be heard by Dane, and the fact that she was leaning to the right, toward the direction of his seat, he would have noticed. His dark eyes left the TV screen to meet Kelly's. He was poised, expressionless.

"I saw that you had dropped them and it was convenient to do so," he replied brusquely, focusing his attention back on the film. Kelly pursed her lips. To her, he wasn't making any sense.

"But wasn't that a bit kind of you — even if it was convenient?" Dane's eyes didn't leave the screen this time.

"I guess."

"Then why would you . . ."

"Kelly, would you like me to apologize or something?" Dane shot back when he looked at her again, his eyes narrowed. Their peers were talking among themselves since the teacher had left, and Dane was thankful for the increase in volume; no one would be paying attention to the irritation that rose in his voice. "Just accept it for what it is and leave me alone."

"What is this game you're playing?" she murmured, studying him once again, making Dane dig his nails into the fine khaki material over his kneecaps. Kelly's brown eyes were set on his, looking shadowed through the dark room. She wasn't afraid

37

of him. Never was.

"It's nothing, I promise," he answered finally, managing to get it out through gritted teeth. Kelly reluctantly backed down, watching him shift his body more toward the TV and away from her. She wouldn't push his buttons further, knowing his potential for making a scene, getting them both in trouble.

Kelly wondered if he really meant that. It was never nothing with Dane and her. Kelly sighed; she was so confused. So anxious. She struggled not to allow the burning question out in the present circumstances. She could always catch him in the hall, but then maybe they would be interrupted again. She was about to burst, she could feel it. After a few minutes of watching the monotone video on literary devices most used in modern literature, Kelly's curiosity sparked again. Before she knew it, she was leaning his way again.

"So why were you in the hospital, anyway?" Maybe she could find out why he was acting so—out of sorts? Kelly saw him tense, but he didn't turn to face her. He took a moment to collect himself, pulling off the calm look that was beginning to annoy Kelly.

"Is that any of your business?" He then turned around, looking her square in the eyes with a smug expression. "Let's just call a truce and agree not to talk to each other anymore." All those years Kelly had wanted a truce with Dane, but today it was the last thing she wanted from him. Not before she got real answers from him. Not until he admitted to this new act he was playing on her. It was hard to even consider the idea. Was a traumatic experience really able to change Dane Morris?

Chapter Four

The cold was promising its presence that evening,
giving a brisk forewarning with the cool afternoon.
Kelly hugged her hooded jacket close to her as she
volunteered to get the mail while her siblings opted
for the warmer environment inside.

Kelly hadn't stopped thinking about Dane's return and unusual behavior. He wasn't the same person. There was something very different about him.
She lingered a while longer at the mailbox, trying to
pinpoint the exact transformation or conclusion to
what she had witnessed. Her eyes rose slowly to gaze
at his abode.

The majesty of it transitioned her thoughts to his
elder brother and her fascination with everything about
his existence. Maybe he would drive by and she'd get
a better glimpse of his chariot. He would sweep her
up into it and they'd trail off into his kingdom. One
day she would see inside, and one day she would pick
the brain of its prince.

A magnetic force from the castle tugged at her,
she conceded, voluntarily pacing toward its tall gates.
She'd since forgotten her initial task, allowing fantasy
to consume her to the core. She coursed the side of
the road leading up to the dividing line between her
own residence and his. Before she crossed that line,
the Lexus sedan pulled up, stopping for the gate to
open. Kelly stood in her spot, not releasing her eyes
from its rear window. This wasn't the chariot she had
hoped for. She stared in as if she could see Dane past
the tint and imagined he'd be looking right back at

her. He would be wondering why she was staring at him, she imagined, as those were her very own thoughts. She wanted to look away but didn't. There was too much of a mystery. He had something up his sleeve. Something coming toward her. His unusual kindness to her that day had to be part of his latest scheme.

The only other logical explanation would be that he had been abducted by aliens and his body possessed by a creature of another universe, a creature that actually could demonstrate benevolence. Her disgust surfaced as the view of his vehicle vanished into the kingdom of the Morris estate. She walked away angered at the penetrating hunger of her curiosity.

The glimpse of Joey pulling up added to her dismay, as Melanie was riding in the passenger seat. She mustered up her most convincing smile and waved at them as she walked toward her brother's vehicle. She did like Melanie, she was sweet, but she would steal her favorite brother away.

"Kelly!" Melanie said with glee, departing from the passenger's side. Kelly kept up her smile.

"Hi Melanie. Come to join us for dinner tonight?" Kelly asked. She caught a glimpse of Joey's wink from behind Melanie's back. He wanted Kelly to talk to her tonight. Kelly had forgotten about that detail. She let out a quick, subtle sigh while embracing her future sister-in-law.

"Yes, I just can't get enough of your mother's delicious meals. She is quite the chef, and of course it's always good to see you and the family." The sincerity of her words sickened Kelly. She really was perfect, at least for Joey and by her mother's standards. After Joey came around to embrace Kelly, his bear hug had loosened up her tension, putting her more at ease for her task.

Upon their entrance, Melanie was greeted by Mrs. Johnson and Lisa. Clearly, everyone else had accepted her. Why did Kelly have such a problem with her? She snuck out from all the excitement of the esteemed guest, hopping up the steps to her room. She dropped her backpack on her bed and went straight out to the balcony. She looked toward the Morris estate for some sort of clue to Dane's behavior. At least that was her excuse this time for prying into her neighbor's yard.

Moore's normal means of transportation was parked in the loop already. He must've been home all day, unless he had taken one of his more rare vehicles out. It wasn't likely. She had been studying his routine for quite some time. She knew him as well as her imagination would allow. She'd created his whole character in her mind and even imagined what their first conversation would be like. Their first conversation besides when they met at the park. "Show yourself," she said under her breath, hoping her words would hold some sort of power. She eagerly looked on waiting for confirmation of her what she imagined.

In her mind, she saw a conjured version of herself marching right up to the front door and knocking. Moore obviously opened and asked what had taken her so long. "I was waiting for you," she answered, merging the false reality with the actual one.

"Well, here I am," Joey said from behind her, startling her more than he'd expected. It had caused him to jump as well.

"Hi Joey," she said.

"Hey, how's it going?" he asked. "Fantasizing again?"

"Wondering." She answered.

"Just curious," Joey began. "Why is it that everyone else is interrogating Melanie right now, except you? You are going to talk to her for me, right?"

"Of course," Kelly confirmed. "I was just letting the stampede through, so the coast would be clear. Don't want to get trampled." She smiled, at her self-perceived clever terminology. Joey seemed to be so serious right now, not showing amusement at all.

"I'm not buying it," he responded. "What's up?"

"It has nothing to do with your circumstances, Joey. I just have a lot on my mind," Kelly lied.

"Such as?" She hadn't sold him yet.

"Dane Morris is back in school, and he was acting

41

nice to me today — well, he helped me pick my books up."

"That is odd. So, you are cool with Melanie, then?" As much as Joey veered off subject on his own, he was somehow good at refocusing the subject when his own questions were at hand.

"Of course!" Kelly smiled, more insincerely than she had anticipated. She wasn't fooling him for a moment, but a knock on her bedroom door saved her from further interrogation. Kelly quickly moved past her brother, back into her room and to the door. It was Melanie.

"Hi Kelly," Melanie greeted her. "Have you seen Joey?"

"Out here, my love. Join me on this lovely balcony."

"As romantic as that sounds, it's starting to get really chilly out."

"My love will keep you warm," he responded. Kelly rolled her eyes, even though he was joking, it was still sickening to her.

"Oh gosh," Melanie teased back, winking at Kelly. "You have such a way with words." Melanie chuckled through her sarcasm.

"Hey Melanie," Kelly said in a lowered voice.

"Yes, Kelly?"

"Can I talk to you when you have some time?"

"Yeah, of course. We can talk now if you'd like."

Joey was by Melanie's side in an instant, and the two locked eyes. Kelly felt awkward to be around them, because they certainly looked like they felt they were the only two in that moment.

"Kelly would like to talk with me," Melanie said. I hope you don't mind if we have a little girl talk?"

"Not at all. I am a master at girl talk," Joey responded. "Just ask Kelly. Tell her about Fifi."

"Joey, not now," Kelly said, though she couldn't help but smile. It was a character Joey would bring out at times when Kelly's talks with him would get too girlish. He would whip out his girl voice and over-the-top flamboyance to engage in the conversation. It was his way of saying he was not the right person to talk about certain things, that she should address such topics with Jessica or Michelle. Kelly would always crack up and couldn't get a word in, as Joey would perform an impromptu monologue. She had learned a lot about Fifi over the years.

"I actually would like to hear about this Fifi, Joey," Melanie chuckled. "But now is not the time."

"Okay, fine," he said, pretending to be crushed at the rejection. He waited around a while longer and both Kelly and Melanie just stared at him, silently. "Wait, did you want me to leave while you have this girl talk?"

Melanie rolled her eyes playfully, escorting her boyfriend out of the room. While her back was turned, Kelly readied herself. Melanie made herself comfortable on Kelly's blue disc chair and Kelly sat across from her on the bed.

"So, shoot," Melanie said, leaning forward, fully engaged. Kelly tried to think of how to do this.

"If your boyfriend cheats on you and seems to be completely remorseful, do you give him a second chance, or do you think once a cheater always a cheater? How do you know that you can ever trust him again?" Kelly spat out, fully in character.

"Oh, that is tough. I would always say be cautious. Start out just being friends again, and if you don't feel you can do that, then, I wouldn't recommend it at all. The second time around is always so much harder."

"But, what if he's popular and you two were just so cute together and got a lot of attention?"

"You've got to decide if that is the base of your affection for him or if you two really had something on a deeper level."

"We did, definitely," Kelly assured. Her scenario wasn't so far-fetched. Her first and only boyfriend, Jake, had cheated on her. The only difference was that she had absolutely no residual feelings for him. She couldn't say she liked him all that well in the first place; he wasn't a good boyfriend. "Also, he's my best friend's brother. So, I have to see him whenever I go over to Michelle's house."

"That would be tough," Melanie said with a brief pause. "Kelly, you truly are a beautiful individual, inside and out. And I don't think you should waste your time with someone who didn't recognize that when he had it. You're young; you need to know this. Don't give the wrong guy your efforts. If he doesn't treat you as a princess, then move on. The less your heart gets broken, the better. One day your prince will come in and swoop you away and you'll know it, because everything in life will make sense."

"Is that how you feel about Joey?" Kelly asked.

"Definitely. I can't imagine loving anyone else besides him," she said quickly. That was all Kelly needed to hear. Her mission was accomplished, and she couldn't help but feel fonder of Melanie. She was great for Joey; Kelly always knew that.

"I'm so glad he found you," Kelly said, finally with some sincerity.

Dane felt like his limbs were creaking when he got home from school. His backpack felt like a sack of bricks; it was packed to its limit with books. The amount of catch-up work he'd have to do made him want to get started right away, but he had a meeting to go to. His father and brother would be expecting him downstairs very soon. He walked into his room only to drop the leather bag onto the floor before trudging down the hall to meet his father in the elevator.

The short ride was quiet—as it usually was—as it took them underground. When the estate was designed by his great-grandfather, the underground level was added for secrecy, total seclusion. It was basically a protected oversized basement. Its solid granite walls and padded ceilings made it quite difficult for eaves-droppers and spies. Sure, the home was built beside the Johnsons for the purpose of spying on them, but they knew how easily it would give their opponents a look into their own dark secrets.

It was a constant battle of one family upper-handing the other, though it had diminished in recent years. There hadn't been a threatening confrontation between the main families in almost two decades. On the surface, it appeared as though both families had created a world where there was a place for each other without crossing paths. What it actually meant was that each had gotten more strategic in its approach.

When Dane and his father arrived underground, they sat themselves at the dark meeting table in the main meeting room. Moore was already sitting down. Moore was first to arrive at every meeting, just to show their father his commitment. Dane avoided his brother's eyes and sat at the left of his father, as he usually did, and looked down at his folded hands.

This "family activity" used to be everything to Dane, before the hospital. The meetings involved all things Aponlean. All had been discussed and taken apart at this table. A new theory, plot, plan, possibility — anything that would bring the Morrises closer to their ancestral kingdom. To find Aponlea and restore its glory. And Dane used to love it. He loved to study and observe the family's collection of Aponlea's remaining artifacts. He loved the rare times he'd win erudite arguments that would end in a pat of approval on his shoulder from his father. He loved to sit alone in the family library and flip through ancient Aponlean texts. He loved to be brought on "business trips" across the world. But now, Dane couldn't bring himself to care. It seemed the coma had brought him a cynicism regarding Aponlea that clung to him without any give.

Now, he wanted to see the world beyond the perspective of his family's. That was a desire he never had until he'd woken up in a hospital bed. Before the hospital, everyone outside of his family was misguided and ignorant. Dane used to think he knew everything he needed to know about anything. Now he felt he didn't know nearly enough. He didn't know other cultures. He didn't know other religions or viewpoints. He knew nothing besides what he was born into: a dark, sheltered, empty life.

"The Alliance is pressing for Richard's whereabouts. They want him dead," Mr. Morris began.

"You would think — with how intelligent the Stanforces make themselves out to be — they would see the stupidity in this logic. It seems they've taken a backseat to the Normans." The descendants of Morr, Sta'an, and Norm made up the Alliance. The Normans were the ruthless hit men, handling the dirty work in the group. And they weren't very good with much else. The Stanforces were known for their intellect. They studied the science behind ancient Aponlean devices. "I've convinced them against it for now, but it doesn't buy us much time."

"Even less with Uncle Vince around," Moore said under his breath. Mr. Morris raised an eyebrow on his otherwise expressionless face.

"Would you like to speak up, Moore?"

"Yes, I would. I don't like how involved Uncle Vince is. He's bound to slip up and reveal that we have Richard's location."

"Dishonoring my brother is dishonoring the Great Morr. He has just as much claim to the Great Morr as you do."

"Until you hand over what is rightfully mine," Moore said. Dane looked up at his brother, knowing full well Moore's eyes had intensified at the sheer mention of receiving the family's honor. It had been passed down through generations until it met Mr. Morris. There wasn't an official age that the honor was to be passed down to the eldest son, but in recent years eighteen had become common.

"I haven't determined yet if it is rightfully yours, as you say. I do have two other children." Their father loved to taunt Moore this way. Both Beauty and Dane knew it would go to Moore, but Mr. Morris would hold onto it for as long as he could. Dane saw the annoyance in Moore's eyes, though Moore fought hard not

46

to show any disrespect. He kept silent.

"Back to the Alliance. Martin Stanforce wants to move into the neighborhood once they finish up in Spain. Dane, you remember Drew and Bryan?"

"Yes sir." Dane recalled the twin brothers. They were pretentious and egotistical. The Stanforces were known for their love of science and even scratching the surface of Aponlean technology, which was far advanced from any known discoveries. Dane never got along with them, but his father was oblivious to this. When they were kids Mr. Morris thought they played along like good little children. "When are they moving?"

"Not for another year or two. They're still working on that hot spot they found, making advances on the minefield they uncovered. If they can crack the technology through the devices they've found. It's a possible location of Aponlea, or it will lead to it anyway."

"Aponlea is mystical, not scientific," Moore disagreed. "Its doors will only be reopened once all the prophecies are fulfilled. Schernols first, then Aponlea."

"Right, Schernols," Mr. Morris added, as if remembering the wonder of them. The man displayed no evidence of excitement on his face, but Dane knew he was beaming inside.

"Nadia's informed Vince that Richard's kid has been talking about a big revelation." Dane couldn't help his own excitement, having a feeling where this was going. He figured Moore already knew, since he and their cousin were very close. There was no doubt that Nadia told Moore everything before telling her father, Vince.

"She says Richard has cracked the code of the Sceptra and has found the first Schernol."

"Why would she tell him that and not us?" Moore asked immediately. Dane looked at his brother. He was surprised that Moore didn't know.

"Because he's her father and just as much a part of this as we are," Mr. Morris answered plainly before intensifying his voice. "If you can't get it through your head that in this family blood comes first, then maybe you can be on the outs. I will not have division in this household." Moore sat back in his seat and seethed.

"A Schernol? Would that mean we might be in possession of one soon?" Dane attempted at soothing the tension, although he too was still intrigued enough to hear more about the Schernol. No one in the known history of the dark bloodlines had recovered a Schernol after the exile.

"Yes, son," Mr. Morris couldn't help but crack a slight smile despite his serious composure. "Nadia's informed Vince that Richard has cracked the Aponlean language's second meaning and therefore the Sceptra is spewing out all sorts of answers."

"So, we steal it back. I'm sure we can crack the code ourselves," Moore said, his voice suggesting he was begging.

"How far have you gotten with that, Moore?" Mr. Morris asked, his voice still low, but with an edge of impatience.

"Nowhere, sir. There really doesn't seem to be a second meaning to it."

Dane watched in silence as his brother and father continued with their mild argument. Dane was anticipating an explosion from his father. Moore was so eager and persistent, but his father seemed to have a supernatural patience about the process of uncovering the secrets of Aponlea. Perhaps it was because he had been at this for more than half a century and Moore less than a quarter. Dane was sure his father had been through so many let downs in his life that he learned to wait, to count the chickens after they hatched. That would be something Moore would need to learn.

"Now, interpretation with the new code is lengthy, but he has just gotten to the first Schernol and knows its location," Mr. Morris began again. "It's the silver one."

"That's the one Morr fought with," Dane decided

to speak again.

"Can we tell Captain Obvious over here to shut his trap," Moore glared at Dane. "Is there ever anything useful coming out of Dane's mouth?"

"Perhaps you both can remain silent while I continue with the rest?" Mr. Morris steadily rose from his chair with his hands pressed firmly on the black table, his jaw set. It was instantly quiet. "Nadia's updating us frequently, so once she gets the location of the Schernol from Richard's kid, we will know and make the appropriate plans to go to the location." Mr. Morris moved his hands from the table. Dane looked at him for either dismissal or further information. "That's enough for today. Be sure to pray. Times are approaching that our forefathers had been waiting for. If we find enough favor with Radehveh, maybe we will live to see the ingathering."

"Yes, sir," Moore agreed. "I think Richard knows we have him tapped." Moore was following after his father as Mr. Morris made his way back to the elevator. Dane stayed further behind.

"That's impossible." Mr. Morris stated evenly. Moore quickened his pace to walk beside his father, like a faithful apprentice. Dane often felt invisible among the two of them. He didn't understand why he had to be at any meetings; his thoughts and questions were rarely acknowledged anyway.

"He hasn't mentioned anything about this Schernol thing on the tapes," Moore insisted.

"Who would he be talking to? Himself?"

"I don't know, but I don't think we should treat anything we get from him as significant and credible."

"Look, Moore, the information we got from Richard last week was viable and beneficial," Mr. Morris said, pausing in his step to look at his son. Moore shook his head.

"He's not an idiot, father; he's going to lead us on. He let us figure out a lesser to secure the greater," Mr. Morris pressed his lips together, blinking. He started walking again, and Moore waited for an answer, catch-

49

ing up with him when he started to quicken his pace.

"You're giving the man too much credit, Moore."

"He stole the Sceptra after it had been in our possession for fifty-eight years, and up until three years ago he'd been successfully nonexistent to the Alliance for nineteen years."

"He's been lucky in the past, unfortunately. But nothing stays hidden forever," Mr. Morris said, entering the elevator nearest to them. Moore joined him inside; he pressed the button to shut the door. Dane hurried in before the doors closed on him. "The tables have turned—we have the lead."

Dane could tell that Moore didn't agree with his father in this subject, but Moore stubbornly conceded. "It's only a hunch."

Chapter Five

The next two weeks passed rather swiftly for Kelly. Besides her date with Melanie proving to be a success, she really hadn't done much. After the joining of the seals, her family went straight into wedding mode. All other family crises had to be put on hold. Although there were moments when she enjoyed the preparations, she still wasn't ready for the pending absence of her favorite brother.

She was already getting a whiff of it, what with his being tied up with wedding plans. Five minutes of his time ended up dissolving into his love-struck rants about Melanie. Kelly found herself straying away from Joey, fearing she'd get asked to participate in another cake tasting, try on another dress, or anything to do with the wedding. Kelly often wished he'd leave the planning to the bride like most grooms would. He wanted to be right by Melanie's side in every decision that was made, even if it meant neglecting his responsibilities as co-owner of Gilby's, constantly relying on his trusty partner to see to his duties at the drop of a hat. With despairing realization, Kelly's beloved venting buddy was diminishing.

There was so much she wanted to talk to him about, like Dane. Dane had continued to refrain from his usual cruel pranks and tricks. The fact that he hadn't done or said anything menacing to her for such a long time since he'd been in the hospital scared her more than any of her other trials. She was losing her alertness for his next move and feared that her guard would soon fall completely, leaving her exposed to a possible unexpected strike from him. This made Kelly groan as she slowly headed to her fifth-period class, shaking her head to rid all the conflicting thoughts.

All these thoughts churned with unrest in her head, something subconscious was poking her, an alert in the midst of them, notifying her that if she walked any slower she'd be late. That was the last thing she needed, more trouble. She sped up, passing up various students in the quickly dissipating crowd in the hallway, blurs of plaid, burgundy, and beige, and white lockers blending together as she began a jog.

Everything was a conglomerated mess to her eyes. It was as if her brain wouldn't let her identify anything or anyone around her. She had one goal, and that was to get through this day as quickly as possible. The quicker she could get through it, the faster her problems would just fade away, or so she'd hoped.

Although she wasn't paying attention to her surroundings, somehow the repetitiveness of the daily school schedule made her stop at just the right classroom, making it seconds before the bell. Quickly, she took the only remaining desk, and once again, it was right beside Dane Morris. She figured this would be the case, since there always used to be an empty seat beside Dane's, because no one wanted to be subject to his heartless glares — that is, whenever he was in the mood to meet eyes with the poor soul. If she wanted the window seat she often had in the far left corner of the middle row, she'd have to get to class much earlier.

She looked longingly at the now-occupied seat before sitting down, wondering why the sun seemed to caress the student sitting there and why the colors around it were more vibrant and appealing than the blandness she was trapped under now. Why was her imagination playing such malignant tricks on her?

Not realizing that her pretty face was expressing every thought going through her head, she sat down. For that brief moment her wistful, unrelenting imagination shadowed her reality, but as shadows move with the light, this somewhat peaceful one swayed as she sank in her chair. Her head, which was ready to meet with the comfort of the wooden desk before her, wasn't allowed to rest, so her hand held it up, forcing her to bare with her thoughts.

"Are you alright?" The question that almost slipped passed her attention barely touched her ears and broke her out of her trance, but it wasn't quick enough for her to respond to it, let alone see who asked it, so the question was repeated. Conscious but bleary, she turned to her left. She managed a muffled "Huh?" in response.

"Just wondering if something was wrong, that's all. I mean, you haven't been yourself lately." The speaker's voice was laced with a mysterious emotion, one that most would identify as concern. To Kelly, it was hard to place it with someone like Dane, especially since she hadn't ever heard anything like it come out of his mouth. In her opinion, it didn't suit him at all; she wished he'd refrain from showing real emotion.

"I'm fine, just been busy lately." She was too mentally and physically exhausted to make a smart remark, so she didn't question his concern. If it was enough to suffice the conversation she saw coming, then she'd let it go.

After a long enough pause, he blurted out, "With what?"

"It's not really any of your business," she snapped on impulse, a little louder than intended. At first, she felt justified by her response, but when he cast his eyes down to his desk, almost shamefully, Kelly was disgusted. She wished he'd stop acting like someone he wasn't.

"You're right," he answered with thinned lips. "It's none of my business. You've just seemed down lately, and I was starting to get concerned."

Kelly was taken aback, not just by the calm in his voice, but also the sincerity. When she realized her heartbeat was quickening, she pushed the hopeful thought as far from her mind as possible. The last thing she wanted was to attribute positive human qualities

53

to Dane. He'd always be inhuman in her mind, and she didn't want to see anything different from him. There was her stubbornness for you.

"Um, thanks for caring," she said, resisting the urge to mutter "or whatever" and forcing a mocking friendly smile. Dane didn't seem convinced. Kelly felt miserable when she saw his dissatisfied face still looking at her. Surprisingly, though, he shifted in his seat and turned his attention to the front of the class respectively.

Kelly looked aimlessly up at the ceiling and began to imagine whether it were possible for Dane to be different. Maybe whatever put him in the hospital resulted in damage to his brain, stimulating a section of it that he never used, the section that held kindness, care, benevolence, self-control, and the other nice things Dane was void of. Whether or not this was the case, one thing was certain: Kelly's curiosity — her most predominate quality, which often seemed a curse, and often overrode many of her emotions, common sense, and logic — had unfurled and expanded.

There was a mystery to be solved about Dane. Had he actually changed, or was he pulling the biggest act yet to completely humiliate her? She'd only know if she continued to play along, as unpleasing as that sounded; that way she'd have a better chance of finding out what was really going on. One thing was for sure: there was no way Dane was going to ever see her with her guard down.

With a sudden rejuvenation about her, she faced Dane and feigned hesitance. "Sorry if I sounded harsh. I guess the main thing is my older brother is getting married, so he just hasn't been around much lately. And we've always been so close. Besides, you know how rushed Aponlean weddings are."

"That would be tough, but I wouldn't know. I'm not particularly close with either of my siblings." Dane's eyes may have been looking toward the front of the room, but it seemed his voice was aimed right toward Kelly.

"Just Moore and Beauty, right?"

"Yeah, I mean Beauty and I were close up until a few years ago. She's been different ever since a traumatizing breakup. She doesn't really open up about it or anything else these days."

Kelly didn't really care about Beauty; she had only brought up her name to not seem so eager about Moore.

"And Moore?"

Dane swallowed hard, biting his tongue. The face he made was reminiscent of his old self.

"We don't get along that great. Never have. Don't ask me why." Kelly could see his discomfort with this topic growing. It didn't surprise her when he changed the subject. "How many siblings do you have again?" he asked.

"There are seven of us," Kelly answered, annoyed at the change of subject. Perhaps if she did fake a friendship with him, she could finally have a way into the world that plagued her deepest curiosities. Kelly was unsure of what to add. It was strange having a decent conversation with him. He also seemed to be stuck, as he redirected his attention to the lesson. Starting a friendship at a slower pace was fine with her. She didn't know how long it would take her to be comfortable with it.

<hr />

Mrs. Johnson's famous tuna-stuffed mushrooms filled a giant plate at the center of the dinner table, along with assorted home-cooked sides she made with it. It happened to be Kelly's favorite, and she would gratefully have eaten two or three helpings of it if it hadn't been for the empty seat across from her father's. The main dish's creamy sauce complemented everything so well, filling Kelly's nostrils and awakening her unsatisfied hunger, but she was conflicted, and the faint rumble in her stomach didn't sound demanding anymore, but mournful.

Everyone was at the table except for Joey. He was

at Melanie's parents making preparations for the wedding. This had become a regular thing, and Kelly knew that from now on, dinner with him would be a rare occasion. His seat would be empty for a good while, until after the wedding, when Mike would rightfully take his place. Still staring at Joey's empty seat, she tried to cheer herself up by reminiscing on the most memorable dinners her family had had. That only made it worse. As her eyes panned the whole family at the table, she already knew that future dinners were going to be bland without Joey. He seemed the family's only source of light and laughter. Everyone else was either too serious or too young. The only ones who were fun were the ones who fed off of Joey's fire, and without that fire, well . . .

Even Jason was keeping his annoying remarks to himself. Since there was no competition for humor anymore, Jason simply ate his food just to be able to leave the dinner table. It was the first time in Johnson history that the dinner table had been almost completely silent, save for the clinking of silverware, the chewing of food, and Rita's sorry attempts at starting group conversations. All attempts produced one-phrased answers, nothing worth further discussion.

It now looked like dinner would be the longest time of the day for Kelly to endure, even longer now that she had no desire for food. How was it that everything else breezed by — even school — but this particular hour of the day felt like an eternity of wasted time?

Kelly wondered if anyone else felt the same way she did, and when she glanced at each face, their inanimate, bored expressions answered her question. She looked back hopefully at the open arch that led to the spacious foyer of the front of the house, and with a fragment of a wish that Joey would burst into the dining hall — as was his nature — with that magical smile of his, surprising them all, saving the evening. Imagining it even made her smile, and she could hear his inviting voice let out a single remark that would garner the laughter of every single being in the house,

56

the smiles that would suddenly appear on their faces at the mere sight of him.

Her smile ultimately faded as she turned around in her seat, fiddling with her fork and nudging a stuffed mushroom with it. She could feel her father's gaze on her, probably wondering why her plate was still untouched. Gaining attention slowly from the whole table, Kelly forked a petite amount of tuna and forced herself to eat, chewing slowly and carefully. When eyes were off of her, she stared off into a vast arena of ruefulness, moving away from the existence of her surroundings, forgetting her food once again.

A sudden movement from the left of her brought her back quickly. It was Lisa turning back behind her. Kelly's heart leaped and she almost gasped Joey's name, certain he'd walked in, but it was no one. Lisa turned back to her food with a pout very visible in her full lips. Kelly's heart beat with overwhelming warmth. She poked Lisa softly with her elbow and Lisa met sad eyes with her. Kelly gave her an understanding smile and kissed the side of her head. She took another bite of her stuffed mushroom in a better mood; her sister was looking for the same hope she was.

After dinner, Kelly found herself in Jessica's room. Unlike Kelly's room, there wasn't a single object out of place. Everything was in order, alphabetized and color-coded. On her walls were all the latest teen heart-throbs, plastered everywhere. She may have been very structured but was boy-crazed nonetheless.

Kelly was almost unsure of where to sit so as not to disrupt her sister's order.

"You can sit anywhere." Jessica could see her dilemma, her voice laced with congestion. She coughed. Kelly still looked around a little more before moving her desk chair out and facing the bed. Jessica was splayed across it holding a novel, *Geeks and Theater Freaks*.

"What's up, Kelly?"

Kelly didn't know what to say. She was just used to visiting Joey in his room and talking about any and everything.

"Missing Joey?" Jessica knew her sister better than Kelly realized.

"Yep," Kelly responded, still unsure of what she would talk about.

"It'll be alright. I'm here for you whenever you need me. But you're going to need to start knocking." Jessica coughed a few more times.

"Thanks," Kelly smiled. "Are you sick?"

"Just a cold. I feel fine, just a slight runny nose and a cough." Jessica placed her book down and sat up.

"So..."

Jessica wasn't used to Kelly being so silent.

"Any guys you wanted to talk to me about? Are you still interested in Steven, or was it Joab?"

"That was like middle school," Kelly said making a face.

"My bad, I've been out of the loop lately with you in that area."

"No one worth mentioning."

"That's good, because you shouldn't feel like you need a guy or anything. We're young and have a lot to accomplish," Jessica said. Kelly looked at her amused at her trying to sound wise. It was just last week that she had had a major crush on a classmate.

"You got over Aaron quickly," Kelly smiled.

"You know, I fell for a moment of weakness, but I am back up. To singlehood and to womanhood!" Jessica crossed her hand over her heart.

"We'll see how long that lasts," Kelly chuckled. Jessica was known to be boy crazy.

"Kelly, I am serious. Have you ever taken the time to really think about your life and where you'd like to be in five years from now?"

"Yes, graduated from high school and enrolled in college," Kelly answered quickly.

"That's good, but what do you want to do with your life?"

Kelly had thought about it at times. Often she was unsure, but felt she didn't need to be as she had

58

all the time in the world. Other times, she had an inner inclination desiring to do something great in life. She wanted her name to be remembered like John's or Peter's. She didn't think it was very likely and didn't know too much about Aponlea in the first place, but still that thought popped up from time to time.

"I don't know," she answered. "I'm only fifteen."

"That's no excuse, Kelly. I had my whole life mapped out at fifteen."

"Including who you wanted to marry, right?" Kelly mocked her knowing full well who her crush was at that time.

Jessica rolled her eyes. "Fine. If you don't want to have a serious conversation with me, maybe I'll just talk to Zach."

"Oh, have fun with that one," Kelly laughed this time.

"He is actually a good listener," Jessica said.

"I can see him tuning you out while working on one of his projects."

"He actually challenges me and helps me be more practical about certain areas," Jessica defended.

Kelly sighed, "Go ahead, Jessica. Tell me your life plan."

"Okay," Jessica pulled up a chart she had made. It had her life mapped out until the age of sixty-five. This would be a long night.

Dane was hesitant to knock on his sister's door; it was rare for him to visit her room. It didn't help that he knew she would be occupied with her packing.

When he did push himself to knock and was let in upon Beauty's short welcome, Dane got straight to the point.

"Why are you moving out so soon?"

"Dane, you knew this was going to happen." Beauty responded quietly, continuing to place items into boxes. Her face, like every face in his family, was blank and lifeless.

"You've wanted to do this, sure, but you were never going to; you're as bound to the tradition as the rest of us."

Dane stood next to her, and she was suddenly occupied with some unpacked belongings behind her.

"Well maybe I needed an extra push."

"What has pushed you to leave, Beauty?"

Dane could hear Beauty's breath hitch across the room. He watched her as she continued to appear busy. But then her body stiffened, and she set down whatever was in her hands. She slowly lowered herself to the ground. A delicate hand passed over her mouth as she tried to choke down a sob. Dane was stunned at the sight of seeing his older sister cry. He didn't like it one bit. Beauty never forfeited her control.

As much as Dane wanted to comfort his sister, he didn't know how he could. He was rooted to the foot of Beauty's bed, rubbing his thighs awkwardly. Had he been hugged or comforted more by his parents, Dane might have been able to put his arm around his sister. But even at a time like this, physical comfort was too unfamiliar.

Beauty stood up and moved to sit beside Dane on her bed. She sat there, tensed up, still trying to hold in an inevitable breakdown while tears were streaming down her face.

"The hope I used to have," she began with a trembling voice, "has come to an end. I'm sure of it." She struggled to breathe through sobs, but she was losing. "I can't take it anymore, Dane. I'm not wanted here. I never was. It's better this way, I think."

Dane looked at her, and Beauty met his understanding eyes. "Maybe you're right," he replied gently. "Maybe this is what you need to be yourself again."

Beauty scoffed at him between sobs. "There's nothing left for me, Dane. Moving will just make life a little less unbearable."

"Beauty, there's more to life than the messed-up world we were raised in. If I didn't believe that, I would've ended it all a whole lot sooner."

"I know that," she nearly shouted. "I knew what it was like and now it's gone. It's really gone. It's gone!"

"Beauty," Dane said softly. Beauty was in complete hysterics, bent over and balling the ends of her dark dress with clenched fists. She sounded strangled with the intensity of her tears. Dane's eyes widened with fear and concern. He took his shaking sister by her shoulders and held her in his arms. He stared ahead at her room, with all its boxes and its lack of good memories while Beauty cried into his shirt. He didn't ask again.

Just overnight, snow fell again, covering almost every bit of color God created, leaving a magnificent scene of pure white.

Jessica was sicker than she expected and was sentenced to bed rest by her mother.

Kelly and Jason stepped outside to icy wind blowing mercilessly at their faces, though they were covered generously in winter coats and scarves. Reluctantly, they made their way down the driveway to their bus stop up the street. Today was one of the days Joey would've driven them to school, but he'd forgotten, being tied up in wedding preparations. So instead they were walking and waiting for the bus in this weather.

Kelly was shivering, fighting with her protesting body as she tried to keep up with Jason. They could have been in a heated car by now — Joey's heated car or even their mom's if she had known Joey would forget; instead she was off running errands with Lisa. But now they had a grueling ten or fifteen minutes to wait for the bus to arrive. And just a little more snow overnight would've been enough for a snow day, but the two of them weren't fortunate enough for such things.

Not even off the driveway, Kelly felt like throwing in the towel. Her short brown hair blew across her face as she looked up at the sky, watching the falling flakes of snow, pleading to them for some sort of miracle.

She stayed there until the low roar of a black Lexus sedan pulled up in front of her at the edge of her own driveway. It was odd, what had just happened, like her thoughts had just been read, because as the window of the backseat rolled down, warm air poured out at Kelly's face, teasing her. She wanted more of it. The voice that followed was almost heroic.

"You guys want a ride?" Dane asked, except "guys" wasn't the right word. Jason was already off the street. With his hands shoved deep in the pockets of his red winter coat, he hiked up his backpack and walked faster.

Kelly had never been so happy to see Dane before. She quickly pulled down the thick scarf covering her mouth. "Yes," she blurted breathlessly.

"No," Jason shouted down the street immediately after, like a contradictory echo. He looked at Kelly incredulously. "Kelly, what are you doing?"

"I'd rather ride with him than be uncomfortable from this weather," Kelly said, watching Jason stalk back to the driveway. Dane's chauffeur looked calmly yet cautiously at the approaching young man.

"Young sir, would you please consider . . ."

"It's alright, Mason. He wouldn't dare do anything stupid," Dane murmured confidently, obviously amused.

"I would rather die by any means than ride in the same car as him," Jason shot back and began to tug his twin sister around the automobile and away from it.

"Suit yourself," Kelly began, forcing her release from his grasp and heading back toward the door. She felt bad for his aghast expression because she knew what he was thinking.

"Kelly, you are not riding with him! Have you forgotten all the years of your life up until now?" the voice that came out of him was strangled with anger and disbelief. Kelly shrugged.

"I don't want to freeze, Jason. Besides, our bus's heater sucks," she said, ignoring the stern warning on her brother's face. She waved at him before getting in the car. "I'll see you in school."

Jason's eyes darted past her and into Dane's, but his glare was broken after the power windows rolled up, revealing nothing but their thick black tint. The car sped away, leaving Jason no time to kick hard at the back bumper of the expensive car.

Kelly's eyes lowered as she embraced the warmth surrounding her, though they immediately shot open as she realized what she had just done. Her face was drained of all color, looking full of regret. Dane easily picked up on what she was thinking about.

"He'll get over it," Dane said in a low voice. Kelly just looked out the window.

"You don't know my brother," Kelly said sharply, looking at him now with frighteningly serious eyes.

"That's true," he agreed. She looked silently at him, and Dane looked back at her. Her eyes showed the wonderment of what he must've been thinking. Neither of them said a word, allowing silence time to settle in. Kelly's mind singled out one particular question that had been boring itself deeply inside. "Who were the ones making sure my life was perfect?" Kelly couldn't find the words to ask it out loud. The ride was already awkward for her; she didn't want to rehash their last fight. She would need to ask him in more neutral territory. Then there were questions about Moore she could ask, but she didn't feel there was enough foundation established for her to pry.

"Have you ever wondered about other cultures or religions?" Dane asked.

"Um, no, not really." Kelly straightened in her seat, turning her head back toward Dane. "Have you?"

"Not so much in the past. I've always been taught other cultures were inferior to the Aponlean race and other religions were out of the question."

"Did your hospital stay change your mind on that?" Kelly was excited to have a glimpse into the result of his traumatizing experience.

"Yeah," Dane said, as if that would be his only answer. They were back to square one: silence. It didn't last as long as the last time, as Dane began again, "Can I show you something?"

"Uh, sure," Kelly responded. She watched as he picked up his backpack and dug through the front pocket to pull out a little book. He handed it to her. The words *Holy Bible* were inscribed on it in gold. Kelly looked up at Dane with confusion. "Are you a Christian now?"

"No," he answered. "But open to the second page." She scrolled through and saw his name written out and then the date January 14, 1999. That was nearly five weeks ago. Dane would've been in the hospital. Was this the answer she was looking for? Did this have to do with his change in attitude? "I didn't write that."

"Who did?" Kelly asked.

"I don't know," Dane answered, permitting another brief pause. "It was left on my bedside when I woke up from the coma. The hospital had no records of any visitors. None of my nurses had seen anyone come by. I've been trying to figure it out."

"That's strange," Kelly said. "And your family didn't see anyone?"

"I had no records of any visitors," Dane said in a more bitter tone. Had his family not come to see him once in the three weeks? Kelly didn't feel comfortable with replying to that. "Have you read it?"

"No, I've been too afraid to. I've even been afraid to keep it in the house. I've kept it in the maids' house."

"Afraid of Radehveh?" Kelly asked.

"Somewhat, but more so . . ." Dane stopped. "Some other people in my household."

"Moore?" Kelly pressed. Dane didn't respond; instead he readied himself to exit the vehicle. They had arrived at their school.

Chapter Six

Kelly loaded the books she didn't need for her next class into her locker, lightening her load. Sighing heavily, she closed the locker door only to find Jason in front of her, eagerly awaiting her full attention.

"What is it, Jason?" she asked, even though she knew what he was getting at. She could see it in his face.

"I want you to stop talking to Dane."

"Alright?" she said slowly, trailing off.

"I'm serious. I don't want to see him hurt you anymore." Kelly felt he was overreacting, as they hadn't talked more than a handful of times.

"Believe it or not, I do care about you, Kelly."

Kelly's attitude softened, though annoyance could still be traced in her voice. "Jason, look. The only time I ever talk to him is in the one class I have with him . . ."

"Which is now," Jason finished her sentence, looking her straight in the eye. He wasn't playing around, and Kelly knew it, but she felt brave enough.

"Why, yes, actually it is, and you're going to make me late for it, by the way," she told him with a slight smirk on her face. Jason fumed.

"You're lucky I didn't tell Mom about you riding to school with him yesterday," he growled through gritted teeth. Kelly shrugged with a straight face.

"It's not like I've been hanging out with him outside of school or anything, so I really don't think you should be worrying,"

"Kelly, your talking to him period is already ab-

65

normal enough. And you think I should just go with the flow of things and watch?"

Kelly looked around. Fortunately, Jason's voice hadn't risen to its full potential, and no one turned to see what was going on between the two siblings.

"You honestly believe he's changed?" he asked. His voice was softer, but uneven and strained. Kelly looked down, pressing her lips together, because she knew that what she was doing was dangerous, and she was messing with her own brother's head.

"I don't know, Jason," she started quietly. "But it is not like I am trying to be his best friend or anything. Sometimes — not all the time — we briefly chat in class. I rode with him one time, yesterday, so you are hugely overreacting."

"You forget, I am also your twin and I know you. You may use his sudden behavior shift with a plan, either to get back at him or to satisfy your curiosity about the Morris estate," Jason suggested. He did know her well.

"I appreciate your concern, baby brother, but I really must be getting to class." Kelly quickly dashed off to avoid further arguing. She knew Jason would be fuming at her blowing him off, and adding the baby brother comment on top of it all didn't help. She did need to get to class, though.

She ignored Jason's last statement, even though she'd heard it loud and clear. In the back of her mind that was exactly what she was planning on doing. She hadn't thought about it in depth, but it was a strong desire she had. The intrigue of Moore was driving all her actions at this point.

As they did every day, Kelly's eyes trailed away from Dane, heading straight to the seat she'd been unfortunate to end up in for weeks now. She unwillingly sat down, seconds away from another lecture.

"Tough day?" Kelly should have expected the voice by now; Dane had been quite observant lately. He started to find things to say when she walked in. Sometimes she wished he'd go back to talking to his followers, like Cyrus. Kelly shook her head slowly when she looked at him.

"It's just Jason," she said, pulling out a notebook and a pen from her backpack. "He can be so frustrating sometimes."

"I can understand sibling issues," he said, chuckling lightly.

"That's right." Venting that felt good, and Kelly was joining him before anything registered. Dane and Jason never got along. Though Jason had the typical stubbornness of a brother, he was still very protective of her. He had had to take care of his sister a few times after she was in utter tears at something Dane had done.

Their teacher interrupted both of them, silencing them. Kelly fumbled for her pen and flipped through her notebook until there was an empty page, posing as if she was now prepared to take notes. Dane immediately apologized and opened his book. Kelly was embarrassed, but she still managed to share an amused look with Dane when their teacher's back was toward them.

She looked past his smile and straight to the small bruise above his eye; she didn't remember it being there yesterday. To stay on the safe side, she decided to pay attention for once, taking real notes, and asking relevant questions that pleased the teacher. Luckily for her, half of the period was dedicated to a group lesson that day, so Kelly conveniently teamed up with Dane.

"What's that from?" she asked when they had connected desks to work together. At first, Dane was confused, but when her eyes floated above the right of his forehead, he understood.

"Oh, this?" he said, pointing at the bruise incredulously. "It's just a battle wound."

"Battle wound, huh? From who?" Kelly asked, holding in her laughter. Dane was concentrating on their answer sheet. It was for the chapter review that Wednesday; he was already a good quarter through the whole thing while others were noisily flipping through their books for answers.

"Cyrus." It wasn't a mumble of shame. In fact, Kelly was certain his tone was quite triumphant.

"Well, what happened? Aren't you two best friends?"

"We were," Dane said casually, "before the accident, but since I've been back, our interests only clash now."

"So he hit you over a disagreement," Kelly guessed, and Dane stopped his steady writing to laugh.

"I don't know. I mean, Cyrus and I had a strange relationship to begin with. Before, our amusement was only in others' discomfort—wait, maybe I'm being too subtle. It was more like, we took pleasure in the agony of others, whether it was mental, physical, or both," he paused to look up at Kelly with softened eyes. They were almost apologetic. "As you well know, I wasn't fun to be around," he chuckled nervously to relieve the dark tension between them, Kelly thinking back on past memories of the unforgettable things he'd done to her. Dane went back to the chapter review in front of him.

"We didn't hang out or talk much, anyway," Dane continued after a short while. "All we did was devise schemes and play them out on people, promising to have each other's' backs in the process. Since I don't have an interest in that anymore—and it disgusts me to know that I once did—I started acting in defense of a few students he was foolishly picking on. Cyrus, being the violent and rage-driven guy that he is, wanted to shut me up for getting in the way and not being on his side. So, when he had the time, he sneaked up on me in between classes and threw a punch at me, but just once,"

"Only once?" Kelly asked eagerly.

"Of course. I took over from there," he answered quite calmly. "Should I have let him think he could get away with it, start up a whole new daily routine for him? I wasn't going to accept what he did and walk away from it without teaching him something, even if that meant literally knocking sense into him." Kelly was astonished. She couldn't find anything to correct him with because the action he chose didn't sound wrong. She hated Cyrus anyway, so she was pretty satisfied with what he'd said.

"Is that why he isn't here?"

Dane nodded.

"Imagine coming to school looking worse than your victims usually do. No one will take him seriously anymore, and I hope it shows him something," he said thoughtfully. Dane's demeanor suddenly changed. "Hey, Kelly. I wanted to apologize for all the stupid pranks and tormenting over the years. I shouldn't have treated you or any other students that way."

"Oh." Kelly didn't know how to respond. She wasn't quite ready to forgive him. He was right—it was all still so fresh. If Moore weren't in the equation, she wasn't so sure she would be talking to him all this time.

Kelly grabbed her pen and doodled on a blank sheet of paper. "Dane, why don't you and Moore get along?" It was almost like she was testing him.

Dane stirred in his seat. Kelly remembered this was a hot topic for him. She needed to know why Moore was off limits. She needed to know more about him. Her infatuation with him was becoming unbearable.

Kelly saw him stiffen, just as she'd seen him do the last time she brought up Moore. When he didn't reply but continued with the review sheet, answering the questions with ease, Kelly sat back in her chair, certain it was a subject she wouldn't break him on.

"You really want to know?" Dane asked after everyone else was starting to prepare for class to be over. They were still seated together, desks connected. Kelly had drawn a full-page maze on her once-blank sheet of paper—something she and Michelle did whenever they were bored and in class together. Dane had already turned in their review sheet, while most of the other students had to finish it for homework. It had been silent between her and Dane for that long.

"Yes, I do. I'm curious, but if you don't want to talk about it . . . "

She trailed off, standing to move her desk back to its appropriate spot. Dane was gathering his books.

"Why don't you come over today? We can talk then," he said with an even voice. Kelly definitely wasn't expecting that. Excitement swept over her at the thought of being inside his palace, but she was also hesitant about being in it with him. He was already frighteningly unreadable; it was dangerous. Unsure of what to say, she weighed the pros and cons, deciding she'd ask Michelle to come with her so it wouldn't be so awkward. How she was going to make that happen she wasn't so sure.

"I guess I can do that. My mom will be coming home late today anyways," Kelly reasoned.

"I remembered you telling me that. She's helping your brother and his fiancée fill out the last of their wedding invitations, right?" Dane asked. Kelly nodded. He was a great listener.

"Do you mind if Michelle comes, so I can get around Jason's questioning?" Kelly asked, adding the Jason bit off the top of her heard.

"Uh, yeah, I guess that's a good idea," he said. The bell rang seconds later, startling Kelly enough to make her jump a little in her seat. Hurriedly, she got up and slung her backpack over her shoulder, feeling strange. She was invited to visit Dane's house. She wondered what she had just agreed to. She left the classroom, looking back only to exchange quick glances with Dane before disappearing out of the classroom without a word.

This was almost unreal. She had waited almost her entire life for this moment. To set foot in such a forbidden place was so thrilling. She could feel how wrong it was, but that only made her want it more. What if she finally had that conversation with Moore? Maybe it would play out how she'd always imagined it. How on earth was she going to convince Michelle?

Kelly spotted Michelle in the hall after sixth period and ran up to meet her. Michelle brightened at the sight of her friend. Kelly gripped Michelle's shoulders with pleading eyes, and Michelle's lips poked out in an exaggerated frown. She knew the expression all too well.

"What is it this time, Kelly? I hope we're not breaking into Jason's locker again. I don't want to find any more moldy leftovers hidden under his messy pile of books."

"No, no, no, it's not that," Kelly corrected breathlessly.

"Good. Hey, speaking of Jason, I've been meaning to talk to you about something."

"Oh, well, me too, but you go first," Kelly said, wondering why Michelle sounded so serious all of a sudden.

"Jason and I were talking earlier, and what he was saying makes a lot of sense. He now has me convinced that you talking to Dane isn't a good move at all." Kelly stared with unbelieving eyes at her best friend, blinking slowly with a deadpan expression. This was absolutely the last thing she wanted Michelle to be saying. She wanted to laugh hysterically at her luck.

"I totally agree with you," Kelly lied, and Michelle, not seeing it, was pleased to have the disagreement avoided.

"You do?" she asked anyway, unsure her ears had heard right.

"Yes," Kelly replied, sighing, smiling wearily at Michelle. "Which is why I'll be ending these games as soon as possible," Michelle gave her a wary look.

"What's going on?" she said slowly, her fingers touching Kelly's arm. Kelly sighed. Michelle read people way too well. "The Kelly I know cannot be so easily convinced when driven by curiosity," she stated, smirking playfully at her friend.

"Michelle, you're my best friend and I value what you say to me. In fact, you could actually be able to help me end this little affair quicker," Kelly said, her mind concocting things to say as she went. Anything to succeed in getting Michelle to come with her. Michelle narrowed her eyes.

"There's a catch. What is it?" she demanded, face expressionless, lips parted with anticipation.

"Come with me to his house after school today, and I'll end it there," Kelly said quickly. When Michelle didn't move, Kelly knew her reaction wasn't going to be a good one.

"You're out of you mind, Kelly. He invited you over?" she choked out, eyes wide.

"Yes."

"And you're actually considering going?"

"I already did that, yes. And I'm going."

"You expect me, a Peterson, to partake in this insanity?"

"Michelle, I've taken your advice. The least you could do for me is help out," Kelly said softly, inching closer to Michelle, who was backing away a little.

"Kelly Nicole Johnson, this doesn't even compare to my little bit of advice, and you know it. I don't want to be involved with this madness. Period." Michelle's voice was shaking audibly. Kelly knew she'd gone too far to begin with, but it was worth another try.

"Michelle," she started gently, pleadingly. "I really need you to do this for me. I have to be able to tell Jason that I'm riding with you."

"I can't. I won't. It would go against everything I was ever taught, growing up a Peterson—against everything you were ever taught growing up a Johnson, Kelly."

"I know," Kelly whispered, and her mind was already conflicted by those words about herself and Dane. She was going against everything. Michelle didn't have to remind her. "But I've always wanted to know what it was like to be inside of his house — ever since I was little, Michelle. This is the only time I've ever actually been invited to see inside it, and my Mom will be out long enough for me to accept. I promise you, if you come to his house with me, I'll do everything in my power to never communicate with Dane Morris again." Kelly believed that statement to be true. She'd know all she wanted to know about him, his house, and his brother. Once that was revealed to her, she would end their "friendship."

"I'm sorry, Kelly, but I'm not setting foot inside his house," Michelle said firmly. She had her mind set, and Kelly looked down at her feet in defeat, until she had a sudden reviving thought.

"What if he gives you a ride home after he picks us up from school. That way I'll still be riding with you, and you wouldn't have to go to his house." she said animatedly. It had to work. She had to say yes to that. But she didn't answer for a while. She lingered on the suggestion while looking at Kelly. Kelly's face showed nothing but desperation as she returned Michelle's uncertain stare.

"Michelle," she pleaded softly.

"Fine, I'll do it. But don't expect me to say anything to him. If you get caught, you better not drag me down with you," she rambled. Kelly nearly tackled Michelle with an excited hug.

"Of course, I'd never do that to you," Kelly said, squeezing her. Michelle patted her back absently.

"You owe me big time, girl."

"Anything," Kelly said quickly with a huge smile on her face. "Thank you so much, Michelle. You know I love you, right? You have no idea how much . . ."

"Yeah, yeah," Michelle said, loosening herself from Kelly's embrace. Her brown eyes were sorrowful. "Please don't flatter me. This is against everything I believe."

Kelly looked down, biting the inside of her bottom lip.

"I don't want to make you . . ."

"If it'll stop this whole thing between you and Dane, I'll force myself to be fine with it," Michelle said, then insisted they head to their last class, not wanting to speak any further on the matter. Kelly kept silent, not wanting to ruin the agreement that

Chapter Seven

Dane was leading Kelly and Michelle to his car. Mason, his chauffeur, stood beside the closed door of the backseat, waiting for them at the school's round-about entrance. Michelle clutched the thick sleeve of Kelly's winter coat tighter, almost hiding with embarrassment. Kelly ignored her antsy behavior.

"Do you think Jason believed us?" Kelly whispered to Michelle as they got closer to the black Lexus.

"Yeah, I'm pretty sure he did. I could see the relief in his eyes when I let him know the whole situation with Dane was over," she said, then exhaled with disgust. "I feel so dishonest," she muttered.

"That's good. Now, hopefully, I won't have to be hounded by him when I get home," Kelly said, slightly relieved. They reached the entrance, and Dane waved the chauffeur off when he made to open the front passenger door for him. Instead, Dane opened the backseat door for Kelly and Michelle, gesturing for them to get in with a genuine smile on his face. The two girls exchanged looks before getting in. Dane got the door for himself in the front seat, and Mason rounded the car, back to the driver's seat. Dane twisted his body to face the backseat, smiling subtly at Michelle.

"Hello, Michelle," he welcomed softly. Michelle's lips were tight and straight. They twitched into somewhat of a returning smile, but she looked out the window a few seconds later, acting disinterested. When Dane took the hint and twisted back to the front, Michelle leaned to Kelly's ear.

"I thought we agreed that I wasn't going to be

talking to him," she whispered, more like hissed, to Kelly.

"I'm sorry. I didn't know he would even acknowledge you," she whispered back. They were on the road now, headed across town to Michelle's house. Kelly wasn't sure whether she should strike up a conversation with Dane or Michelle, or neither. Maybe it was best to let it be a silent ride. She hated the awkwardness but felt that talking to just one of them, excluding the other, would only make matters worse.

Kelly felt the car stop, close to dozing, but when Michelle nudged her, she opened her eyes and sat up, looking around. They had arrived at the front of her house.

"I'll call you in an hour," Michelle told her, her eyes set and serious. "You should be home by then, right?" She glared up at the rearview mirror, where Dane was looking, giving him a warning.

"We'll see," Kelly said softly, smiling. "I'll see you tomorrow." The car drove off when Michelle made it to the door and Kelly watched as her mother let her in, catching a glimpse of the Lexus with a wary expression. Kelly hoped she wouldn't question Michelle about it.

"That was unusual," Dane said, breaking the silence in the car, referring to Michelle's glares at him and secretive whispers to Kelly. Kelly smiled tightly.

"Yeah, sorry about that."

Dane just shrugged and twisted back in his seat, not bothering to start up anything while they rode comfortably in the luxury car. When they pulled into their neighborhood, Kelly inched closer to the window. They reached the gate and Mason peaked his head out of his rolled-down window to put in the security code. The gates opened and Kelly watched in awe as the car pulled into the large, stone-cobbled driveway she'd seen Moore pull up on. His car was parked in the loop and the Lexus sedan pulled up right in front of the doors, parallel to Moore's car. Kelly couldn't take her eyes off of it at first.

The green lawn stretched around the massive house, with luscious trees and flower bushes aligned neatly and artistically in the right places around the home. Kelly gasped when she caught sight of the house, and Dane tried hard to hold back a smile.

The exterior walls were of pale, aging stone, and tiny vines had grown in between the crevices, adding character to the house. Kelly noticed the shadows that loomed there, though, which gave off a weird feeling, but she was overwhelmed and amazed at the overall effect.

Dane opened the door for Kelly when he got out of the car, and Kelly was still staring at the house, lips parted, frozen in an expression of wonder. This was it. All those years staring from her balcony, longing for this moment. Dane cleared his throat to remind her of his presence, and Kelly's glazed-over eyes flicked to his at once, breaking out of her trance.

"You coming?" he said, amused. Kelly quickly grabbed her backpack and got out of the car, walking around it and up the stairs that led to the entrance. Dane hurried to catch up with her while Mason left to park the car in the five-car garage hidden farther down the driveway.

Two pale marble pillars stood before the main entrance, reaching as high as the second story of the home, connecting with the decorative roof above it. Kelly ran her fingers over one of them while Dane opened the door slightly, slipping his frame through its crack and signaling Kelly to wait a moment. When he saw the coast was clear, he opened the door for her. She stepped inside, her boots emitting a resounding echo the moment they landed on the shiny marble floors.

"Wow," she breathed, whispering. "This place is beautiful." The foyer was an expanse all on its own, with its ceiling and walls matching the almost golden marble of the floors. Two rich staircases facing opposite of each other were decorated with fresh greenery. The plants must have been tended to daily to look so green and healthy.

"The house is my mother's canvas. She's constantly refurbishing it. And when she's not doing that, she's planting in the garden, ordering new arrangements, or planning new themes for the coming seasons. It's pretty annoying," he explained in a hushed tone.

"It's pretty rad," Kelly corrected.

"Now, if you see anyone at all, hide, duck behind something," Dane looked around at the amount of space they were in without any objects to hide behind.

"I don't see that working," Kelly said, looking at the same obstacle he was.

He gave her a vague tour of the house, not able to reveal every nook and cranny of it, of course, for it held restricted secrets she wasn't allowed to see. Kelly wanted to just soak it all in, but Dane was on edge the whole time. He thought of the danger she should be wary of. He avoided most rooms and all of the upstairs, eventually leading them down to the recreation room.

"In here will be safe," Dane started. "No one in my family has time for fun."

"That sounds about right," Kelly joked.

"Would you like something to drink? A snack, maybe?" he offered. Kelly waved it off. She seemed too distracted by her surroundings.

"You don't happen to have lemonade, do you?"

"Yes, actually. That mini fridge over there has water, soda, and lemonade," Dane said, pointing to a small refrigerator.

"Why is that fridge stocked?"

"My mom has the maids make sure each fridge in the house is stocked, rotating out all the food and drinks."

"Oh, great." Everything was just so foreign to Kelly here. It was the polar opposite of her house.

"Dane!" An echo rang down the hall. Dane's eyes widened. The voice didn't seem near, but it would be if he didn't act fast.

"Can you wait in here and just don't do anything till I get back? I mean, you can watch TV or play a game, but do not leave this room."

"Yeah, sure," Kelly said.

"Okay, I'll be back." He left the room. When he was midway down the east hall he called out. "Coming, sir."

"In the main office," his father called out.

◆———◆———◆

As soon as Dane was out of the room, Kelly made her way out of the room, peering out first to make sure the coast was clear and watching where Dane went. She made her way down the hall, not entirely sure where she had gotten the nerve. The danger of it all was driving her every move.

She was soon right outside of the office Dane had entered. Earlier he had gestured to this area, but hadn't taken her to it. Kelly could hear voices from inside. She inched closer, pressing her ear to the door.

"Yes, sir?" Dane asked.

"Nadia called. The Schernol's in Puerto Rico. The exact location isn't pinpointed yet, but it should be within the next three weeks," Mr. Morris informed his son. "Moore and I will be going alone, so that you don't miss any school. We'll be staying with some of our Puerto Rican relatives."

"Okay, sir."

"I wanted you to know, since we will probably leave abruptly as soon as the final information comes in."

"Is that all, sir?" Dane asked, and Kelly realized she had a long distance to get back to the rec room. She wasted no time, scurrying back down the hall and into the room. What on earth was she just thinking? Her heart was pounding to the point of discomfort. She quickly sat on the couch, turning the TV on.

Dane entered barely a second after she had turned on the TV. Kelly's eyes didn't move from the screen

78

as her heart continued to race. She hadn't fooled him.

"Did you . . ." Kelly turned her head toward Dane as he spoke. "Leave the room?"

"No, my show comes on at this time," Kelly answered, keeping her eyes on the TV. Dane sat down beside her. She managed to keep her voice even, but couldn't keep her heart from pounding out of control. She had followed him out there and heard the brief exchange.

"Did you still want that lemonade?" Dane asked.

"Oh, yeah," Kelly said and jumped at her opportunity to move away from Dane. She knew she hadn't fooled him. She grabbed a glass bottle of lemonade from the fridge and returned to the couch. "My favorite," she said sheepishly.

Dane had his head in his hands, looking straight down at his shoes, and Kelly took a seat beside him. She saw that he was tense. He knew. Dane looked up at Kelly eventually, dark eyes wary. "You have no idea what you're getting yourself into." Kelly didn't respond. "Do you know what could've happened if they caught you?"

"What are you talking about?" Kelly asked, not knowing why she was still trying to hide what was so obvious.

"Look, if you are going to be over here, you need to respect some things. Eavesdropping on anything to do with my father or brother is putting your life in danger."

"Got it. Sorry," Kelly said with no conviction.

What happened to her lying skills? She could lie easily to Jason, but not Dane. Maybe she wanted him to know. Her heart was still pounding. She had to fight hard to keep her hand from shaking. What was she thinking when she followed him down the hall, listening to a conversation she knew she shouldn't have? What was up with her these days? She was acting irrationally. But she had to do something to stop this longing that had sprouted. Now that she was in the house, she needed more than ever to see Moore in person.

"Kelly," Dane looked her square in the eyes. "You don't know my family." Kelly listened, waiting for him to go on, but it seemed he was done. What was he going to say? What about his family? Give me details of the things they did. Maybe then I'll stop, Kelly thought.

"Dane," Kelly began and found herself pausing longer than usual. The rest of the question was burning to be released, but she waited for an approval.

"Yes?" Dane asked.

"The last time we talked before your hospital stay, you said something about 'They' would make sure I had a perfect ending. Who are 'they'?" Kelly asked.

"They?" Dane had a bewildered face. "Um, I don't know. I don't remember some of the things leading up to my health scare."

"But you have to remember if there are some people looking out for me. If you knew anything about them, you would've known before that talk."

"Maybe I was getting ready to play a new trick on you. Make you think up some crazy conspiracy." Kelly searched Dane's eyes as he said that. It would make sense, but it didn't satisfy her. She wanted to believe those words. She tried to sense any deception, but she wasn't one for reading poker faces, especially that of a Morr. She wanted to press him more but held back. There were plenty of other things she was curious about.

"What's a Schernol?" Kelly's head turned to face Dane. Dane wasn't expecting that question.

"You mean you don't know?"

"No," Kelly shrugged, genuinely clueless.

"The Schernol are the shields the twenty men fought with in the Aponlean Civil War," Dane answered.

"Oh." Kelly's mind raced with a million questions; she tried to slow down to figure out which one to ask next. "Who were the twenty, exactly?"

"You do know you are a descendant of one of the

twenty men, right?" He was in more shock than after her first question.

"Well, I know they are our ancestors, but not much beyond that," Kelly answered with eager eyes, begging him to start teaching her.

"I thought all descendants would know, especially a Johnson," he said, still awestruck.

"No," she answered. She was getting annoyed. Couldn't he just answer already?

"The twenty were twenty men exiled from Aponlea, a mystical realm . . ."

"Mystical realm?" Kelly said, pretending to scoff, but inwardly wanting it to be true more than ever. "Sounds a bit . . . ," she trailed off.

"Hey, I don't know how much of it is true. I'm just telling you what I've been taught. Anyway, the twenty men are who we descended from. Me from Morr, you from John, then there's Michelle, Peter . . ."

"Why are we enemies? What's the reason?" Kelly interrupted.

"I'm sure your family will tell you differently than mine, but I was taught that Morr was next in line to be king, and John stole that from him. Long story short, Morr fought with nine great warriors and John fought with his own. The fights became destructive, too destructive, and Radehveh kicked them out. So to this day, the Morrises, who came from the bloodline of Morr, only associate with other families that come from one of the nine warriors who fought by his side." he explained.

"Why only nine each?"

"Because there are only twenty Schernols. Morr recovered ten, John recovered ten."

"Right, the shields. What's so special about them?" Kelly asked. She felt like a child just learning how to speak and wanting to know everything.

"They're magic shields. Whoever possessed them had more power than a typical Aponlean. If you possess all of them and put them together, you make one powerful shield called the Prostasia. This shield, of course, is much bigger than a Schernol and gives you power to do about anything; therefore if you possessed it you'd rule the kingdom," he finished. Kelly lit up a little, they had mentioned the Schernol in the office. It was the first time she had learned about the Schernols.

"Why don't we have powers now?" Kelly asked.

"I'm starting to wonder if it is a myth derived from true events." In that moment Dane's eyes looked as eager as Kelly's to know.

"What does your family say?"

"They say that once they were removed from the mystical realm all powers muted, and only when all the Schernols are recovered and the Prostasia is made will the doors of Aponlea once again open. Then all descendants will be allowed back in," Dane explained. "Once inside Aponlea, we will have powers again."

"You forgot to mention that the one to do that has to be from the bloodline of Morr," a smooth voice from behind Dane said. Kelly couldn't see the speaker so she whipped her head in his direction, in the direction of the door. She froze in her seat. It was Moore. He laid his dark eyes on her. Her own eyes widened involuntarily with a combination of fear and delight. This was the moment she was waiting for. Moore was here in front of her, speaking, and she was paralyzed.

"Hello, Kelly," Moore said, breaking the silence that ensued for too long, and his gaze hadn't left hers during that time. He knew her name. Maybe he remembered their exchange as children. Kelly forced herself to respond.

"Hi," she choked out in barely a whisper. What was wrong with her? She was going to kick herself later. This was not how she had planned it in her head numerous times.

"Giving her a history lesson, are you?" Moore said to Dane. He had made his way in front of the two and sat in the lounge chair beside them, his eyes still on Kelly, boring into hers. Kelly couldn't take her eyes off of his, and she hated it. She felt as if he

82

were somehow mystically locking her gaze with his.

"Just a brief rundown," Dane replied brusquely. "Is there something you wanted?"

Moore looked utterly amused. "Well," he drawled, lingering. "I thought I heard you talking, and I wanted to make sure you weren't losing it." A corner of his lips tugged into a half smile. Kelly looked down. She couldn't bare it anymore. She could see Dane from the corner of her eye. He was getting irritated.

"Thanks for your sudden and insincere concern, but I am not crazy. I am visiting with a friend, so you can go about your business now," Dane growled.

"By 'friend,' you mean a Johnson," he responded, looking to Dane briefly. Fear struck Kelly; the repercussions of her being there seized her mind. She wasn't allowed over there by either end. Looking back up at Moore, his look was unreadable. He didn't seem to be angry or threatening as he should be. "Sorry, Kelly, it's just as an unwritten rule that we don't normally allow descendants of John over. There's sort of been this rivalry spanning centuries between our families. We don't want our secrets getting out, now do we?"

"I can leave, if . . . if you want me to?" Kelly stumbled over her words.

"No, it's alright. I can keep a secret," Moore said. "I have nothing planned for the rest of the day. I'm all yours if you have any questions," he said. Kelly's heart rose. This was more than she could handle, everything she could have wished for. Someone needed to pinch her, because she had to be dreaming.

"No, she doesn't," Dane spoke up, interrupting Kelly's coming response. She did have lots of questions. She wanted to ask so badly. "I was only giving her a little history lesson."

"So I've heard," Moore said, ever so quietly. He glared at Dane before turning back to Kelly to continue. "I have a collection of books on our history in our library, if you'd like to read any of them. Unfortunately, you can't take any of them home with you, but you're more than welcome to stop by any time.

You may want to call first, not sure how my father would be with you over. Dane, did you give her our number?"

"Yes," Dane answered with annoyance.

"Let me give you my cell phone number. It will be more secure." Moore looked for a piece of paper. Dane nudged Kelly. He looked at her incredulously.

"Well, actually, Dane pretty much answered all my questions," Kelly said, quickly, regretfully. Moore's grin was lopsided, remaining in a moment of silence before standing from the seat.

"That's nice to hear. At least he's good at something," he said, making Kelly let out a nervous laugh. Moore looked at Dane again, bringing fear to his brother that actually showed on his face this time. His eyes were so cold, the most distrustful eyes on the planet.

"I guess I'll leave, then. Kelly," he said, nonchalantly looking back at her when he stopped at the door. No, stay! Kelly thought, wishing her vocals hadn't been seized by fear. "If you're curious about anything that comes to mind, I'll be in my room." he offered in that smooth voice. With another smile, he left the room, leaving Kelly and Dane in silence.

Kelly sank in her seat, feeling giddy and light.

"That was strange," Dane said in a very low voice, and it seemed both he and Kelly were sharing the same thought.

"It was strange to you? He's not always like this?"

"No, he isn't. He was . . . being open with you. He knew you had listened in, I know it, but he didn't lash out at you," he said, ending with a shuddered breath. Kelly tapped at the glass bottle of her barely touched lemonade. She was replaying the whole scene, making sure it was secure in her memory.

"Oh . . . that is strange. He doesn't even know me."

"Yeah," Dane's confusion was evident on his face. "He keeps secrets from even my father. But he willingly offered to answer any of your questions."

"Right, so what was wrong with me getting his

number, in case I do have these questions?" Kelly asked.

"Well, remember earlier I said you don't know my family. I would like to reiterate that. They don't play by the rules. There's a lot of stuff and people they are involved with, and getting involved in their affairs is putting your life in danger. And they don't let things go away. For example, some guy took something from us almost seventeen years ago, and even though they took out his wife and all that time has passed, they haven't given up on their search for him."

Kelly was beginning to feel she knew too much already. The fear that had caused excitement all this time was starting to cause uneasiness. But she knew she could never unlearn what she had learned today. It only made her want to know more. Aponlea had become interesting to her, and she was suddenly very patriotic.

"Dane, why are you telling me this, and why did you invite me over here?" Kelly asked.

"I don't know," Dane admitted. "I don't really have any friends at the moment. I kind of spent my early high school career making sure of that. And sometimes you just need someone to talk to."

Did he call her a friend, or was he saying he wanted to be friends with her? Did he not realize the complications of such a friendship? Although she had been encouraging it all this time. She had felt for him the day she rode in his car. This was all just messing with her head. Did she even know if she could trust him at this point? It had only been a few weeks.

"Oh, well, do you actually think that we can be friends? I mean given our circumstances?" Kelly asked.

"Well, why did you come over today?" Dane asked.

"I wanted to see your house," Kelly answered bluntly. She felt almost too bluntly. She felt ashamed of her answer. "I don't mean to sound harsh, it's just hard to view a friendship happening, given our history."

"We can grow from our history to create a better

future. I'm a different person, and I never want to go back to who I was. And I think that being friends with you can help me achieve that."

"How?"

"Because when I am around you I see that there's a better life than what I grew up in." Dane adjusted his posture and looked in Kelly's eyes. "You've been so curious about my home life and family and have idealized it for reasons beyond me, but I have always looked at your family with the same intrigue. I see laughter and light over there. You and your siblings joke and are there for each other. I used to wish to spend at least one day as a Johnson." Dane's answer astonished Kelly. Peering over into the Morris estate, she never would have guessed that any of its inhabitants would be looking over into her environment. Her astonishment manifested in muffled laughter. "Ironic, right?" Dane smiled.

"Yeah," she agreed, looking past him. Her thoughts were racing. There was just so much to process and take in. This was not what she had envisioned for her first visit, that's for sure. Dane arose from his seat, placing his hands in the pockets of his khaki uniform pants. He strode the area of the recreation room that held the air hockey and pool tables. Kelly watched him from the couch.

"Kelly, maybe . . ." Dane paused a moment in his speech, but not in his pacing. Kelly's ears were perked, waiting for the conclusion. "What if our friendship is what it takes to start a change for our people?"

Kelly didn't know how to answer that. "But what would be so special about us? I'm just one of many Johnsons, and the same for you from your family," she responded.

"Both of our fathers are the current honored ones of our lines. If that isn't a huge statement, then what is?"

"Listen Dane, I didn't have a near-death experience. I just want to get by in school right now."

"I'm not saying we start a revolution, just a friend-ship."

"That in itself is very risky," Kelly responded. "I have a clean record right now, and I'd like to keep it that way." She was charmed by the idea. She enjoyed being under the radar, having a routine and knowing what to expect to an extent. But every ounce of her being loved the thrill of the unknown. She had played it safe all of her life, but with today's events, she felt she had been missing out on something. The adrena-line of it all was too enticing. She could never fully go back and ignore what she had learned today. "I'll think about it tonight and get back to you tomorrow in fifth period."

"Sounds good to me."

"I should get going now, though." She stood and walked toward the door. Dane quickly caught up to her, opening it for her and leading the way out.

Chapter Eight

Dane came back from walking Kelly out, gazing up at the spacious interior of his home. He had so many unanswered questions. He related to Kelly's eagerness to absorb all the information she had just been given. He just wished there was someone he could rapid-fire his questions at.

His family was always so strong on serving one's purpose in Radehveh's plan that finding his own now seemed a fundamental need. Nearly tasting death had awakened in him such an inner hunger, but he couldn't pinpoint what it was for. Was it for friendship, companionship, truth, or purpose? He didn't know.

The one thing he was sure about in this moment was that something was drawing him toward a friendship with Kelly Johnson. He felt somehow he needed her and that maybe in some way she needed him.

Dane found himself in the kitchen. He was so deep in thought that he had been on autopilot and needed a drink. He took a bottle of water from the fridge and closed it. When he did, he had to do a double take. He had thought Adelina was doing the dishes at the sink, but now it looked to be his mother. And She was washing them by hand instead of the dishwasher.

"Mom, why are you washing the dishes?"

She didn't answer right away, as if she hadn't heard the question. Dane was ready to repeat it or ask another when she finally answered, "It reminds me of my mother." She didn't look at Dane when he asked. She had been avoiding eye contact with him since his return. When she did look at him, her eyes looked beyond him, never directly into his own. "And the life I had before all this." Dane couldn't help but stare at her, trying to will her to look back, so he could see her expression, see her eyes, understand what she meant by that.

"Before all what?" Dane asked.

Mrs. Morris turned around, leaning against the sink, looking off in one of her dazes, looking past Dane again. "Aponlea," she answered. Dane had never stopped to think about how his mother felt about all this. She was not raised in the Aponlean lifestyle, since she was not an actual descendant. When Dane looked up at her eyes, they looked weak and almost tortured. She looked as though someone else was trapped inside of her, begging with her eyes to be free. He had never noticed this about his mother before. He was never taught to give such attention to feelings or the well-being of others. Emotions were something his family tried to move past and beyond; everything was goal-driven. Stay focused and don't let feelings get in the way. Concern for others was demonstrated through Vanni and Adelina and sometimes Beauty.

"Are you okay, mother?"

"I'm sorry, Dane," she looked as if she snapped from her trance. "I haven't taken my medication today. You'll have to excuse me."

"But are you okay, Mom?" Dane asked again, not buying her response. His mother finally faced him. Her eyes didn't appear to have any life in them.

"I'm okay, son." She quickly turned from him as if she were ashamed. She returned to washing the dishes, and after remaining there a little longer, Dane accepted her answer.

When Kelly got back on her property, her dad was pulling up. He was home early, earlier than her mother. He pulled up beside her as she was on the driveway. She waited for him to get out.

"Kelly, what's going on?" Mr. Johnson asked,

placing his arm over his daughter's shoulder.

"Nothing. I just went for a walk to clear my head," Kelly said, not bothering to hide her pensive tone.

"What's the matter, sweetie?" Mr. Johnson asked while opening the front door.

"I'm just overwhelmed. All the wedding plans, hardly having Joey around. Everything's so strange now." Kelly followed her dad in. Everyone was in their rooms except Lisa, who was out with their mom. Kelly followed her dad as he headed to the back of the house, toward his office.

"Yeah, it can be tough. I had a few more siblings than you and remember when things started changing. Even though I was the oldest, I was the one to inherit this house, so I never actually left. I had to watch as each of my younger siblings left, one by one." Mr. Johnson made an unexpected turn as he knocked on Zach's bedroom door. "Come in," Zach called out. Kelly watched her dad as he entered and followed him in. Zach was working on putting together some sort of device — Kelly couldn't tell what. She never could. But when he always finished a project and showed her the result she was astonished every single time.

"Sorry, Kelly, I have to talk with Zach a moment. You can stay if you'd like." Kelly nodded and waited, looking around at his room. He shared it with Lisa, so half of it was full of toys, the other full of technological devices. "What are you working on?"

"Lisa wanted walkie-talkies, so I said I'd make us some."

"I see," Mr. Johnson said. Kelly wanted to laugh: she could see her little sister asking him. "Have you started on the device I gave you?" Zach sighed heavily. He picked up a large metal disc from the back of his desk.

"Yes, well, sort of. I don't know how. It's just a disc and there's nothing to take apart, no data bumps on it. It just seems like a dangerous Frisbee," Zach ranted. Kelly looked at the disc with wonder. She was now curious as to what it was. Zach was right,

90

it wasn't like a TV or VCR that could be taken apart. It didn't have the dimensions of a CD. To the naked eye, it looked like a flat, metal plate.

"Aponlean technology is always seamless. If you can figure that disc out, you've figured out the base of Aponlea's science. You'll have a whole new array of devices you can make, far beyond anything modern science has discovered."

"Dad, it's impossible. There is no way this disc does anything. There's nothing to figure out."

Kelly was so eager to touch it. If it was an Aponlean device, it was hundreds or even thousands of years old — she wasn't sure how old Aponlea was. It didn't look aged at all. Kelly hoped her father would show the two of them what the device did.

"You've got that book on Aponlean I gave you?" Mr. Johnson asked.

"Yes, but linguistics is not my specialty," Zach answered, going to his bookshelf to pull the book down. He held it out to his dad.

"You hold onto that," Mr. Johnson said, cracking a smile. He suddenly seemed like an enthusiastic child. He picked up the disc and held it with two hands in front of him. He jerked it toward himself and then placed it back on the desk. Kelly couldn't believe her eyes. Inscriptions began to appear. Symbols were now inscribed across it. Zach was amazed too and looked at it.

"Those are its instructions. They are in Aponlean, so you'll need to make that a specialty."

Zach stood awestruck.

"Now, I gave you that much, you can figure out the rest. I know you can. You've got a gift, son, and I want you to use it."

"Yes, sir," He said, mouth still agape. He sat down with the book and started reading. Kelly wanted to read it too.

"You ready, Kelly?" Mr. Johnson asked as he began to head out of the room. Kelly ran up beside him.

"Dad, what was that?"

"It's an ancient household appliance that my mother gave me years ago. I want Zach to figure it out, so I won't say what it is exactly. I want each of you to use your gifts for the good of our people."

"What's my gift?" Kelly asked.

"Well, Kelly," Mr. Johnson welcomed her into his office. "You're an inspirer. You have the gift of motivating people. If you're not careful, the dark side of that is manipulation for selfish gain. Focus it on rallying people in unity for the good of Aponlea."

"That's it?" Kelly was hoping for something more tactile. The unity part hit home with her previous conversation that day.

"That's huge, Kelly. Picture Aponleans wandering aimlessly, never accomplishing anything, because they are each going their own way. You can connect their efforts. Once unified, a group of people with one mind can accomplish just about anything. Your gift is very special." Kelly sighed, and Mr. Johnson couldn't help but laugh. "You're not using your gift yet, Kelly. Once you do, you will see the fulfillment you get from it. There's nothing like it."

"I'll take your word for it," Kelly said. It was strange that all her life she hadn't cared much about Aponlea, but with all the recent events, she felt it was very important to learn more about it. "Do you have another Aponlean book?"

"You want to learn the language?"

"Yes. I want to learn everything. Can I ask you some questions about Aponlea?"

"Of course. But right now I have to work on some things. I came home from work early to do so."

"Oh, okay."

Mr. Johnson pulled an Aponlean book out of a desk drawer and handed it to his daughter.

"Here."

"Thank you, Dad."

"You're welcome. Now remember what I told you. There are two ways to use your gift. Remember John and Peter." Kelly nodded and ran to her room with the book, excited. Maybe learning the language would help her figure out some things. For the first time after school she didn't have the urge to head straight to her balcony upon entering her room. She had a decision to make by tomorrow, and she had a little bit of homework to do.

Chapter Nine

Fifth period came in a blink of an eye. Her father's words fell flat when Kelly first heard them yesterday. But as she tried to read the language book, she could only meditate on his words. It was like he was speaking to her situation so accurately and had told her to side with Dane. She may have been reading into them too much, but to receive such a word after the proposition presented to her had to have meant something.

She hadn't given much thought to destiny in the past, but it was now a topic she dwelt on. John and Peter rose to the occasion, and here an occasion was being presented to her. She couldn't just let it pass by.

"Hi Kelly," Dane greeted her once she had taken her seat.

"We can be friends." Kelly didn't like to beat around the bush.

"Okay," was all he said before the bell rang. The two appeared to be focused on the day's lecture, but Kelly knew their minds were far from it. She was thinking all sorts of things. She had just agreed to be friends with her former nemesis. Was she getting cold, letting her guard down to being hurt. What if this really was all just an act, his greatest prank yet? He would humiliate her beyond recovery and she'd be ruined. Her gut told her that wasn't true. There was something happening in her life. All these events happening so back-to-back had to mean something.

She wouldn't try to pinpoint it just yet. She would let things play out more to find out what this all meant.

"Beauty's moved out" were Dane's next words

after a completely silent class period. He was loading his notebook into his backpack, as was Kelly.

"A new adventure?" Kelly said, not entirely sure of how to respond.

"An escape from the torment." Kelly hadn't expected such a dark response. She had to adjust her outlook on life for the Morris family.

"She wasn't . . . abused, was she?" Kelly asked in a hushed tone, stopping in the middle of zipping her bag.

"Not physically. My dad's always resented the fact that his firstborn was a girl and never treated her as such."

"That's terrible. What's so wrong with her being born first?"

"Nothing. It's just the way he is," Dane flung his bag over his shoulder and waited for Kelly to go before him.

"How old is she?"

"Twenty-one," Dane answered.

"Why didn't she leave when she turned eighteen?" The two of them were walking in the hall towards Kelly's sixth-period class. It was on the other end of school from Dane's next class, but that didn't stop him from escorting her.

"That was around the time she fell apart. She could hardly function in our house, and I couldn't imagine her on her own at that time. She thought she would move in with her boyfriend at the time is what she told me, but they went through a pretty bad breakup."

"What happened?"

"She won't give me details, really. Just that she had all her hope in that relationship, and when he was out of the picture, she had nothing to hold on for, except maybe getting that relationship back."

"So, she still isn't over it after three years."

"She's had a rough life. I don't know if that is the only factor to her pain. I try to be there for her, but my family's not good at opening up."

"Except you," Kelly commented in front of her next class.

"Only with you. You make it easy to, being so open yourself."

"Thanks," Kelly said awkwardly, not sure of how else to answer. "Well, you're probably going to be late now."

"Won't be the first time. Mrs. Cross appreciates my grades over my attendance."

"Look at you, a teacher's pet?" Kelly teased.

"Right, well, I'll not make you late." Dane turned to leave. He wasn't so amused by her comment. He said he envied how the Johnsons joke with each other, so she would need to help him along with that. Kelly smiled as she headed into class.

A wedding. That's all that was discussed in the Johnson household. It's all that was thought of and prepped for the last three weeks now; Kelly had been counting. Mainly because this would be an Aponlean wedding, one the family would be arranging for the first time since Mr. And Mrs. Johnson's wedding. It was the only reason they were planning so urgently, too, because they wanted to keep the Aponlea tradition of having the ceremony two months after the joining of the seals. Unlike the traditional American wedding that normally takes months to plan for one big day, an Aponlean wedding had three days. Both families had to learn so much in the last three weeks, memorizing all the whole Aponlean wedding process, reviewing how the three days would be played out. Imagine the pressure.

The first day the female and male guests would be separated and advice would be given to the bride and groom. There was also celebration going on. The bride and groom wouldn't see each other until the ceremony of the vows.

Kelly had been to five extravagant weddings in her life, and only one of them was a traditional

Aponlean one. Even though she was only five when she went, she still placed no other one above it. The traditional Aponlean wedding — from what her young mind could remember — was her favorite by far. She was even more excited to relive the experience, but the mild negativity about the whole thing still had her spirits low occasionally.

According to tradition, the bride and four maidens would be given extra care three days prior to the wedding, which included full-body treatments at the spa and dinners fit for royalty. They'd be catered to every moment of the day. Kelly couldn't wait.

She was packing for the getaway in her room, deciding which outfits were the cutest. She couldn't help but wish she had gotten Moore's cell phone number. She had been replaying that day over and over again, imagining herself asking him all sorts of questions. Reliving the moment distracted her from the self-criticisms of how she blew such an opportunity. She couldn't see herself going back over there any time soon. At least, she hadn't been invited back over yet.

Moore. Why was she so fascinated with him? What was it about him that paralyzed her in his presence, but motivated her in his absence?

A knock interrupted her thoughts. Kelly called for the person to enter, expecting any one of her siblings besides Joey. To her delight it was her oldest brother, three days before the beginning of the three-day event. Kelly's face lit up, although Joey's looked worn out and irritated.

"Kelly, I hope to never go through this sort of thing again!" He moved her chair from the corner, sinking down into it, resting his head on the back of the chair staring up at the ceiling.

"Go through what?" Kelly asked, unsure of what he could be talking about.

"An Aponlean wedding," he said, his eyes still fixated on the ceiling.

"Then don't get divorced and you won't have to worry about that." Kelly moved closer to him to provide some comfort.

"That's for sure," he sighed. "You wouldn't believe the politics involved" He sat up and began with more passion, "First off, I consider myself American, not Aponlean, for the record. Maybe, Aponlean-American, or however you want to word it, but I bleed red, white, and blue and I'd like to keep it that way. My children will not recite the repetitious prayer at dinner. We will be football and hotdogs all the way and . . ."

"Joey, what happened?" Kelly knew if she didn't stop him now, he'd keep going and never really get to the point. She'd never seen him so upset in her life, except for the time their father shipped him off to boot camp.

"I thought marriage was about love, you fall in love and that's that, but apparently not when you happen to be the oldest son of one of the most prestigious couples in Aponlean history. Turns out Mom and Dad's marriage was strategically planned." Joey was now looking his sister in the eyes.

"Really?" She hadn't heard that side of the story before.

"Yeah. I thought they just fell in love and that was it, but nothing's that simple when it comes to the politics of Aponlea."

"Joey, you're killing me here. Please tell me what happened!" Kelly pleaded.

"I will tell you what happened. I just came from a three-hour meeting with the Aponlean Council, which Dad's a part of, to discuss the acceptability of my marriage. We spent a good deal of time determining the percentage of purity in Melanie's lineage, as in, from the direct line of Jacob through the honored children. Turns out she's only five generations out from the direct line of Jacob; her great-great-great-grandfather was the honored child, and on her mom's side, seven generations up was one of the honored children from Thom's lineage. Why does all this matter? Because, as it turns out, you and I are perfect breeds."

"Perfect breeds?" Kelly repeated, delighted with

the term.

"So Dad is from the direct line of honored children from John as was Mom's dad from Jacob. This is a big deal, because as you may or may not have known, Jacob was the prince of Aponlea, but John, not being of royal blood, was selected as the heir to the kingdom by the king. Basically, it is expected that one of us will take the throne if Aponlea is ever rediscovered. That would be the case if any of this was real." Joey leaned his head back again. His head was hurting from all this talk.

"It is, Joey," Kelly asserted.

"Aponlea is a joke. It was probably made up by a group of men who wanted to fool a generation into believing in something more than reality. That is why the existence of such a civilization is not in any history book in any place in this world."

"There are plenty of history books. I know someone with quite a collection."

"An obsessed descendant, no doubt. Be careful, little sis. The obsession will ruin you. Some of my former Aponlean friends, who apparently were selected for me by the Council, got in deep with these fabrications and it never ended well for them." Joey stood, walking over to Kelly's bed and sat. Kelly joined him, leaning against his arm. Joey moved his arm around his sister. "Six days, just six days, that's what I have to remind myself. Then it'll be my family and we will have no part of this. Maybe we'll move, since New England seems to be the place of Harbor for most descendants."

"Joey, please don't!" Kelly protested.

"I won't. I'll be fine in six days." Kelly was determined that he didn't mean what he said about Aponlea. He was just stressed about all the pressure. After his honeymoon, he'd be back in the bliss he had been. Kelly was sure of it.

A shrill sound ripped through the walls of Dane's

room and broke him out of his thoughtful trance of staring at the ceiling. He shut his eyes; he should have been unmoved by the sound. A scream wasn't uncommon in the evening. It was only his brother paying homage to Radehveh. Moore had a small statue of the god with a moat around it, where the blood from his sliced hand would pour into. There must have been something of dire importance that Moore was in petition for, for him to be doing this now.

Moore's screams pierced through the air again and Dane winced. He didn't want to think about that practice. It was something he always felt was asking too much. He was never as dedicated as Moore was. He got off of his bed and left his room.

He skipped steps as he soared down the stairwell, just as quickly being hit with another sound he hated, the pained voice of his mother.

"You pushed her away — she wants nothing to do with us!" his mother screamed at his father.

"She's twenty-one. She wants to live a little." Mr. Morris's voice had a calmness to it that just didn't work.

"You're so blind! How do you not see that she hates you?" Mrs. Morris's voice quivered. Her tears could be heard in her voice.

"Calm down, Vivian." Dane's father's voice was still even, though stern and authoritative. He hated to raise his voice at his wife, though she was quick to show her emotions. She hadn't been taught to suppress them as the rest of the family had. "Have you taken your medication?"

"That's what you think this is about?" she shot back. "You know, I didn't have to take anything before I married you!"

"I've given you everything, Vivian. You're acting irrationally. You've always been treated as a queen."

Dane made it to the back door by the time his father spit out those words. He left his parents to argue in the kitchen and went straight for the housemaids' house. Vanni and Adelina were still working, so they were not home. Dane snagged the spare key from the plant hanging by the door and let himself in. He often used their place as a safe house. As soon as he entered, he felt peace engulf him. There was something pure about their place that wasn't present anywhere else on the property.

His head cleared of all confusion as he sat on their sofa to ponder. He laid his head back to just gaze up as he had been doing in his room. Was there any hope of his family being restored? That was the first topic he started at. He quickly responded with an audible "No." What happens if I get caught hanging out with Kelly? he thought. "I'd get shot by Mr. Johnson. Hm, not so bad considering my future."

Is she worth it, though? "I think so," the last thing he uttered out loud to himself. That thought gave him a rush of peace.

To pass some time, Dane roamed the quaint living area of the house. There was a picture of him hung up on the wall. He had to have been about five years old. He was eating a watermelon, topless on a picnic blanket. Vanni and Adelina were with him. He moved closer to it and examined it. There was a little phrase printed at the bottom of the picture in Italian. Below the phrase read "Salmi 37:4." He was curious what that meant.

Dane moved around the room rapidly reviewing his familiarity with the place. He went to the book-shelf fully stocked with all sorts of books, mostly in Italian, but a few in English. He ran his fingers down the line of them until he got to the second shelf, where he pulled the book he had hidden there. He pulled it out, going from a squat to sitting on the floor in front of the shelf.

He held out the Bible in front of him and looked at the cover a moment. He flipped through to the page that had his name on it and tried once again to iden-tify the handwriting, but with no success. He turned a few more pages to the first section: Genesis. He couldn't get past "In the beginning" before slamming it shut. He didn't know what kind of harm reading further would lead him to. He pushed the book back on the shelf.

Dane got back up and walked around some more. The pool. The pool would be nice about now. He could go around the back way of the property, avoid the chaos inside. He needed something to get his mind off of Kelly.

◆———————◆———————◆

Three days of utter bliss for the girls being pampered. Three days of shopping sprees, spas, fine dining, yachts, and five-star hotels, and best yet, no school. Kelly got to know Melanie's two sisters very fast, and Melanie was beginning to feel like an actual sister. Kelly loved the time away.

She felt complete freedom. No curfew, no real rules, just girl bonding and amusement. She could get used to this sort of thing; maybe she should find other Aponlean girls getting married, befriend them enough to be one of their maidens, and live like this the rest of her life.

The pampering was a vacation from everything but her thoughts. Moore popped in her head frequently.

After a cute romantic comedy in the hotel to wind down from the busy day, Kelly headed to her room. Since it was right beside her sister's, she decided to knock. She hated to be alone and seldom was, growing up with so many siblings.

"Come in!" Jessica nearly sang through the door. Kelly couldn't remember a time when Jessica was so happy, except when it came to something to do with her crush. When Kelly entered she saw her sister splayed across the bed as if she collapse backwards in excitement. She kicked her legs in a happy dance.

"Someone's in a good mood." Kelly jumped on the bed next to her.

"How could I not be? These are the best three days of my life." Kelly laughed at the amount of amusement her sister exuded.

"Tell me about it. Maybe, we can sneak Mom's credit card and just spend the rest of our lives like this?"

"Ha. If only." Jessica sat up and Kelly followed. The two girls scooted back to lean against the headrest.

"Jessica, can I talk to you?" Kelly got serious.

"Of course! As long as it's happy. I only want to enjoy this time."

"Well, it's just . . . I wanted to ask you what you thought about Aponlea, I guess."

"What do you mean?"

"Like, do you believe it's real?"

"Why wouldn't it be real?"

"Well, I was talking to Joey and he doesn't believe it is. He says it's made up by some people long ago who just wanted to fool a future generation."

"He's probably just messing with you," Jessica shrugged.

"He was very serious. He said it's not in any of the history books and so therefore not real."

"That's just because non-descendants are not supposed to know. Kelly, we're living proof that it's real."

"What about the actual Aponlea, the country? Do you think one day we'll return there?"

"Is that what Dad or Mom says?"

"I don't know. They never talk about it, only 'Do this, it's part of the Aponlean tradition.' Tradition this and tradition that, but no history, no future."

"Kelly, why does it even matter? If it's real, it's real. If not, no harm in that."

"Because, if it is real, one of us will take the throne of Aponlea." Jessica stood. She couldn't understand the urgency in Kelly's tone. She paced a moment.

"What are you talking about?"

"Joey said that apparently Mom and Dad were selected to marry so that one of their children would be the king or queen of Aponlea once it is reopened."

"I guess only time will tell."

"And you're okay with that?" Kelly asked eagerly, wanting some sort of answer, but not sure what.

103

"You're not? What are you getting at, Kelly? What are you looking for?"

"I . . . I guess I don't know," Kelly admitted. Why did it all matter? Why was she so curious all of a sudden about something she had been surrounded with since birth? What was the answer she wanted? Maybe a purpose, something to strive toward. She was only fifteen. Did she really need to find her life's meaning so early on? "Never mind."

"Come on, enjoy this vacation with me!" Jessica said, trying to lighten the mood.

"You're right." Kelly smiled outwardly, but the wheels hadn't stop churning in her head. "Can I sleep in here?"

"You have a nice large bed in your own room and you want to make me surrender half of my own?"

"Yes," Kelly made her puppy dog face.

"Sure! It'll be like when we used to share a room."

"Yes, and you kept getting on me about tidying up."

"Or when we would stay up all night laughing and talking."

"Those were the days!" Kelly agreed.

Chapter Ten

Joey marched down the rich blue aisle through the middle of hundreds of familiar and unfamiliar faces, but still with a genuine smile on his face. He was wearing a traditional Aponlean tunic, just what he'd promised his family — and most importantly, his bride-to-be — he'd wear. He had an authentic sword attached to his belt, a warrior's helmet over his head, and a full bodysuit of armor. He was a reflection of an ancient Aponlean, and this was what they wore on their marriage day. This was a display of the pride he would have had from being in battle. Kelly had seen it all in the dress rehearsal but couldn't help staring from her post at the back of the room at.

"Kelly, get in your position," Jessica said in a hushed voice. Kelly remembered her place and turned to get ready for her entrance. She could still see a sliver of it through the slightly parted curtains.

Joey was at the front now, approaching the round table perched neatly in the circular setup of the elevated platform among the crowd. The platform looked like a giant whitewood gazebo, veiled with free-flowing sheer veils of soft shades of blue and green — like water. That was the theme. In fact, everyone attending was told to wear colors that were similar to the ocean, and the results were breathtaking.

He slowly dismantled his armor, taking off his helmet ever so carefully, then proceeding to take off the rest, carefully placing each piece side by side onto the glass table. Finally, once he was in only the expressive turquoise tunic, feet bare, he pulled his sword from his side. Then his father came up from where he was standing beside Joey, holding his hands out for the sword, reenacting a request for his son to entrust his last bit of security to him. This signified that Joey was making himself vulnerable for one person alone: his bride. An active Aponlean warrior was never without his sword in public unless he was getting married. And even then, his father would be holding the trusty weapon at their side.

Mike, Melanie's father, and her two brothers were holding Melanie up on a man-made carrier where she sat with her knees on a white feather pillow, all the while being veiled in a transparent canopy of light turquoise material. This displayed the groom's awaited love, his treasure.

The boys carried her gently down the aisle. Two pairs of the four maidens walked alongside the left and right of the front of the carrier, hands folded behind their backs, awaiting any kind of service. The guests marveled at the sight. The ceremony was perfectly rehearsed. No one involved had slipped up once. Melanie looked ahead, forcing her eyes to see past the veil to Joey, whose mouth was agape with awe. She smiled, but he was too awestruck to smile back.

Soon, the oversized tent was silent no more, rising to a roar of a cheerful, accordant Aponlean chant, as Melanie's carrier circled around the guests for all to see. Melanie laughed, covering her mouth with a manicured hand.

Once she'd been around the entire room, she was brought down the middle aisle once again and gently lowered to the floor in front of the altar at the platform. The first two maidens, Melanie's two sisters, grabbed each end of the veil and pulled it away, revealing the full vividness of Melanie's blue and green dress of satin, and the enhanced glow of her curly golden hair. Her father approached at the front of the carrier and helped her out while Kelly and Jessica dropped pure white silk where she'd step down, so her bare feet wouldn't touch the bare ground. This signified her purity.

When she stepped down, the gold embroidery from the waist down glittered from the movement. She sparkled endlessly as the lights aligned on the whole frame of the tent reflected off of the gold bangles on her arms and wrists, the gold gems patterned on the pinned train connected to her hair. Natural, cool colors complimented her fair, sun-kissed skin. The embroidery of the lower half of her dress resembled detailed scales, like a mermaid's tail. It was very unlike any other traditional wedding. Definitely unique.

Melanie faced the crowd now, with her maidens to her right. In the next minute, with the turn of the heel, she and Joey were facing each other. Only then had the chants ceased, and the vows began. These vows were memorized and there was no need for a minister. Kelly stood by like a robot on auto mode. She wanted to make sure she'd done everything just as it was rehearsed. The last thing she wanted was to be the cause of a sudden drop of the mood. She wouldn't let her feelings get in the way. When the vows began, she was able to breathe finally; her part was finished. And it was pretty exhilarating, having been involved in such an important event.

But then, the exuberant smile Joey was wearing erased everything. She could have hugged him with thanks, right then and there. The sparkle in his eyes, the joy clear on his face — Kelly couldn't recall a time when he'd displayed such a unique happiness. Joey, of all people, had even more happiness in him to express to the world. He was more than ready to start a new adventure with his very own wife. And despite what this would mean, Kelly couldn't help but feel joy for her brother.

Joey would be the very first spin-off from this generation's Johnson family. From then on, the family would be ever changing. Before long, Mike would find the same fate, then Jessica, then one day, even Kelly, all until it ultimately got to Lisa. Kelly couldn't imagine her five-year-old sister being older than five years old, but she did know that she'd be looking back at this moment one day, wondering how.

———◆———◆———◆———

The ceremony was finished. Melanie and Joey were finally and officially married. In the next tent over, an abundant feast awaited the celebrated couple along with the guests. While professional pictures were being taken of the Johnson family and its new additions, everyone not of the immediate family gathered in the second tent to mingle and find their reserved seats.

Photography seemed the most modernized custom the wedding had allowed; and for Kelly, the longest. She clicked her heels together with her flat gold sandals and tapped her sides with her fingers, ran her hands down the soft materials of her light blue dress. The tent was heated, but Kelly gave the impression that she was cold, though she was only restless. She had one thing on her mind while the photos snapped and that was the Council. She needed to know who they were. She wondered if it would be considered inappropriate for her to approach them. She wondered what their purpose even was.

Mrs. Johnson had demanded over ten different arrangements of portraits. Some involved the Johnson and the Jacobs family together, some with just the Johnsons, some with just the Jacobs, all with the bride and groom. Kelly was ordered to stay through all of them, just in case she was needed for another shot. While one of the arrangements of just Melanie's family was going on, Kelly couldn't help but notice her father off to the side talking with two men. They all seemed to be enjoying themselves. Could they be part of the Council? She had one way of finding out.

Kelly boldly went up to the three of them, going in to put her arm around her father. He pulled her in to a tighter hug. "Here's my ever-curious daughter, Kelly," he said lightly.

"Hello there," the first man said. He looked very similar to Michelle's dad, which probably meant he was of Filipino decent.

"Kelly, this is Angelo Peterson and Eric Thompson," her dad introduced them.

"Nice to meet you both," Kelly smiled, still under her father's arm.

"How did you like the wedding?" Mr. Thompson asked.

"I loved it!" Kelly said enthusiastically.

"She was a maiden, so she got the whole getaway of her dreams," Mr. Johnson added.

"Oh, I see." Mr. Thompson responded with a smile and a wink.

"Nick, I believe a congratulations is in order," Mr. Peterson said. He was shorter than the other two and had a very small frame. The other man, Mr. Thompson had blond hair and was slightly overweight. He wasn't overly tall, but taller than the other two.

"Yes, congratulations," Mr. Thompson added.

"Thank you, Angelo, Eric." Mr. Johnson smiled, looking at the photo shoot with pride.

"And when do you think the next ceremony will be?" Angelo asked with a nudge.

"Well, Mike is freshly eighteen. I don't think he'll get married soon. Unless one of you has a bride in mind?" Kelly looked up at her dad, trying to tell if he was joking or not.

"You did always have a sense of humor," Eric said with slight sarcasm. "Joey's been prepped his whole life for succession to your family's line. He's as perfect as it gets."

"Yes, perfect, except that he has no interest in Aponlea," Mr. Johnson interjected.

"Maybe not in Aponlea, but see how he responds to accepting the inheritance that comes along with it." Angelo looked at Eric and they both laughed.

"That was all my daddy had to say," Eric agreed.

"Naturally, but the responsibility that comes with it. What if we find Aponlea?" Mr. Johnson remained serious. It was a touchy subject.

"Surely, you don't doubt your son's ability?"

Eric asked.

Mr. Johnson thought a moment. "I suppose not. If the time came, he would step up to the plate."

"Then don't delay it too long. I'm not saying you are old, but you won't be around forever," Eric stated.

"I haven't seen either of you two pass the torch over to your sons yet," Mr. Johnson added.

"Rocky's only sixteen, but I am making plans for his eighteenth birthday," Angelo responded. It finally clicked; he was Michelle's uncle. Kelly knew Rocky Peterson, Michelle's cousin, who had come over a few times when she had been at Michelle's house. He was nice, but young. She couldn't imagine him wanting so much responsibility even when he turned eighteen.

"Edward has a little more growing up to do. He has to get a few things out of his system," Mr. Thompson added. Kelly knew Edward Thompson also; he was one of Joey's friends, or former friends. He had gone a little wild with lavish spending and parties. His dad, Eric, had to cut him off and kick him out of the house. Kelly was sure her dad knew of his behavior, but knew her dad had more respect than to bring it up.

Joey was right: all of their friends had to have been planned out. These families were obviously very close. Between these three and the descendants of Michael and Jacob, she was surrounded by her entire life. Maybe the five families made up the Council. She wondered where her uncle was, her mom's brother. He would've had to be the most recent honored child, unless he had already passed the torch to his oldest son, Cohl. Kelly cringed at the thought. She and her cousin did not get along at all. He was so arrogant and prideful. His brother and sister were both nice, but she was always getting into arguments with him.

"Now, do you feel Mike would be better suited?" Angelo asked, showing some concern. "It's not too rare these days for the second-oldest son to be selected." Kelly watched as her dad thought about what to say. She had a feeling he had already thought about that possibility, considering how responsible Mike was.

"Honey, it is our turn," Rita called out. "Come over for the photo."

"Gentlemen," Nick excused himself and headed over. Kelly quickly followed, still thinking about the conversation. She wished a girl could be selected. She could prove herself responsible enough. She wasn't sure what it actually entailed, but from what she did know, she wanted it.

Once pictures were finished being taken, Kelly squeezed her way through the pack of family members to get to her brother and Melanie before they disappeared to the front of the reception tent. Quickly, she tapped Joey's back, catching his sudden attention, and hugged him tightly. He hugged her back with just as much love as he always did, lifting her off the ground. It would probably be the last time she'd be able to do that for a good while. Tears threatened her as a flood of longing for her brother swelled in her heart. When he put her down, Kelly hugged Melanie, so as not to look possessive of her brother, kissing her cheek in greeting. Melanie's eyes were warm and serene. Kelly's new sister-in-law. She was glad it was Melanie.

Kelly's mother had insisted she greet people at the reception, so Kelly unwillingly obeyed, making rounds about the reception tent with Jessica, being kissed and hugged by family members from long distances and greeting guests with smiles that hurt her face. Just when she thought she'd seen to everyone, other family members would call for her, wanting pictures, complimenting the curls in her pinned-up hair, fawning over her dress and nails. What she wouldn't give to sit down right about now; her stomach rumbled angrily for food, as she had forgotten to eat earlier.

Michelle spotted her from the Peterson table and Kelly made her way to it, excited to have seen her best friend. Mr. and Mrs. Peterson wouldn't let her by until they'd gotten a hug. Mrs. Peterson also tested her with the Tagalog she had been teaching Kelly. Michelle bombarded her with compliments and a long embrace, while Kelly gushed over her friend's elegant appearance, touching the signature wooden broach on Michelle's neck, liking the heaviness of it, the smooth glossed finish, and the touch of it on her fingers. Michelle motioned for her to sit in the empty gold plated chair next to her and they sat down. There was a guy around their age sitting across from them, arms folded, looking absolutely miserable.

"So, how are you?" Michelle began softly, hands placed on the flared part of her cyan dress. Kelly just shook her head and rolled her eyes.

"Well, I'm sick of greeting people, that's for sure," she said with a light chuckle, leaning heavily on her elbow, not caring about the exaggerated slouch in her posture.

"I can imagine. I've been waiting for you to get over to my table. You look so gorgeous, Kelly," Michelle added in a high-pitched voice.

"Aw, don't flatter me, Michelle, you've told me already. I should be telling you that," Kelly said, playfully nudging her friend's shoulder. Michelle's long, black hair fell beautifully down to her back, like a shiny sheet blanketing her bare arms and complimenting those dark brown eyes.

"I can't wait until it's our turn for this," Michelle said wistfully, letting her eyes trail across the tent at the colorful sight.

"You want an Aponlean wedding?" Kelly asked, and Michelle chuckled lightly.

"I don't think I have a choice. Neither do you, for that matter."

"That's true."

"But seeing as this is the first one I've ever attended, I like what I see. It looks more meaningful than any other generic wedding. I think I would have chosen one like this either way."

"You'll definitely love the three-day retreat, especially when you'd be the bride, having four maidens at your side, ready to do anything you please. And you'll get so many gifts, gifts of jewelry. And you can't forget the famous carrier you'd be in at the wedding

112

ceremony. You'd be fit for royalty."

"It sounds so wonderful!" Michelle breathed, eyes wide with delight.

"Hey Michelle, is your cousin Rocky here?" Kelly asked.

"Yeah, he's . . ." She looked around. "He must be outside skateboarding. Why?"

"Oh, I just wanted to ask him some questions. It's no big deal." Kelly looked around also, hoping to see something Michelle missed. She did. Zach was at a corner table with some strange object, looking rather amused. Maybe he had figured out the Aponlean appliance. "Michelle, follow me." Kelly was already halfway over to where her brother was. Michelle scurried to catch up.

Kelly sat right beside her brother, who was alone at a table. She looked at the object. It was the disc, but now it had three legs holding another disc above it. The top disc was smaller and had a hole in its middle. "You figured it out?" Kelly asked.

"Yes, it had an 'on' switch," Zach answered, proud of his accomplishment.

"Where?"

"What is it?" Michelle asked.

"It's an ancient Aponlean appliance. It wasn't a physical switch, Kelly. There is a pressure point on it with a code or a certain movement of a finger, and the center and its legs rise up, still without seams. It doesn't make sense. It moves like liquid almost," Zach explained, visibly perplexed.

"Show me," Kelly said. Zach held out his index finger and circled it in a small, seemingly random spot of the device. The legs collapsed like a waterfall back into the disc, which then again appeared solid with a smooth surface, as if the legs and top circle were not even a part of it.

"What on earth did I just see? Are you sure this isn't some sort of alien device?" Michelle asked.

"It is in that it is completely foreign from anything I've ever seen before. Our forefathers must have been

113

geniuses," Zach commented, studying the device.

"But did you figure out what it was used for?" Kelly asked. Sure, she was perplexed like the others, but she took delight that something so unique existed. It meant life was more exciting than she had thought.

"Yes, without too much detail, it's sort of like a microwave," Zach began and swirled his finger in a circular motion on the same spot. The legs shot up, along with the top circle. He grabbed his plate of food. "This chicken is getting cold, isn't it?" he said. Kelly and Michelle quickly felt it. It was about room temperature. He picked the chicken up and placed it on a napkin in the middle of the disc, where the metal legs surrounded it. He moved his pointer finger in a V shape in the same spot and quickly moved his hand. The girls watched as nothing seemed to be happening. Suddenly the chicken wobbled a little bit, but no sound came from the device. Zach looked at his watch and counted down. Kelly tried to see how much time he was waiting, but couldn't tell. He reached his hand in and pulled the chicken out by lifting the napkin and dropped it on his plate.

"Feel it now," he said. Kelly and Michelle touched it and quickly moved their hands away from it. It was hot, very hot.

"My mind is blown right now, Kelly. I just might have to reevaluate everything I've ever known," Michelle said, sinking back in her chair. Kelly's mind raced. If such technology existed, maybe this was the magic the Aponleans had.

"I still haven't figured out the science behind it. If I do, Dad will give me more devices to look at. He's got quite a collection, I'm told," Zach said, eyes intent on the device as if it were his very own treasure.

"Can you possibly explain this to me? Kelly, why are you not freaking out as much as I am about this?" Michelle asked. Kelly laughed, "I am, I promise I am, just inwardly." This was proof enough to her that Aponlea was real.

Dane got out of the Lexus sedan and looked around. This was his first time at his sister's loft since her move.

"I'll call you when I am ready, Mason," Dane called out before heading inside the building. He went up to the second floor. Her loft number was 217. Dane breezed past the other numbers, finding it in an instant. He gave a few soft knocks. The door opened almost immediately, as if she had been waiting by the door.

"Thank you for coming so quickly. I didn't want to be alone today," Beauty said. Dane followed her in. "Do you want a drink or anything?"

"Water is fine," Dane responded. Dane thought back to his sister's call earlier and her urgency for him to come over. "What's going on?"

"Today's just one of the tough days, the toughest," Beauty said with a sigh. When she handed him a glass of water, he was able to see the swelling of her eyes and her red nose. Her cheeks were still moist. He wondered how long she had been crying. "I'm a mess, aren't I?"

"You're recovering," Dane said, offering encouragement. He took a sip of his water and sat on the tall stool at her center table. Beauty just stood on the opposite side, leaning against it.

"I hope. I'm sorry we haven't been as close as we used to."

"It's okay. It's hard to harbor as many burdens as you do. I think you just need someone to be open with," Dane consoled her, trying to be that person for her. She had been holding back so many secrets, and he wanted to know why. He wanted to help her.

"You've changed since your hospital stay. I noticed your first night back. Tell me about that," Beauty inquired.

Dane looked at her, she was avoiding the subject again, but maybe if he opened up, then she would. "Well, it's a funny thing when you come so close with

115

death; nothing looks the same anymore. The things you once thought were important aren't such a big deal, and the things you didn't pay any mind before become your priority."

"Like what?"

"Like genuine friendship, like trust and openness. Like valuing people over tasks or expressing emotion and living in freedom, not holding back." Saying those words was the first time he ever really felt like he wasn't holding back. "And then there's Aponlea, and the quest to find it. I've been losing interest in it. I've neglected so much for it. I should've been there for you and Mom instead," Dane let out a sigh. "Our family's one big mess, and nobody wants to address it."

"Dane, you have been there for me — I've just pushed you away."

"No, I gave up, when I shouldn't have. I should have worked harder at being there for you even when you pushed me away." Beauty didn't respond and Dane didn't follow up. The two just lingered in silence for a while. "I am here for you now, Beauty, and I want to help. Please tell me how I can help you."

"Like you said, our family is one big mess. I should've been born a boy. Dad's made that clear, and now Moore's treating me as if he feels the same. He talks about Nadia as if she is his sister, but won't even talk to me anymore."

"Since you left?"

"Since before that; that was part of the push for me to leave."

"Nadia just happens to be in alignment with his plans at this time, and that's why. I bet when he looks at her, he doesn't see her; he sees Schernols and Richard and Richard's son."

"He wasn't always like that, though. You remember the three of us used to be able to just have fun, and we hid secrets from our parents. And that was when his mind was full of Aponlea and the Great Morr. Something must've happened to him, for him to change like that."

"I don't know what to say about him." Dane's sentence had bounced off Beauty's ears as something else seemed to catch her attention. She was off in her mind again, eyes gazing at the large windows that were at the opposite end from the front door. She walked over to them without saying a word. Dane followed. When he reached her side, tears were streaming down her face again. She was holding something up to her chest. She must've had it in her pocket. It was completely concealed by her hands.

"What is it?" Dane asked.

"A promise ring." Beauty held it out to him.

"Why do you still have that, Beauty?" Dane tried to sound concerned, but he was angered by this. It meant she still wasn't over her last relationship. "Why won't you tell me what happened?"

"He promised me eternity and gave me goodbye instead," she answered through her tears. "That's what happened, Dane."

"Beauty, that was three years ago, why can't you let him go?" Dane asked.

"Dane," Beauty said and turned her head toward him. "My promise of eternity has no end." She clasped the ring in her hands again, before sliding it back into her pocket. "Did you say you learned how to live in freedom after your hospital stay?"

"I learned how to desire that but haven't experienced it yet. I'm still bound by fear."

"Fear of what?"

"Fear of Radehveh, fear of Dad," he answered.

"Me too," she answered. "If you find that freedom, please share it with me."

"If I do, I will. Anything to stop your pain," Dane responded. For the rest of the visit they stared off in silence. Dane felt the need to save his sister but didn't know how without even knowing how to save himself.

Chapter Eleven

"How was the wedding?" Dane asked, seated on the bleachers out back on the football field. School was in session, but now was Kelly's lunch. Dane had insisted on skipping biology in favor of accompanying her. The two needed to catch up after the wedding retreat.

Kelly opted to walk across the bleachers a row down from Dane. She had been sitting all day in classes and preferred to move about. "It was really cool. It feels weird to be back here after being engulfed the past six days. Oh, and I learned a lot of things about Aponlea."

"Like what?" Dane queried.

"Just the origin of different traditions and more about the culture itself. And letting go of Joey wasn't as hard as I expected. I am actually very happy for him. Melanie is perfect."

"I'm glad." Dane just watched as she made another turn, walking in the opposite direction.

"How are things on your end?"

"I visited Beauty yesterday. We're starting to rebuild the friendship we once had."

"That's so good. Siblings make the best friends," Kelly said with a smile. She was still on cloud nine from her experience and could hardly focus. She hadn't even touched her lunch.

Kelly stopped in front of Dane before stepping into the footrest of his row and seating herself beside him. The two positioned themselves to face each other. "About that Schernol I wasn't supposed to hear about?"

"The one I am not supposed to talk to you about?" Dane asked.

"Yes, that's the one I need you to talk about. I haven't been able to stop thinking about it since it came up, and if we're going to do this whole friend thing and trust each other . . ."

"What do you want to know about it?" Even though this is what Kelly wanted to hear, she wasn't expecting it.

"I'm not sure exactly." Kelly wanted to know any and everything about it. She just didn't know where to begin.

"Kelly, I'll get to that in a moment." Dane stopped. Kelly looked at him questioningly, waiting for him to continue. He seemed to really be contemplating something. "I want to be able to trust you. It's such a burden always having to carry secrets. My whole life has been hiding information, and I might just be crazy for wanting to trust a Johnson, but is that something I can do?"

Kelly looked at him a moment in bewilderment. In that moment she didn't know what the truthful answer would be. How much information from him could she handle? She kept telling herself to answer, to say yes. "Yes, yes, yes," her inner desire shouted, but for some reason the severity of the question made her want to give the honest answer. Could he trust her? She could hardly trust herself. When it came to her curiosity and getting answers, sometimes she did the unexpected, but then this time she was maintaining self-control. She didn't offer an affirmative right away.

"Yeah, I don't know who I'd tell. As far as anyone else is concerned, we don't even like each other," Kelly answered. That was something she believed.

"It's not about whether or not you'd tell anyone. It's about whether I can trust you." Kelly understood he meant to ask if he could be vulnerable with her. That frightened her. Just his asking that was making himself vulnerable. She couldn't understand how he could do that with the short time they had been friends.

"I believe so," Kelly answered almost as a question. This was something she would need to take more time to meditate on.

"Well, good." Dane had accepted it. "I'll tell you whatever you want to know. We haven't retrieved the Schernol yet. We are waiting."

"Waiting on what?"

"The right information. The Sceptra was stolen from us seventeen years ago. And now the man who stole it discovered that there are two meanings in the Aponlean language: the surface level, which we read and understand, and the cryptic level. He cracked the code for the cryptic level and has been using it to search for the locations of Schernols. The problem is figuring out what the world was like at the time the Sceptra was written. He found out it is in present day Puerto Rico, but deciphering the exact location has taken him all this time."

"So, if you find the Schernol, then what?"

"It is only the beginning, then we find all of them."

"And when you find them all?"

"Remember, the Schernols combine to create Prostasia, the mother shield? The person who possesses Prostasia is heir to the Aponlean throne."

"If Aponlea is found?"

"It is assumed that also comes with Prostasia." This was so much to take in. Kelly loved this. She was finally getting answers. There had to be a reason for all this. What Joey said about her parent's union, the first Schernol almost being recovered, her friendship with Dane, it wasn't all a coincidence. This was all privileged information that she had. She could combine the information from both lines of descendants and do something with it. She wasn't sure what, but she could feel something telling her this was big. This may be her calling.

"Dane," Kelly began.

"Yes?"

"Who are 'they' for real?" Now that he had become vulnerable she could see whether he was telling the truth before.

Dane sighed. Kelly couldn't tell why. "The Council. They have people protecting your family."

"But they can't guarantee a happy ending," Kelly said.

"They can make sure your family remains unshaken by outside force."

"There are always things beyond one's control."

"You're right, Kelly. I'm not trying to argue. I was just answering your question."

Kelly didn't want to argue either. She often asked questions when trying to cope with new things.

"Thank you." Again her answer sounded more like a question. A barely hostile Dane Morris was a whole lot to get used to.

<hr/>

The seating arrangements at the dinner table were different than they had ever been in the Johnson house tonight. But it didn't feel as alien as they'd thought it would. On an optimistic note, it felt like a refreshing way to move on.

Mike had taken Joey's old seat, as planned, and Jason had taken the seat Mike used to have, at the left of his father. The table was fairly silent, but it didn't have the same mood as the first day Joey had been gone.

A few taps of a glass turned everyone's heads to Mike. He had his glass lifted above his head now, like he was the host of a dinner party. Jason rolled his eyes.

"I now officially call this meeting to order," Mike began in a ceremonial yet joking voice. It wasn't hard to find cheerfulness in his voice—though often serious, he knew how to have fun. "It's come to my attention that dinners without Joey have been pretty dull and gloomy and now, with me in his place, I must take the responsibility of keeping the table lively and fun. He gave me a big task when he left for the real world, and

I promised myself I wouldn't take it lightly. So, with my first day in office, I plan to make a difference. From now on, I'll start by opening the night with a joke."

Kelly and Jason exchanged looks; they were ready to laugh, since they knew Mike lacked spontaneous humor, they were prepared when he attempted to be funny. Everyone at the table tried to hide their smiles, afraid they'd burst out laughing before the joke began.

"This isn't an inaugural address, Mike, it's a dinner table. Loosen up on the speech, dude," Jason said, unceremoniously picking up a chicken wing from his plate and tearing off half of it with his teeth. Kelly snorted at his remark, and Mike ignored it like the mature boy he was. Kelly was surprised; his mock speech almost sounded exactly like something Joey would have done.

"Be quiet, Jason. It's better than silence," she defended him. Her parents silently agreed.

"Since Mom made chicken, tonight's joke will be more suiting," Mike continued with a smile. He folded his hands together and looked around. "Is eating chicken with your fingers good manners?"

Kelly found the question pretty random, but when she saw that he was waiting for answers with an amused spark in his eyes, Kelly caught on: this was his joke.

"No it's not," Jessica said, eyeing Jason as he ate shamelessly with his fingers. One side of her lips twitched upward into a grimace, and she forced herself to stop staring at the disgusting sight, hoping not to lose her appetite. She daintily cut some meat off the bone of one of her chicken wings with her knife and fork; it took almost a whole minute for her to finally get the piece in her mouth. Kelly had been watching. It was also about how long the room was silent once again.

"Actually," Mrs. Johnson began, regaining everyone's attention from their food, "I think it's okay. There are some foods that are meant to be eaten with your fingers, hence the title 'finger foods.'"

"Exactly. I agree," Mr. Johnson said, nodding once. He rarely spoke when he ate, a man of few words, but he was amused and wanted to know what his second eldest son was getting at.

"I also agree with mom," Kelly added, already clearing her plate and reaching for the basket of extra wings.

Lisa was looking eagerly at Mike, waiting for the answer, eating her chicken with her hands. Jason was looking annoyed and impatient, so much so that he didn't bother voicing his opinion. And Zach hadn't answered either. He already knew the joke.

"The answer's no. You shouldn't eat your fingers at all," Mike finished, trying to suppress the quiet snickers behind his closed mouth. Lisa started laughing loudly, probably because she didn't fully understand his joke.

"Wow, that was incredibly corny, Mike," Jessica said, taking another bite of her chicken. She still laughed, as did everyone else, and it was quite boisterous.

"I second that," Jason said.

"Hey, Lisa thought it was funny," Kelly said. Mr. and Mrs. Johnson laughed some more. Zach ate silently. Mike looked like he'd given up.

"Well, I tried," Mike said, giving up his professional posture for a slouch as he went back to his food. Lisa leaned his way even though he was beyond her reach.

"It's okay, Mike. My teacher told me that whenever you fail, you are one step closer to getting it right!" she said triumphantly, feeling important. Mike was hiding his expression with his face toward his plate, but he softened with a smile at his baby sister's words.

"Ooh, you just got burned by a five year old," Jason said, bursting into a fit of cackles. Mike's smile disappeared from his face, and Mrs. Johnson gave something like a warning hiss at Jason that shut him up immediately. Kelly and Jessica exchanged looks, pleased with their mother's acknowledgment of Jason's unacceptable behavior.

Kelly felt a rush of joy as Mike, despite his embarrassingly lame attempt at creating laughter, had succeeded to an extent, which had brightened the mood that night. His lack of humor was his charm, and Kelly was beginning to imagine that this was exactly what his family would be expecting every night. She felt even better as he looked around the table. Mike had brought smiles to their faces that night and was rewarded with the fading gloom that had spread thick around the large Johnson home in Joey's absence.

When everyone started dissolving into their own conversations, Kelly shut herself off again. As soon as she wasn't distracted by the other things around her, her thoughts were soon plagued with unnecessary stress. She had told Dane he could trust her, but could she trust him? What if he was telling her these things to gain her trust and ultimately wanted information from her? How could she ever know for sure? She didn't want to live her life in paranoia, that was for sure. She would trust him and live with the consequences. She decided that was a better option than having her guard up all the time.

"Dad," Kelly began leaning toward her father's end and almost in front of Lisa. Though Kelly's voice was soft, Mr. Johnson heard her call and gave her his attention.

"Why don't we discuss Aponlea more here?" Mr. Johnson looked at his wife, deciding how to answer. Lisa looked at her dad, waiting for an answer, although she didn't really understand the question. The rest of the siblings were still holding their conversations, not paying attention to Kelly's question.

"We do all the traditions," Mr. Johnson answered. "You and your siblings haven't really asked many questions about it."

"Joey told me about a conversation he had with the Council . . ."

"Joey shouldn't have been discussing any conversation he had with the Council," Mr. Johnson was quick to interrupt. This drew a few more ears to the conversation. All of the Johnson clan were now fully attentive to Mr. Johnson.

"Go back to your conversations. Quit being so nosey," Mrs. Johnson commanded to no effect.

"It's okay, Rita," Mr. Johnson started. "If you kids want to know more about Aponlea, we can start discussing it at the dinner table. We haven't focused a lot on it because your mom and I have both witnessed the downfall of those descendants who have become obsessed with certain aspects of Aponlea. We didn't want to see any of you heading down that road. But it is our history and it is important, so if you have any questions, I want you to feel open to asking."

"Who's the Council?" Jason asked as soon as he saw his father had ended.

"The Council is made up of honored descendants of John, Tom, Jacob, Michael, and Peter. They meet and discuss the future of Aponlea and how to keep things in order. They keep you safe from those of the dark bloodlines. They act as sort of a ghost government for our people."

"Why don't they form an official government and make us an official people again?" Kelly asked.

"One day they will. We have to wait on the prophecy first. Aponlea, the land, must exist first."

"Where is it?" Jason asked.

"We haven't found it yet, nor are we really sure of what it is. It could be a physical land occupied by a current nation, or it could be a mystical realm only to be opened once the prophecies are fulfilled."

"What are these prophecies?" Kelly jumped in, with one of her many burning questions. She had her next few lined up if his answer didn't spark more.

"Well, things need to be lined up. The armies are to be at a certain number and a descendant must have the right lineage. Certain artifacts must be unearthed and aligned . . ."

"There's an Aponlean army?" Jason interrupted.

"Yes. There will more than likely be a battle be-

125

fore Aponlea's fulfillment. Let's not forget there are the dark bloodlines eyeing the same power and corruption Morr had."

"Where are they?" Jason asked.

"They're everywhere. Their identity cannot be revealed until it's their time."

"Dad, it's one of us, right? The descendant with the right lineage?" Kelly asked eagerly.

"Ye —"

"It's Joey, Kelly," Mike responded. "It cannot just be handed to anyone." Mike seemed to know all of this already. He didn't ask any questions and he lacked the enthusiasm shared by the other siblings.

"Mike's right. Joey is expected to step up," Mrs. Johnson finally chimed in.

"But does Joey want it?" Kelly asked.

"Does it matter?" Mike retorted. Kelly wasn't used to this side of her brother. He seemed to have some sort of chip on his shoulder about all of this. "He needs to rise to the occasion as Dad has been instilling in us our entire lives."

"It is Joey's expectation, though he doesn't seem to be ready yet. I know one day he will be," Mr. Johnson agreed. He didn't seem so confident about his own words. Joey did have a certain stubborn streak. It all boggled Kelly's mind as to why Joey wouldn't jump at the opportunity: she would. Anyone in their right mind would love it. Rule a kingdom, lead a people into their destiny. "Remember this isn't about just one person, though. Aponlea isn't about elevating individuals. It is about individuals working together. It is about unity. Everyone working together for the greater good."

"Yes, now, let us all work together for the greater good of cleaning this table." Mrs. Johnson was less comfortable talking about such things, Kelly could tell. "We can discuss more at tomorrow night's dinner. Jason and Kelly, it's your turn to wash the dishes."

Kelly forgot that detail, and she wished her mom had also. She wanted to ask so many more questions, but it would have to wait. Patience and waiting were not her specialties. She began helping Jessica clear a few plates and once they were in the sink began washing.

Stillness had full supremacy over the Morris's dinner. Dane sought any sign of livelihood in his family members. He didn't understand how they could sit there eating together without talking. They wore a mask of peace, but the atmosphere was far from it. He now wondered how for so long he saw no problem with everyone holding back all emotions or thoughts, ignoring that there was a problem. He hadn't seen it before, because he grew up with it as the norm. Now seeing the detriment of it all with Beauty, and the opposite of it all with Kelly, his eyes were fully open.

He wanted so badly to open his mouth, to bring peace to his family. He wanted to convey his mother's pain to his father, try to help him understand. He wanted his father to see that he would still be loved if he showed vulnerability.

Now that he had had a taste of freedom by holding nothing back with Kelly, he felt an urge to continue it and speak out to his family. He wasn't there yet. He was still paralyzed by fear.

As Dane watched his mother, father, and brother depart in different directions, he knew he had missed an opportunity. He caved. It was strange. All this time he thought he had lived a fearless life. He was never afraid of anyone. He never backed down from a fight, but maybe that was all an outlet for the lack of liberty in this part of his life.

"Are you okay, Master Dane?" Vanni asked as she took his dish.

"Huh? Yes," he responded, getting up from his seat. He walked out of the kitchen with the burden of his thoughts. He caught a glimpse of Moore at the door as he arrived at the stairwell. "Moore!" he shouted without thinking. His heart raced as his mind caught up to his pending actions. Moore looked back in question as Dane made his way up to him.

"Where are you going?"

"Is that your business?" Moore shot back as if in an interrogation.

"No, I mean. I was thinking, it's been a while since I went for a ride," Dane said. Moore looked at him blankly.

"Don't you have some schoolwork to do or something?" Moore asked.

"Nothing I can't finish later on tonight," Dane responded.

"Come along, then," Moore said, not holding the door behind him. Dane quickly made it past before it shut and got into the passenger's side of the car. They took off at high speed, soaring out of the neighborhood and into the street. Moore's gear shifting was effortless and his fear of collision nonexistent. His flight down the road simulated a hover vehicle.

"How are things going with Kelly?" Moore asked right as Dane had finally adjusted to the speed they were pushing.

"Um—well, good, I guess?" Dane answered.

"I mean are you gaining any insight?"

"That wasn't really the goal. I mean you saw what kind of questions she was asking. I don't know what I could gain from her."

"That's what makes it even better, she won't know what information is beneficial to us and will have no problem. Things should slip out that we can use."

"Why were you so nice to her?" Dane asked, subtly veering the subject.

"Now's not the time to wage a war," Moore responded.

"Surely, escorting an intruder out of your house isn't a declaration of war," Dane said.

"Kelly is hardly an intruder." Moore took a sharp turn, upsetting Dane's balance and posture.

"You offered her access to our library and entrance to your room. You won't even allow me in there."

"It was a gesture, a strategy."

"With what intent?"

"Are you falling for her?" Moore asked, agitating Dane a bit. He was beginning one of his head games. Dane didn't want to play along.

"She is attractive, has a cute little figure. Surely in all that time you have been spending with her . . ."

"She's pretty, what of it?" Dane broke in, not wanting him to continue.

"You're so weak. She would've been broken by now if it were me. Did you see how she was paralyzed in my presence?"

"Yeah, she was terrified."

"She was enamored."

"Don't flatter yourself."

"Does she ask about me a lot?" Moore asked. She did. Dane hadn't paid much mind to that before. He had been too stirred up by the mere mention of his brother's name that he hadn't noticed the pattern before.

"I don't want to talk about her anymore."

Moore let out a hushed cackle. He knew he had achieved his goal with Dane. Dane was too upset to care about his victory. "Where are we going?"

Moore didn't respond immediately. Dane was close to repeating the question.

"You know it's strange you asked to ride with me," Moore said. Dane looked at him, an eerie feeling flushing over him. "Dad took me on a similar ride when I was around your age. A little younger, actually."

Dane didn't really want to hear anymore. He regretted asking. He regretted going. Had he forgotten the monster his brother had become?

"He asked me if I was ready to become a man." Moore made another sharp turn, decreasing speed slightly. He began to shift down. "I told him I was." The car was now at a soft roll. They turned into a small neighborhood, and Moore turned off his headlights as he cruised down the quiet road. The streetlights were minimal. "He took me to a scene of the Norman's. It was pretty gruesome. I felt the same ill feeling you're probably feeling right about now.

"They had a man strapped to a chair; he had been tortured. They told our father that he had squealed and was of no more use to them. Dad said we had come at a perfect time and took a gun from his suit jacket and handed it to me. I was nervous and asked him why he wanted me to do something the Normans were supposed to take care of. And then he told me that I couldn't truly encompass the spirit of the Great Morr without a little blood on my hands."

Dane was feeling full on sick in that moment. He used every fiber of his self-control to keep him from vomiting in Moore's car. Why did he do this? He could always jump out of the car and walk home or find a pay phone and call Mason. He looked down at the door handle and readied himself mentally, but physically was unable. His body had turned to stone in his fear. He couldn't move.

Moore pulled into the driveway of one of the houses. "Are you ready to become a man today, Dane?" Moore looked right at him. He had Dane's full attention, yet Dane couldn't move or speak. Suddenly his arms and hands became free, and he cupped his mouth, holding back his sickness.

Moore looked a little disappointed, before reaching over Dane to the glove compartment. He pulled out a pair of black leather gloves and pulled them over his hands. "You're not getting sick in my car and if you do on the sidewalk, it'll tell the cops you were here." Dane was able to swallow and push back down what had been rising. He put his hands down, again frozen. Moore then took a gun out and twisted a silencer on it before vanishing from the car. "Run!" was all Dane could hear in his mind, but his body wouldn't allow him. He squeezed his eyelids shut, hoping to alleviate the nausea. He'd hoped it would transport him somewhere else, but it didn't.

He reopened them to see Moore walking out leisurely holding a small bag. He looked unfazed by whatever he had done inside and reentered the car. He tossed the bag on Dane's lap and placed the gun back in the glove compartment before backing out. Dane didn't let his hands touch the small leather bag. He just let it rest on his lap. He didn't have the slightest curiosity of its contents. He wanted no part of whatever had happened.

Moore didn't say another word to Dane on their trek back home. Once the car was parked securely, he swooped the bag back up and went inside, leaving Dane still in shock in the car. Dane finally managed to get out and went straight to the maids' house. He swung the door open and stumbled into the bathroom, knees hitting the floor to desperately hover over the toilet. He retched and heaved until his ribs burned. Sobs choked him into hyperventilation.

He was done. He had to get out of that house. He had to break all ties to his bloodline. If that was what it meant to be a true descendant of the Great Morr, he no longer wanted it. Tears poured out without ceasing, releasing his anger, confusion, fear, all the emotions he had suppressed for so long. How could he get out of this? How would he break free?

He knew one answer was to go back to Moore's car and end things the way Moore had ended the life of the occupant of that house. That was an option. Dane was so drained from the release of emotions that he couldn't fathom gaining enough energy to do that. He wondered how long it would take Vanni and Adelina to finish up inside. He didn't know what time they actually retired. They could also be running errands. He didn't want to be alone right now. His thoughts turned to Kelly. He could call her and she would come over. He knew she would risk it if she knew the distress he was in. He also knew that if she was caught it could mean they wouldn't be able to sneak around anymore. There was Beauty, but he didn't want to cause any more burden for her. He had no one.

Dane paced around the living room praying Vanni or Adelina would return. It was already ten o'clock —

how had they not retired yet? He couldn't sit still. He didn't want to allow his mind to dwell on what he had experienced. He went over to the picture on the wall, of him eating the watermelon. Why couldn't he go back to that day and speak through his child self? He would tell Vanni and Adelina to take him away. He would tell them how evil his family was and that it wasn't safe for him. The three of them could run away.

Salmi 37:4. What did that mean? He remembered an English-Italian dictionary on the bookshelf. He went over to it and pulled it out. He looked it up.

Salmi—song, Psalms a book of the Judeo-Christian Bible.

Dane without hesitance pulled out the Bible he had found in the hospital. He had no fear as he opened it, flipping to find that book. It was easy to find the Psalms as it was placed in the center of the Bible, and a piece of paper was lodged in the crease of the exact page he was looking for, Psalm 37. He unfolded the paper and found a handwritten note on it. It was in the same hand as the writing at the beginning of the Bible with his name on it. He read it and headed straight for the maids' telephone and dialed the number on it.

"Hello, is Jordan there?" He asked. His heart was rising from the adrenaline rush he got from reading an alien religious text. It was all about a God other than his family's. "Hi, this is Dane Morris. I'm sorry for calling so late, I—just, I got your gift."

Chapter Twelve

Even though it was risky, Kelly was glad Dane had invited her to his house after school. She managed to leave in his car without being seen by either Jason or Michelle and was now at the main foyer of the Morris home once again.

The welcoming warmth of the main foyer thawed out Kelly's stiff limbs as she ogled the house's interior. The place still hadn't ceased to amaze her. But Dane stiffened. He heard the sound of two pairs of expensive shoes clacking on the marble floors, coming their way, and his hand reached out to snag Kelly's arm, poised and ready to hide.

Kelly noticed the sound too, so she didn't protest when Dane pulled her to a safer spot, out of plain view. They both peaked out from the thick marble column under the left staircase, and Kelly caught sight of Moore in a tailored black designer suit. He walked at a quickened pace with a traditional black leather suitcase identical to his father's.

"I told Mason to leave the car running," Moore announced urgently, as they turned to the right corridor.

"Don't rush," Mr. Morris said, checking his watch. "The Schernol's not going anywhere." He was slightly behind Moore.

"Where is Dane?" He looked around, and Kelly was terrified they would be caught. She remembered why she hadn't been over there in so long.

"He's probably already in his room. He doesn't care about this stuff," Moore said, arriving at the front door. He paused as his father was catching up to him. He looked back as if he sensed something. What if he sensed me, Kelly's mind raced. A chill went up her back as a thrill did through her veins.

"What is it?" Mr. Morris asked after he had gotten to the front door.

"I was making sure I wasn't forgetting anything," he answered and opened the doors. The two made their exit.

"That was close," Dane whispered.

"Yeah—close," Kelly managed. Moore had known she was there, she knew it. He sensed her, he just had to have. Moore was hard to understand, and that was what bothered her. Kelly closed her eyes, remembering his chilly yet enticing looks, wondering whether she should be scared out of her mind or flattered. When she opened her eyes, Dane was out of their hiding spot, standing out in the open with his hands in his uniform jacket, perplexed.

"Where are they going?" Kelly asked, standing with him, staring down the corridor.

"Puerto Rico," he said quietly. Kelly stared back at the front door, longing to follow after them, to see this 'Schernol.' Suddenly Dane grabbed her hand and started pulling her toward the back of the house.

"Come on. Let's get out of here," Dane said with a smile. He must have noticed her longing look.

"Where are we going?" Kelly asked, pulling her hand from his and following after him.

"I want to show you something," Dane said looking behind for a moment. Kelly shrugged and followed after. They ran through the lawn of what seemed to be a never-ending backyard. They swiftly passed the maids' house and a few more buildings Kelly couldn't identify. They seemed to be running toward the gate to the forest behind the estate.

"We're almost there, I promise," Dane assured her once they were on the other side of the fence. He slowed down a little as they made their way through the trees. Kelly tried to imagine what could possibly be back here. Her legs were getting tired, but the mystery of it all got her excited.

They approached what appeared to be a tree house, though one could call it a tree mansion for its size.

"Why would you build a tree house so far from your house?" Kelly managed to ask between breaths as she realized this was their destination.

"Well, there isn't really a forest any closer."

"But there are trees all over your property."

"Yes, but a tree house didn't fit in with my mother's ideal image of what she wanted her castle to look like," Dane replied pushing forward. "Besides, it was nice getting to spend time with my dad at a good distance from Moore."

Directly beneath it, Kelly gazed up at the monstrous size of the fort. It could pass as a real house for at least two people. And it was beautiful; the mauve color cracked in places and some of the railing was broken off, but otherwise it looked fairly well maintained. "Were you planning on living out here or something?"

"What can I say? My family doesn't settle for second best, and once my Dad and I built it, my mother had a field day with her interior design skills." Dane called down from the front door of the fort. Kelly quickly went up the spiral staircase. The inside was gorgeous, filled with furniture fit for a king. Cobwebs showed either that this was the first time in a long time Dane had come out here or that he wasn't one for taking care of things. As she took a seat at Dane's request, her mind went back to Moore and Mr. Morris. She had to come up with a way of going over to Dane's house again when they got back. It would be hard with Jason.

She knew Jason was just waiting for her at home with a full on interrogation. Maybe she could run away and live in this tree house.

She couldn't wait to see the Schernol. It had been on her mind, in her dreams and her waking thoughts; her curiosity had never been so rife. The only thoughts that seemed to distract her from it were her thoughts of Moore. She wanted to see him more often, to talk with him as they had in the recreational room. He was the one giving her the mysterious looks, wearing a face so unearthly beautiful and acknowledging her with it. Who wouldn't go weak in the knees when meeting his rich dark eyes? Yet she couldn't explain the exact feeling she had for him. He still gave her chills.

"Lemonade for the lady," Dane said playfully, a smile plastered on his face. Kelly looked at him warily. He handed her one from the mini fridge inside the fort. He must've remembered her fondness of the drink and planted it there earlier. All of that wasn't strange to her; it was his joking and his smile. She'd never seen him so cheerful or playful. "It's your favorite, right?"

"Yes, thanks," Kelly responded taking the drink from his hand. She watched him as he pulled a bottle from the fridge and sat down. He was so full of life right now; there was something different about him that she couldn't pinpoint. "Are you okay?"

"Yeah, great. Why?" Dane asked.

"You're just acting strange," Kelly said slowly. She couldn't think of a better word to describe it.

"A lot has been going on in my life lately."

"Such as?"

"I just finally feel . . . free." Kelly sat up and looked at him, urging him with her expression to continue. "Free from the fear of my family, of Radehveh."

"You don't fear Radehveh anymore?"

"No, I don't even believe in him anymore. I follow the God of Israel."

"But you're Aponlean."

"Yes, but I found out this God accepts people from all nations. I don't know too much about Him yet. All I know is since I accepted His son Yeshua into my life, I've felt free. He saved my life."

"When did this happen?"

"The other night. I finally opened the Bible and found a note from a fellow student named Jordan. I called him up and he shared with me..."

136

"So, you found out who visited you, who left the Bible?"

"Yes. So, I don't know how to explain it, but Jordan just seemed to know what I was going through and answered all the questions that had been burning on my heart about life and purpose and I accepted it. I felt a release and a presence come over me. Like, God's presence, and I never knew I could experience that with any god."

"What do you mean by presence?" Kelly asked, fully engaged.

"I can't explain it, Kelly. It just happened. I just knew this was what I was longing for. I knew that He was real. He is real; His love is real."

"Well, um, good for you." Dane knew exactly what to say to render Kelly speechless. Her responses never seemed so limited until she started hanging around him. As much as she wanted to keep her guard up, Dane's transparency was growing on her. She liked being around him and witnessing all the changes he had gone through. She liked his unpredictability.

***

Kelly crept past Jason's door towards her own. As soon as she opened her bedroom door, she saw him, arms crossed like a disapproving parent's. Kelly stiffened.

She knew her mom had gotten home before her but was so busy in the kitchen that she would expect that Kelly would be in her room doing homework or studying.

As soon as she reached the middle of her room he had her in a loose hold.

"Ah, Jason!" she screamed, trying to wiggle loose. "Let go of me!" She stepped on his foot, but Jason didn't budge.

"Where were you?"

"Hanging out," she said with a strained voice, still trying to struggle free of her brother's grasp.

"Hanging out where? And with who?"

"None of your business, Jason. You're not Mom."

"Yeah, well, I had to cover for you with Mom." Kelly stopped struggling. Her arms went limp like noodles, and her backpack slid off her back and onto the ground. Had he actually done that for her? He kept her from getting in serious trouble?

"Wait, you did that for me?"

"Yeah . . . it was a one-time situation," he said. Then he let go and Kelly faced him. "Now you can pay me back by telling me you're not hanging out with Dane, especially not at his house, and you won't be doing it again," Kelly sighed wearily.

"Hey, what are you two doing?" Jessica asked in the doorway. She must've glimpsed the scene going on from the hall on the way to her bedroom.

"Nothing. Just talking with Kelly," Jason said.

"Really? Because it sure looked like you were strangling her," Jessica said, entering the room.

"You know siblings, they do that sort of stuff," he turned to face Kelly. "I'll take that as a deal." Jason said, shaking her hand and then exited, but not before giving an agitated glare to Jessica. Jessica just shrugged it off, walking over to Kelly, who was now seated at the corner of her bed.

"What was that about?" Jessica asked.

"Jason being annoying — oh wait, being himself," Kelly said sarcastically.

"He'll grow out of it," Jessica tried to comfort her. "Mike was the same way, nagging and just mean."

"Yeah, but by fifteen Mike had grown out of it."

"Some guys need a little extra time to reach maturity. Has he even reach puberty?"

"I'm pretty sure he has," Kelly laughed.

"Kelly, did I hear you two talking about Dane?"

"Dane? Oh, as in Dane Morris? No. There's this new kid in one of our classes named Thane."

"Nice try, but you and Jason don't share a class." Jessica widened her eyes at Kelly with a smug look of "tell me everything" plastered on her face.

"Can you keep a secret?"

"As long as you tell me you don't like him in a romantic way or anything."

"Ew, no!" Kelly made a disgusted face. "We have been talking."

"Talking?"

"Well, hanging out."

"Why?"

"Because of the mystery of it all."

"Oh, Kelly, you and your curiosity. What have you gotten yourself into now?"

"I haven't gotten into anything. I've just been hanging out with him and finding out answers."

"They aren't answers you could be finding out from Dad? He'd probably be less prone to lie," Jessica suggested.

"Dane's not the same person anymore. He's changed."

"Hm, well, remember how earlier I promised I would keep it a secret?"

"Jessica! You can't tell anyone," Kelly pleaded.

"But this could be risky. He is a descendant of Morr, after all, and you seem to be ignoring that fact and trusting him. The moment you trust someone from Morr is the moment you become a sitting duck."

"I am not stupid, Jessica."

"Maybe not, but naïveté is just as dangerous," Jessica added. Kelly thought a moment of what she was doing. It very well could be dangerous. She couldn't trust Moore or Mr. Morris and Jessica had her starting to doubt she could really trust Dane. How had she let her guard down so much without even realizing?

"You're right," was all she could say.

"So, I won't have to say anything if it stops." Jessica put out her hand and Kelly shook it. She wasn't sure how binding that handshake would be. She had to see that Schernol, and nothing would stop her from that.

Chapter Thirteen

Kelly was ready for her third visit to the Morris estate, but the stakes were high; now she had to get past Jessica and Jason. She walked out of her room casually and headed downstairs. She went through the dining room, where Jason was sitting at the table. She knew he was there, partly because it was the room where you could see the most going on. Kelly rustled his hair with a smile and he grumbled when she did.

Next she went through the swinging doors and saw her mom preparing dinner. She looked like she had just started, so Kelly had some time, plus Lisa was at ballet and she would need to pick her up soon. Kelly went into the fridge to grab the pitcher of lemonade and poured herself a glass. She had almost forgotten to put the pitcher back, but her mom reminded her.

She tried to think of how to go back out there and sneak out without Jason getting on her case. She knew he was just waiting for it. If she headed to the back, he'd question her and possibly follow, and he had a clear view of the front door.

Kelly carried the drink out of the kitchen and smiled at Jason as she passed and headed back up-stairs. Once back in her room, she sighed.

"You're forcing me to do this, Jason," she said, opening the door to her balcony. There was a large tree toward the left end of the balcony, near Jessica's door. Kelly sighed deeply, walking over to the spot closest to one of its branches. She climbed up on the white railing and swung her leg over the large branch, pulling her body around it, hugging it.

She scooted herself down the branch toward the tree itself. Once at the center she eyed her options, there were several branches that lead close enough to the ground to jump from them without getting hurt, but they were a bit of a distance from the one she was currently on.

Kelly turned over, so that she was sitting up on the branch now. She tried stretching her leg toward one of the lower branches, measuring the distance. She could make it; she'd have to give herself enough of a boost, but she was certain she could. Oh, why did Jason have to make her life so difficult? Why did the Morris estate have such a hold on her? Why did her curiosity dictate her actions so much? She couldn't blame those things; it was Aponlea. Aponlea was calling her. She stood up, keeping balanced by holding the tree trunk. She grabbed a slender branch above her with both hands, dangling as she stretched her legs down toward the lower branch. Her feet were just above it when she released herself, her feet quickly keeping her steady. She dropped to the lower branch. Once stabilizing herself she crouched down in crawling position to get to the other end of the branch, where it thinned and was close enough to the ground to jump from.

Once on the ground, she went in the back way, following the Morrises' fence far beyond her backyard. The back gate that they went through to the tree house was usually unlocked, and from there she would make her way past all of the guest houses and the tennis court to the back of the main house.

◆

As she followed Dane to the game room, watching his back, her thoughts went to minuscule matters like his perfectly pressed jacket. If he always talked about how his parents weren't ever around, how did he keep his uniform so clean, ironed so professionally? Did he know how to do all that himself?

When they were closed away in the room, Kelly

idled by the door while Dane circled around the lounge chairs to the soda and juice bar. "Dane, who irons your uniform?"

It was a very random question. Why Kelly wanted to know confused the girl herself.

Dane looked up, showing a look that Kelly found most comical. He straightened up, holding a juice can with both hands. "Uh, well, my housemaids do," he answered.

"Oh," Kelly made herself comfortable in the bucket seat she considered her favorite — the only one with a footrest. Dane sat down with a smile on his face. "What's with the smile?" she asked warily. He shrugged, still smirking. She looked away, mentally beating herself for suddenly finding him attractive. It had to be hormones, though since he'd been smiling more often it did bring a certain charm to him.

"Nothing," he said, moving to sit across from her.

"Okay?" she questioned, looking at him a while longer.

"Wanna play some air hockey?" Dane asked, brushing it off. Kelly lit up. She loved playing that game and always wished she had one in her own house so she and Joey could play.

They ended up playing for a whole hour. Kelly won a few times, but Dane, being competitive, won enough times to make both of them forget about keeping score. Kelly used the time to ask him more little questions, which Dane actually enjoyed answering. She learned a lot about Adelina and Vanni, where they came from, how they'd been with the family ever since Moore was born. They meant a lot to Dane apparently. She also asked him what his days usually consisted of, which seemed pretty dull and boring to Kelly. She even asked him what hobbies he liked. The boy had none, but he mentioned wanting to start playing the guitar.

When it started to get quiet, he urged her to ask more questions. "Ask me anything."

"What was Moore like when he was young?"

Regret immediately showed on his face. But he did answer, giving Kelly the most condensed and vague reply imaginable.

"He was . . . different. Quiet. Very antisocial."

"What do you mean by different? How different?"

"I can't really explain it, Kelly. I didn't hang around him much."

"Oh come on, even as a kid? You guys didn't play with each other?"

"Maybe, it's hard to remember him back when he was a decent brother," Dane said, and when the puck came his way, he shot it a little too hard; the puck went flying over the table. Dane apologized, but Kelly just picked the puck up off the floor and put it back on her side of the table.

"It's alright. Happens all the time," she said. And it did, but she had a feeling Dane didn't do it by accident. It may have been out of anger instead. She didn't ask any more questions after that and kept quiet until the game was over.

"Dane, can we go to the library?" Kelly asked eagerly. She had been wanting to see it since Moore had introduced the thought to her.

"Yeah, of course."

Thick marble columns arched before an open room filled with an unimaginable number of books. Some of the shelves could only be reached by special ladders that were attached to them. The tall wooden sliding doors were wide open. Kelly was drawn to the expanse of the room in an instant.

Most of the books were leather-bound, aligned, and lettered in silver. Kelly was enticed by the beauty of them. She started running her fingers over the ones she could reach, wandering along the many aisles of bookshelves that filled the large room. Dane stood at the entrance watching her.

She stopped at the sight of a thick, age-worn book encased in glass. It looked to be hundreds of years old, and it was lying flat on a silver half-pillar, which was the shape of a perfect cylinder.

"The Great Morr," she whispered, her face inches from the pristine glass. It was the title of the book. Its silver letters were blinding as it caught the light from the display pillar, but she couldn't stop looking at it. Below the wide pillar was an open compartment with a more modern copy. Kelly's hungry fingers grabbed hold of it at once and started flipping through it. She couldn't believe her fortune.

"This must be an important book," Kelly said, eyes glued to the pages.

"That actually might be good for you to read. You can see how horrible Morr was and how his ethics have been passed down through many generations. And since my brother is his star pupil, perhaps you won't be so in love with him."

"I am not in love with Moore." That finally got her attention away from the book.

"Is entranced a better word? I saw the way you looked at him and how you light up when you ask about him."

"I am just trying to figure him out."

"Go ahead and keep reading that book. That's all you need to know. Pure evil."

"Maybe he's just misunderstood."

"Are you forgetting that I grew up with him?"

"But we're different with siblings."

"Yeah, we're our real selves."

Kelly was starting to get frustrated. The topic was obviously one they would never agree on, so it was best to drop it. She knew he was right but couldn't understand why she wanted so badly not to believe him. Perhaps he was right that she was entranced by him.

"So, tell me some important artifacts," Kelly smiled trying to ease what little tension was brought about by their former conversation.

"You already know about the Sceptra and the Schernols. Um, there's the Samorik," Dane answered.

"What about the Sam-thing?"

"The Samorik is a small device, but very important. It morphs the Schernols together to become the Prostasia."

"Right, Prostasia, rule Aponlea."

"Yep."

"Great! So we should find the Samorik!" Kelly knew it wasn't that simple, but eagerly wanted to find it.

"You're right. It should be easy enough too," Dane said, with a hint of sarcasm.

"Yeah?" Kelly joined.

"No, Kelly. Nothing is that simple. That is why people have been searching for hundreds of years and have found nothing."

"Except a Schernol. Times are changing," Kelly genuinely believed that.

"You have got to be the most optimistic idealist I have ever met," Dane said, looking amused.

"That's not hard to achieve in your eyes, when you come from a family like yours."

"Touché. Still it is refreshing."

"What can I say, I believe in the impossible."

"And that's why you're beautiful," Dane said, looking Kelly straight in the eyes. She felt a little embarrassed, but longing at the same time. Dane quickly added, "Your ideals are beautiful. So, tell me, how do we find this Samorik?" Dane flicked his eyes elsewhere.

"I don't know. One of these books should have the answer." Kelly looked around also, not sure how to feel about his blunder.

"Wait!" Dane seemed to be onto something. "I've got it," he said, heading over to one of the bookshelves. He pulled a book from the shelf and held it up, looking at its cover. Kelly waited for him to tell her what it was. She couldn't help but feel some excitement. "This is the Aponlean section."

"What is it?" She finally asked, not giving him much time to tell her before her question. She paced over to him, trying to look at the cover. He playfully held it away from her.

"This one is called Where to Find the Samorik.'" Kelly's face sank, but she still found amusement in his teasing.

"You know, I do not appreciate your sarcasm." She pretended to be very offended.

"You're right. I am sorry," he smiled, placing the book back in its place. Kelly had her arms still folded, facing away from him. Dane went up to her, placing his hands on her shoulders. "How can I make it up to you?"

"I don't know if you can. Of all the mean pranks you've played, this has got to be the worst," Kelly said, still maintaining her offended tone. Dane came around to face her.

"I'll go to the ends of the world, to prove I am truly sorry."

"Some lemonade will do." A smile cracked on her face.

"Some lemonade it is," Dane said and headed out of the library. Kelly went back over to the case and pulled out the modern copy of The Great Morr.

She felt an urge to read it nonstop until she reached the very last page. There were terms, places, interactions that she'd never heard of before, that were probably explained. Maybe if she did read it, she'd be able to speak with Moore on a more equal level. A smile took hold of her lips.

Around the same time her smile dissolved, there were voices growing in volume as they got closer. Two voices. The familiar sound of those expensive shoes was headed to the library Kelly was standing in the middle of, washed with the light bouncing off of the silver pillar, revealing her like an open display for all to see.

The footsteps were approaching much quicker than she'd expected, and her brain wasn't working fast enough. Instinct took over, and she shut the book, shoved it back in its compartment, and ran as far from the center of the library as possible. Leaving it wasn't an option at this point; Moore and his father had entered the room, standing right where Kelly had been seconds ago. Thankfully, they hadn't noticed a presence. Or that was what Kelly thought.

Kelly sat, leaned against one of the tall bookshelves, completely paralyzed. Terror had seized every inch of her. She'd encountered Moore before, but never Mr. Morris, and that frightened her. She tried hard not to pant after her recent sprint and managed to breath without sound. Her heart pounded beyond control, though.

She heard them conversing at the center, where the displayed book lay. She couldn't hear them over her pounding heart and the worries clouding her mind. She did hear someone approaching the shelf she was behind. He was on the other side. She turned her head and saw his shoes: it was Moore. He wouldn't see her unless he bent down to get a book at the bottom. The one he grabbed was at the top. He was soon back in the center of the room with his father.

Kelly looked between a few of the books. They had the Schernol up front, she was sure.

Moore fished through the front pocket of his slacks and pulled out a jewel-encrusted key. It caught the light of the silver pillar, producing bright beams of light that flickered through various parts of the library, including Kelly's eyes. She blinked a few times, and continued to watch. She placed a hand on her chest, alarmed by the rapid rate of her heartbeat. Since she was both panicked and excited, it seemed her body couldn't keep up with itself. She gripped the edge of the bookshelf she was hiding behind, feeling herself sway dangerously to the side. She became dizzy and squeezed her eyes shut.

Come on, not now, she told herself, exhaling through her mouth. She chanted it in her head until the sensation disappeared. Now was definitely not the time to faint, not just because it would reveal her presence, but also because she wanted to listen in and see the thing that many had spent years searching for.

The key opened a compartment Kelly didn't even know existed in the silver pillar. A door slid open, revealing another book. This one was small, slightly bigger than the palm of Moore's hand, but it was thick.

Kelly watched as the two looked through the two books, examining the object they had just obtained. She still couldn't see the object itself. They took the books and the object to a black-stained, wooden table by the sitting area of the library.

Kelly stood, walking toward the corner to get a better look. She pushed two books away from each other slightly, enough for her to peak through without revealing herself. She leaned her body against the rest of the shelf, trying to see the object. She needed to be higher. Kelly looked down and carefully stepped up on the bottom shelf, holding herself up with the shelf she was just looking through. Moore's eyes suddenly shot in her direction. Had he heard her? Mr. Morris certainly hadn't — his attention was on their prize. Moore looked back to the books in front of him.

"The last step is to bring the machine in," Moore said, nonchalantly.

"Or we could bring it to the machine," Mr. Morris corrected.

"We'll still need the books. It'll be easier that way," Moore persisted. "We've got nothing to worry about."

"I suppose." Mr. Morris stood up, still looking at the device on the table. Moore looked Kelly's way again and winked before heading out of the library. He had seen her. Her heart began to race again. Mr. Morris followed his son.

Kelly was frozen stiff. She went limp with relief, plopping onto the floor. Had Moore just left her in the library alone on purpose? Or was she just hallucinating? She figured she had a tendency to do that. She had gotten dizzy earlier. I must be dreaming, she thought, because this is way too good to be true.

Whether it was a dream or not, now was her

time. She needed to see it. She didn't have much time. Eventually Moore and his father would also be returning to the library. Her heart raced, causing a burning sensation to build within her ribcage. The adrenaline, the pressure — it was too great. She stood up, stumbling on her feet because of her numb ankles, gripping the nearest bookshelf for balance. After that she found it hard to move, feeling a strange sense that she'd cheated someone.

Hundreds of years, numerous men fought for this object, and here she was, a fifteen-year-old girl, about to look at it with her own eyes, with no one to watch her, to keep guard. Most who'd seen it spent their entire lives searching for it, probably like Moore and his father had. And imagine the times they'd failed to produce anything out of the searches. Kelly just happened to be in the right place at the right time. But she still didn't feel worthy. She didn't even know a quarter of the object's history. Was she mocking those who'd searched before her? It was an uncomfortable thing to think about, but she eventually clenched her fists and willed herself to move.

She had to remind herself that she was already up, that Moore hadn't ratted her out. That had to mean he wouldn't mind her looking at it, right? The tantalizing glance he'd given her before blocking the view between him and his father was like a repeating tape in her head. He was obviously toying with her. He knew she wanted to see. And if he knew that, he wouldn't have left her in the library with the Schernol to herself if he didn't want her to see it. For whatever reason, Kelly had no idea. Things were working out too easily for her today. Was that even a good thing?

Quickly, she limped across the open space, passing the silver pillar to the wooden table where the Schernol lay open and vulnerable for hungry fingers like hers to take — or worse — to steal. But Kelly had no intention of stealing it; she just wanted to feed her aching curiosity. There was no harm in that, was there?

Her mind was too entranced and awed. The in-

149

tricate design drew her eyes to its incandescence. She realized too late that her hands weren't gripping the object tightly enough as she barely grazed her fingers across the aged engravings. That was when she dropped it

She was too busy panicking over the dropped treasure to hear the faint sounds of footsteps approaching. Reflexes took over finally, and she picked it up before it could make another sound, slapping herself inwardly for letting panic affect her motor skills. She almost screamed when she felt something prickle on her palm; the Schernol had pinched her skin as it moved. Its middle was rearranging itself as it lay face down on Kelly's palm. She flipped it over quickly, her face contorted with confusion and alarm. She wasn't expecting this at all. A cube probably slightly larger than Kelly's hand rearranged itself out of the Schernol's middle and right into Kelly's hand, smooth and cold, gleaming in Kelly's dark brown eyes.

Footsteps got louder; the Schernol took its normal shape immediately, but it didn't take the cube back with it. Everything just went from fortunate to disastrous. She had broken it!

LOUDER.

No time. Kelly shoved the cube in her front hoodie pocket and placed the Schernol back into the cushioned suitcase with uncontrollably shaking hands. At least it had taken its original shape. They shouldn't notice, she chanted in her head as she dashed behind the closest bookshelf, but it revealed her other side, where Mr. Morris and Moore would be entering from. Hearing their voices now, Kelly lunged to the corner and squeezed in between two leather lounge seats. She shook; she bit back sobs and hugged herself. They were in the room now, and Kelly prayed they wouldn't notice.

Dane was with them now. She could hear his voice join into their conversation. He knew she was there — if only he could rescue her. She waited with agonized anticipation, but they went on about further business

150

and future plans — they were still on the subject of the Schernol nonetheless. She eyed the exit, noting that maybe if she was quiet enough, she could creep out of the place without them seeing. There were bookshelves to keep her well hidden on the way. But again, she had to be silent, and she didn't know if she could trust herself, not when her nerves had made her actions jerky and unstable. Being on the verge of hyperventilation wasn't going to help either; her vision fogged in and out.

But she couldn't bear to stay any longer. Moore and his father had dangerous tendencies. She didn't want to think about the punishment if she were caught. Breathing became difficult even at the thought of it. She squeezed from between the seats. She'd planted a step forward, but her jerky movements caused her to trip right where she was. Her knees hit the ground hard, elbows also, and she froze, eyes as wide as saucers, mouth agape. It was over.

"What was that?" Mr. Morris said, more alert. Kelly closed her eyes, she couldn't watch. She wished she had never come here. She wanted to be far, far away. They would see it was broken, and then even Moore wouldn't forgive her.

"I'll go check it out," Dane said. Kelly felt a little relief.

"No, I'll see," Moore spoke up, and the fear returned to Kelly. "Stay with the Schernol; you haven't seen it yet." Kelly could hear his steps were swift, allowing no time for Dane to argue. If only the powers of her ancestors would engulf her and make her invisible. She wasn't invisible. Moore was looking right at her. He swiftly put a finger to his lips when her head whipped up toward him. She immediately closed her mouth and held her breath.

Kelly was cowering under his shadow. Moore could see that she was visibly shaking. He knelt down slowly, as silent as a poised jaguar hunting, and took Kelly's shoulders with his hands, lifting her upward as easily as a blanket. He watched her eyes as they

151

rose together, forcing herself to breath normally, silently. He didn't look dangerous then. He didn't look threatening. His hands were gentle and supporting. She actually calmed as she drank in more of his dark, subdued beauty. She watched his smooth neck lift up, gazed at his Adam's apple as it rose and fell when he smoothly said in the direction of his father, "It's nothing. A book fell from the shelf. Dane must have had something to do with it." Moore looked back at Kelly with a satisfied smile.

He let go of her and gave her a nudge forward, pointing to the exit before heading back to his father and Dane.

"You can't even do that right," he muttered to Dane. Kelly made her quick and dazed escape.

Kelly made her way to the game room and went to the farthest corner from the door, sliding her back down against the wall. Her knees were bent up as she hugged them and tears uncontrollably fell from her eyes. Her heart was pounding worse than before, her face flushed. She wasn't trying to cry but couldn't help it. What was she doing there?

Suddenly, everything everyone had warned her about became real. She wished she could just teleport to her room or anywhere besides here. She wished Joey would appear and comfort her, or even Dane. She felt safe with him. She could finally admit it to herself. He was the one person she could be completely honest with. She knew he cared; his "'new person" act was not an act at all. He really was a different person, and she wanted him there with her now.

At least one wish came true as he came into the room and got down to her level. She moved herself to be in his arms, sobbing all the more. He didn't say anything, just held her. All fear melted away as her guard went down. She was vulnerable to the one person she didn't want to be vulnerable to, but she didn't care. She wanted to remain in his arms always. This moment had to last forever; they were completely connected.

"It's alright," his voice soothed her. "I will never let anything bad happen to you. No one will ever harm you. I will make sure of that."

Kelly still couldn't speak, but felt no need to. Neither of them needed to say more. The moment was best appreciated in silence. She knew they were thinking and feeling the same thing. They would be there for each other always.

Chapter Fourteen

The cube was warm in Kelly's hands. She was now lying in her bed, having taken a shower and changed into her pj's for bed.

"I wonder what it is," she murmured to herself. It wasn't as intricate as the Schernol itself, but it still had those oceanic designs she'd seen on the main piece, only bolder and less defined; everything else about it was simple. It felt good in her hands, and she found herself squeezing it occasionally to relieve her stress. It was smooth, pointed at the edges. A perfect cube. As Kelly felt the box between her fingers she felt comforted somehow.

She stared up at the cube, holding it above her as she lay in her bed. Did Mr. Morris and Moore even know it existed? She wondered. They didn't sound like they knew much about the object. Did the book tell them it had something inside it? It had to; the book explains everything about the Schernol. Why wouldn't it?

Staring intently at the piece in her hand, she let her imagination run wild, her eyelids growing heavy. She wondered what it would be like to have watched the great battle in its time. She could imagine it more clearly, now that she'd seen the very shield they would have fought with. She knew firsthand what it felt like to hold onto a Schernol.

Just then, as she thought that, she curled up and drifted to sleep.

The Glimpse

John could tell. Peter wasn't going to give good news. They'd both briefly escaped the battlefield to a makeshift meeting ground where hundreds of John's soldiers had gathered only hours ago to plan strategies and sequences. Those soldiers wouldn't be coming back. Not ever.

"Almost all of our men have joined with Morr," John said, closing his eyes. He couldn't expect loyalty when they hadn't trained as his men. They were the soldiers of the king. The king was now dead, and to ask them to choose him, not an heir by blood, over Morr, who had captured all but three Schernols, was too much, it appeared. "We don't stand a chance, John. If we accept Morr as king, maybe he'll have mercy on us."

John let out an anguished groan and placed his head in his hands. A chair scraped along the stone floors of the meeting chambers in sync with John's distressed mind; paintings lifted and adjusted themselves; John's bloody sword shook violently in its sheath; the very table he was sitting at lifted a few inches in midair before dropping back down. He had made a promise to the king. He would've been sworn in as Aponlea's next ruler had Morr not murdered the king before he could declare his successor to the people. Only the king's two sons and trusted advisors, all of whom were dead, except Jacob, the king's eldest son, knew of this. Jacob had refused to fight until now, cowering for his life.

"Sir, what do you suggest we do?" Peter asked after there had been a considerable silence. They hadn't even been fighting for a whole day yet, and most of their men had been slaughtered, their natural abilities completely blocked by the Schernol's shielding powers. He followed John out into the open air, into the thickness of defeat, and watched his leader lift pleading eyes to the sky.

"We still have three Schernols."

"Three Schernols against the other seventeen - not to mention thousands of ruthless men."

"Is Tom still with us?"

"Yes, sir, but . . ."

"Give him one. The three of us have held on this

long, and the faith we fight with will bring us the victory. Gather seven other men who have not turned over to the other side. Pure men, the ones who trained alongside us before this civil war."

"Alright, sir. I've known you long enough to trust you in a dark path. I will fight by your side even if it's just us two. I'll go retrieve them."

"And, Kelly, that was just what he did. He found seven courageous men, strong and pure men. You see, the purity was the key. The sense of loyalty to what was right was what gave them their strength. When you fight for greed or selfish ambitions, you're limited to what you can muster up in yourself. But when you're fighting for someone, for something, your strength comes from all directions."

"What happened next?"

"Those very men fought their hearts out."

John used guerilla warfare and strategically led his men to defeat many of Morr's men.

Peter had slain three hundred on the battlefield and hadn't faltered once. His nine fellow warriors were out of his view, fighting their own swarm of enemies.

A typical battle in Aponlea ended quickly, because everything seemed to move at high speed. Soldiers would dip in and out of existence through teleportation, appearing in front of you one second and across the field the next, in the blink of an eye.

A man of good reflexes and precision survived such a war. You'd have to have your wits about you in order to make sense of weapons slicing the air toward a target and disappearing men. Their war cries would still hang in the air even as a soldier changed locations, making it all the more confusing.

Peter was particularly good at prediction. He would appear behind an enemy one second, attempt an attack, then rotate to other enemies, his body moving in anticipation of their next move.

And then, just like that, a soldier of Morr had stabbed Peter's side. He rolled out of harm's way, ducked and dodged the swings of the horde of attackers, and locked

156

on a new target. As he charged forward, his sword went flying straight to the heart of the enemy who had pierced him. Three of Morr's men came at him this time, including Moy, who had the Sulfur Schernol. He stayed high in the air above the other two and combined his own might with that of the Schernol to give an upper hand to his two men, keeping them power driven.

Despite Peter's efforts, the attackers were able to soar toward him; his power block was unsuccessful. Before they reached him, they stopped a few feet away in the air. Peter thought he had overpowered him, but in a matter of seconds he became aware that something wasn't right. Before he could teleport higher, an electrifying cord had seized his neck by surprise, and the sheer pain of it caused him to release control of his Schernol. The cord had come from another soldier behind him. The white-gold device fell, but it was swooped up by one of the men who had earlier charged at him. Peter held off the jolts of electricity and the tightness of the cord as long as he could with his mind, but if the men succeeded in blocking his power . . .

Kelly was gasping for air, sweating profusely, almost falling out of her bed as she clawed at her sheets with her eyes glued shut. When she awoke, shooting up from her bed, she was too winded to scream. Tears formed in her eyes, as she felt that she knew the fallen warrior who'd died in her dream. Her stomach was churning and she clutched at it, hunching over. Eyes still wide and straining from the darkness of the bedroom, she willed the images away. How had she dreamed something so gory, so graphic? It all felt so real, like she was right there watching.

It felt so real, she thought repeatedly, and she couldn't rid her mind of the strange feeling that it had really happened in history. But how would she have known? She'd never been there. And who was that voice, narrating it? Was she remembering something she'd known years ago?

Her parents had never taught her anything on the history of Aponlea, and they most certainly never told her any stories that included violence. She wasn't

even allowed to watch certain Saturday morning car-
toons because of their mild violence, so where would
she have known it from? Now there was a mystery to
solve. The dream was so vivid and so familiar. She was
there; she had smelled the sulfuric odor rising from the
ground, the faces of John and Peter. Her imagination
had never felt so distinct, so tangible, in all her life.

She swallowed, trying to gain control of herself,
but still she breathed shakily. Her stomach relented,
though, and she straightened a bit, turning to look
at her alarm clock. It was still early in the night. She
squeezed her hands and felt the smoothness of the
cube pressing hard against her palms. She looked down
at it. Maybe it was inducing these dreams somehow,
since she'd seen the silver Schernol that same day. It
only made her feel guilty about having it.

Where can I hide this thing?

She scanned her room, suddenly remembering
the hole in the wall behind her wall-length mirror.
Anyone who tried to lift it wouldn't succeed unless
they ripped it up; only she knew how to move it. She
stepped out of bed, running one hand over her clammy
forehead to remove the hair sticking to it, holding the
silver cube in the other. She slid the middle panel of
the mirror up and slipped the cube in the hole near
the floor. She didn't sense any real threats of room
searches, but she had to be careful, just in case her
mother or siblings came snooping around.

She climbed back in bed and flipped onto her
side, exhaling deeply, feeling slightly better after being freed of the object.

⬥ ⬥ ⬥

"Beauty, I found that freedom," Dane said, sitting
across from his sister in the living room of her loft.
Dane was so eager to tell her that he could help find
the healing she needed. He had the answer, and all
he thought he had to do was share it with her. Then
she could stop hiding away in her loft and experience
life again. Life could be returned to her eyes.

"What is it? A new drug?" she asked. Dane winced at the thought of it. Both she and their mother were on so many medications already.

"No. Hear me out a moment. I gave my life over to the God of Israel, and I have never been happier in my life. I don't feel the burdens . . ."

"Do you want to curse this place?" Beauty said sharply, sincere irritation in her eyes.

"Well, no, but . . ."

"Don't talk about this other god. Radehveh is present everywhere, and if he thinks I have anything to do with another god . . ."

"That's not true, Beauty. I have a Bible in my room right now, have had it there for weeks, and things have been better in my life than they ever have. Look at the life you think Radehveh granted to you. Are you happy? Is it possible for you to be happy in it?" Beauty didn't have a response this time. He could tell she was meditating on his words. "I can finally say I am happy. The name you should be calling to and fearing is Yeshua. He is our salvation."

"Nothing's that simple, Dane. You see how bad things are between me and dad. If he knew . . ."

"Don't tell him. I haven't, not yet at least."

"You would have to have a death wish to tell him that. Dane, . . ."

"Beauty, this is real. I finally found what we were looking for."

"I'll keep your secret for you now, Dane. But if I start to get punished by Radehveh on your behalf, I can't make any promises."

"But, Beauty." Dane looked at her. Why wasn't she accepting it? As soon as Jordan told him, he accepted it right away. Jordan Westbrook, a former classmate he used to bully, was brave enough to leave a Bible and forgiving enough to visit him after all Dane had done to him. He couldn't believe it, but he wanted to. It was just the right time and just the right message. God had heard Dane's pain and his cry and rescued him. Why wasn't Beauty accepting it? She was seeking the same thing he had been. She needed this far more than he did. What was holding her back?

Chapter Fifteen

The weeks that passed did become more comforting to Kelly. Though she didn't go to Dane's house again after finding the cube, they would talk at school and over the phone. They talked a lot on the phone these days, but with anyone being able to pick up the other line, they had to be careful what they said. If anyone did catch her talking to some guy, she had decided she'd tell them it was Jake, Michelle's brother. Everyone knew they had a fling in middle school and she could say they had started talking again.

She also was becoming less and less anxious about someone finding out about the cube. Dane didn't bring it up, and he had told her that his father and Moore were preoccupied with finding the guy they had been keeping tabs on. He had made a run for it while they were retrieving the Schernol. They seemed to be very upset about that, and Kelly hoped it was enough to distract them from ever finding out about the cube.

Still, each day after school, she would check behind her mirror, making sure the object was still there, until the week before spring break, when she was packing for her family's annual cottage trip. She decided she would leave it behind for a week. She did steal it after all, so it wasn't rightfully hers. But then, Moore had probably stolen it in Puerto Rico. She imagined a long line of thefts and didn't feel so bad about her own. It wasn't like she set out to steal it, it just happened. If someone took it while she was gone, the chain would continue. It wasn't a big deal.

Actually, it was a huge deal. Kelly couldn't keep

her mind off it as she sat in the family van. They were an hour out. Perhaps she could say she forgot something and they'd go back, but what would be important enough to go back? What was she thinking? Kelly tried to calm her thoughts. She tried to focus on other things, like the trip and family time.

Kelly glanced at the back of Lisa's car seat, a full head of dark wavy hair limply jutting from the edge of the seat because she'd dozed off from the lull of the rental van's hum. The Johnson family was loaded up in a twelve-passenger van, headed north to their beloved vacation home, a two-story stone-cobbled cottage perched on a beautiful piece of land — a place passed down by Mr. Johnson's father, who had bought the land and built the house with his own hands. It was a token of his success. Mr. Johnson, Joey, Mike, and Jason had just traveled up half a year ago to make a few repairs on the roof, repaint a few wooden panels. It could easily have been taken care of with hired help, but the job was more intimate, Mr. Johnson thought, when he and his own boys did it with their own hands. It was a bonding experience.

The family loved the cottage. They looked forward to spring break primarily because they were able to return to it again. The main thing Kelly was looking forward to on this particular trip, though, was Joey. She missed him. The anticipation of seeing him again had lightened her spirit. She relaxed against the slightly reclined seat, ignoring Jason's cranky protests behind her for limiting his leg space. They were, after all, on the road at four o'clock in the morning; she should have been asleep like the rest. But instead, she stayed awake, too restless to sleep.

Zach had his head on a pillow on Kelly's lap, his small and lanky body still and silent. He usually kept to himself — very private for such a young boy — but since he was a restless sleeper even in his own bed, doing so on the road was almost impossible when sitting up. Kelly absently ran her fingers through her little brother's short hair while she stared out the window, disappointed that she was only able to see the shadowed outlines of bare trees against nothing but a dark, navy-blue sky. If she hadn't already burned out the batteries of her CD player, the scene outside might have been more enjoyable, but she was only stuck with the various breathing patterns of her slumbering family.

"Hey dad?" Kelly chimed quietly, just loud enough for Mr. Johnson's ears to incline toward his daughter while keeping his eyes glued to the seemingly endless highway.

"Sweetie?"

"How long . . . ?"

"Not even close," Mr. Johnson interrupted, suppressing a laugh. "We only left an hour ago, Kelly. You're asking me the infamous 'are we there yet' already?" Kelly bashfully sunk in her seat, watching her Dad through the rearview mirror as his eyes crinkled with his smile. She shrugged.

"Sorry. I'm just bored. It's my lame excuse for something to start up. It's so quiet in here," Kelly said, poking her lips out, pressing the side of her forehead against the cool window. Mr. Johnson took his eyes off his driving to glance up at the rearview mirror, raising an eyebrow at Kelly.

"What is it, Kelly?" Mr. Johnson asked softly, knowingly. Kelly linked eyes with her father, shrugging.

"It's really nothing, Dad. I'm just excited," she simply said. She gave him a smile. She wished she could tell him everything, but she knew better. If he found out she got into the affairs of her family's mortal enemies and stole an important object from them . . . She didn't even want to think of that possibility.

"You have a book to read or something? Zach rigged a pretty cool book light back there; it should be on his lap."

"Good idea," she said, looking over her brother's sleeping body. She picked the book light up and examined it. It was a Zach Johnson creation, alright, made from various other objects. She held open the book she had brought with her, but couldn't focus on the words as her eyes scanned the pages. She was imagining the books in the Morris library. She should have taken one of those. With so many, they wouldn't have noticed, except maybe Moore. He seemed to have some sort of sixth sense when it came to her.

◆———◆———◆

It was early afternoon when the family arrived at the cottage. The first thing the siblings did when Mr. Johnson unlocked the heavy wooden front doors was charge into the place to claim bedrooms. Kelly got the room the loser always got. She'd never gotten the worst of the rooms before — which was still an impressive room, just easily cluttered. She accepted what she got this time, because she was too tired to care. She hadn't slept the whole drive up.

Mr. Johnson and Mrs. Johnson, of course, never needed to claim a room. They were entitled to the master suite for as long as the place was standing.

Kelly opened the door to the room with just her pillow tucked under her arm, wanting to linger in the room a while before having to help unpack the van. The room was on a corner opposite the lake on their property. It had no windows but lots of lights to make up for the darkness and creative furniture arrangements.

Kelly tossed her pillow onto the bed and lay on it. Its down comforter hugged Kelly snuggly. She didn't want to move.

"Tsk, tsk, Kelly. You wound up with the loser's room?" Joey said from the doorway. He soon entered, plopping down beside her.

"First time ever," she answered.

"Wow, what a loser. The first Johnson family challenge and . . ."

"Stop right there," Kelly warned, "before you deal with the wrath of my pillow." Kelly was perched up now, clenching her pillow in action mode.

"Oh, the thought of cushioning cotton dreadfully frightens me," Joey said sarcastically and the two laughed.

"This is going to be good," Kelly leaned against her brother. "A vacation from life."

"I'll tell you something, Kelly. Every day's a vacation from life when you are with the person you love."

"Aw," Kelly said. He and Melanie were the cutest.

"Mushiest person of the year stuff right there," Joey teased.

"You won that a long time ago," Kelly said.

"So, in three short sentences, what's new?" Joey probed. "Nothing long, the Jet Skis are calling us."

"Let's see. I have a rare Aponlean artifact that I am not supposed to. I had a very vivid Aponlean dream that has been haunting me. And I might be spending too much time with Dane Morris, which may or may not be causing me to have feelings for him."

"Wow. I was not anticipating those. I was wanting something more cheesy, like I got an A in science. Jason is still a bother, and there's a cute guy in my English class."

"Two of those are true."

"Since I know how much you hate science, I can guess which two. This will be a good vacation for you. Free your mind, forget everything to do with Aponlea, and never date a Morris; it doesn't end well. That's my advice for you. Now let's get to those Jet Skis." He shot back up and sprinted to the door. He waited for Kelly, who quickly got up herself and went after him.

The Jet Skis were the first attraction the Johnson children took advantage of. They had commenced their annual Jet Ski race; only Joey and Mike had a last-minute game change for their partners. They decided it would be more fun to see which person could get their partner to fall off into the water first. It was a risk Joey was taking with his new partner, Melanie, as he wasn't sure what her reaction would be, but Mike knew Kelly would get over it.

Jason, on the other hand, was intensifying the

ongoing war between him and Jessica. He was relentless with her, and even though he wasn't a part of the planning of this game change, his participation would only fuel the already high burning fire.

Jessica's screams could be heard by the relaxing Johnson parents in the master suite.

Kelly was so excited at the game change. It was the type of sentiment she enjoyed. This was a beautiful break from her ongoing Aponlea interest. Even so, she clung onto Mike as fervently as she could.

———◆———

Kelly had taken a nap after the Jet Skiing competition; the lack of sleep in the car ride had caught up with her. When Kelly woke up, it was close to dinnertime. There were no windows, so she couldn't tell just by looking outside that the sun was setting beautifully over the lake in the back, tinting everything with warm purples and oranges. She only knew the time from the digital clock next to her bed.

She was still lying on her bed, not really wanting to get up. She only had a week with Joey, though, and she would make the most of it. She forced herself up, a little too quickly. She wasn't quite ready to move yet.

Her mind went to the cube that was all alone at her house. She longed to hold it. She had become attached to it. She should have brought it with her. It was starting to aggravate her, though, not knowing what it was exactly or what it did. One of those books in the Morris library had to have the answers. But she was still too traumatized to go back there.

That reminded her: she had told Dane she would call him when she got there. She reached for the phone beside her bed and dialed.

"Hello?"

"Dane, hey," was all she had to say.

"Kelly." She could hear his voice spark with excitement. "How's the trip so far?"

"Different."

"How so?"

"Well, it's good to be with my family and of course Joey, but things aren't the same around him. Getting his attention is hard with him being so in love. I am happy for him, but it's just strange how things change."

"It is," Dane agreed. "A year ago, I wouldn't have thought I'd convert to a new religion and become best friends with my sworn rival."

"It is quite a jump," Kelly chuckled. "That dream is still bothering me."

"Have you had any more?"

"No. I wish. I want to see what happens."

"Just read about it. I can lend you some literature."

"I want to experience it, though. The dream was so real. I was there, Dane. I was watching our ancestors."

"That is something."

"Kelly, come out for dinner," Kelly heard Jessica call out from beyond the door.

"Hey, Dane," Kelly began. "We're about to eat. I'll talk to you later."

"Kay. Miss you."

"I miss you too." Kelly hung up tossing the phone instead of putting it on the hook. It was a habit she knew so well. No matter how many times the battery died she couldn't seem to break the habit.

Kelly could smell the scent of her mom's cooking and knew what was for dinner. It was Lasagna à la Kàra made with Portobello mushrooms and always accompanied by salad with her mom's original garlic dressing and croutons. And of course there would be wine for the adults and sparkling grape juice for the children. Her Mom always made that meal on their first night at the cottage.

Kelly just loved the family traditions during this break; the familiarity of it all was always a solace for her.

Mr. Morris let out a shout in his frustrations in, pounding his fists down on the marble table.

"I told you he was playing us this whole time!"

Moore said, biting back his anger. Dane watched the exchange in the lower level of their home.

"How is it that no one has found him yet?" Dane's father had lost sleep over this. He hated to be out of control and to lose the upper hand was even worse. "Nothing from Nadia? If the boy was so head-over-heels with her, wouldn't he have reached out to her by now?"

"Richard's probably ensuring that he doesn't. Or maybe the kid was in on it the whole time too and played along," Moore said with some sarcasm.

"Nadia would've spotted it," Dane added as his contribution the conversation.

"The first intelligent thing you've said in a long time," Moore said, looking sincere. Mr. Morris thrust some paperwork off of the marble table.

"Find him, Moore!" Mr. Morris commanded. "The hit on his head is useless without someone smart enough to find him."

"What's the point? He's useless to us. We have other matters to attend to. He's bound to slip up sooner or later," Moore said.

"He's not useless as long as he has the Sceptra."

"The Sceptra is pointless. Are you still buying into that hidden meaning nonsense? He played us, sir," Moore emphasized each word in the last sentence, hoping it would get through to his dad.

"There's no way he knew the whole three years. He found out at the end and made a run for it. Why else would he sacrifice the silver Schernol?"

"Do you really think that John and Peter planted a Schernol in a Puerto Rican club? That place didn't even exist back then."

"And?"

"The Schernol had to have been already found and moved there. It shouldn't have been hard to find. Richard used it and the whole double-meaning idea to distract us from what we should've been doing, looking for the Samorik. He sacrificed it to get us off his tail and make us dependent on him so with him

168

out of the picture we would be lost."

"The Samorik, what good is that without the Schernols?" Their father had a point: they would need the Schernols for the Samorik to activate and morph them together. That was the Samorik's purpose.

"I've been doing my own research, father. There has to be more to the Samorik. I think maybe it not only morphs the Schernols but locates them."

"Fine, pursue that, but I still want Richard gone. He's cost us enough time and effort."

"Let the Normans take care of him. Have them make you a video, something we can watch on a rainy day," Moore said.

On their walk out of the elevator Moore stopped Dane and pulled him under his arm, escorting him up the stairs. "You want to do a little trade?" Moore asked.

"No," Dane said without hesitance.

"You haven't heard what I had to offer," Moore insisted.

"And I don't want to," Dane responded.

"What's the matter with you, Dane? Your head's been somewhere else lately. Is Kelly getting to you?"

"Shut up about her."

"Remember our little mission the other night," Moore began, and Dane's brows creased. They were now in front of Moore's room. "That bag had the Samorik in it. You can take full credit for it with dad, even tell him how you ripped it from that man's dead hands." Dane began to feel sick again. He forced his brother's arm off from around him.

"That was all you, Moore. I don't want that on my hands."

"You were my accomplice. You were at the scene of the crime."

"Why are you telling me this? What could I possibly give you?"

"Give me some time with Kelly." As those words left Moore's mouth, Dane dived headfirst into Moore's torso; the impact carried them to the wall at the end of the hall. Next came a few swings in a short succession.

"Stay away from her, Moore." Dane ground out through his teeth. He got a few swings in before Moore was able to process the turn of events. Once he did, he knew just how to recover, dropping to the ground, twisting Dane around so his back would slam onto the hard floor. Moore locked an arm around Dane's neck and tightened his grip, just so he could feel Dane's fear as he squirmed and writhed under him. Moore yanked his brother away from him.

"You think you can threaten me?" he practically spat. Rising to his feet, he dusted his pants and calmly walked away.

Chapter Sixteen

"You ready for battle?" Kelly whispered to Jessica enthusiastically, her cheeks painted with battle stripes identical to her sister's. Hair put up in tight buns, the sisters were crouched low behind a bush in front of the house. Kelly had a walkie-talkie at her lips, ready to speak through it the moment Jessica left her and found a successful hiding place.

"Yeah, I'm ready," Jessica whispered back. She pushed forward on her feet and darted across the open yard. It was risky business, but the others were too occupied with finding their own hiding spots to notice that Jessica was an open target.

"Alright. I'm at my destination," Jessica said through her walkie-talkie.

"Good. I'll update you later," Kelly replied.

"Same here."

But already, Kelly had spotted Joey on the balcony above the front door of the cottage. He was looking ahead. Kelly smirked. "I've spotted Joey, on the front balcony."

"I've spotted Jason. He's mine," Jessica whispered, a sinister edge to her voice. Both her and Kelly's new water guns were filled to the brim with watered-down paint. Both in position for attack, they watched their brothers as they waited for Zach to come into the clearing with Jessica, their chosen target.

"I've never been more ready," Jessica whispered to Kelly, swallowing an excited giggle, happy she'd made a pact with Kelly the previous year after Jason had sold Kelly out on a prank both he and she had pulled. Kelly didn't really want Joey as her target, though. He had a good sense of humor, but he always managed to scheme against her team ten times worse than they had against his. He was crazily competitive. She'd have to be more alert with him until the trip ended—otherwise, he'd get her good.

Kelly knew Jessica was pumped. She'd been waiting for years to finally get back at her brothers for all the stuff she'd had to put up with. It became her own tradition to expect something from them every year on their vacations, her only peace being that it was just one prank. Now, she was one step ahead of them. If she shot Jason with her water gun a good bit, she'd have the funny story to tell for once. The last thing on her mind was how they'd get her back. No one was going to rain on her parade.

Waiting on the opposite side of the house, behind the woodpile used for bonfires, was Melanie. She had her target set on Mike. How the scheming sisters got Melanie to plot against the guys, including her newlywed hubby, was quite simple. She didn't think it was fair that all four brothers were attacking just Jessica. After all, she had two older brothers herself, so she knew firsthand how Jessica felt.

They only had two walkie-talkies, so Melanie had to sit still until her two sisters-in-law began the attack. She waited for the call they'd give her. All they needed to happen was for Zach to come out the front door to inform his brothers that Jessica was nowhere to be found. And soon enough, Zach came sauntering out the front door, yelled out that he wasn't the enemy—so they wouldn't accidentally shoot him—and proceeded to step out into the clearing. He looked up at Joey, pushing up his glasses, to tell him that he couldn't find the eldest sister, and the attack began.

Kelly aimed and shot Zach square in the side, since he had the best chance at escaping—with his little strategic self—then aimed at Joey. While she was doing this, Melanie and Jessica were on foot, shooting at their targets. Jason and Mike attempted to get

172

them with their water balloons, but the girls dodged them easily. The girls had the advantage.

While all this chaos was happening, they didn't notice the paint splatters on the house itself. After the guns had run out of fuel, the girls ditched them and broke into a full sprint, as the boys still had balloons in their satchel bags. The ground was muddy from the previous night's rain, and Jessica had slipped a few times already as she made her way toward the lake.

Joey jumped down from the balcony with three balloons tucked in one arm. He charged toward Kelly. She could hear the heavy pounding of his boots gaining behind her. Screaming, she changed velocity, jerking herself to the left, toward the lake with her sister, but Jason was hot on Jessica's tail. With an amused roar of victory, he lunged at her and pinned her to the ground.

"Got her, HA-HA!" Kelly heard from behind her. She laughed at Jessica's frustrated screams as Jason stubbornly kept her bound for longer than he needed to. Kelly bounded for the long boardwalk down the lake, but she skidded to a stop when it abruptly ended with nothing but the calm, dark waters below. She turned around and Joey was a good distance away. He had stopped running also, but he was tossing one of the water balloons up and down in his free hand with a playful smirk on his lips.

"I can't believe you sold me out like that. Why would you want to double-cross the master?" He threw one and Kelly jumped out of the way, almost falling into the water. She came up a bit so she wasn't standing right on the dock's edge.

"I'm a woman of my word and I gave her my promise. Sorry it had to go down this way. You weren't my primary target," she said impishly. Joey played around with the second balloon in his hand.

"Wasn't your primary target, huh? That's strange, because your water gun was aimed right at me." He threw the second one and missed again.

"It was supposed to be for Jason, since he sold

173

me out last year, but you happened to be in alliance with him, so . . ."

"An alliance you were in as well, I thought." He stretched out to throw the last balloon.

"Once Jason compromised it, it became no more," Kelly said, clutching the gun more securely.

"Alright then. So be it." He threw the last one, getting her on her collarbone, near her shoulder. The nasty-feeling paint dribbled down, seeping into her black shirt.

"So . . . you got me. We're even now, right?"

Joey stroked his chin, coming closer. "Let's see. I'm pretty much drenched with paint and you have a small splatter on your shirt," he said, breaking into a run, sweeping Kelly off her feet and holding her over the edge of the lake.

"You wouldn't!" she screamed, laughing uncontrollably, tightening her grip on Joey's neck.

"Give me one good reason why I shouldn't?"

"We can rebuild our alliance," she offered.

"Oh, whatever's convenient for you, eh?" He extended her further over the water. Kelly shrieked. "A little water won't hurt," he said and rocked her over until there was enough momentum to toss her in. She let go of his neck and screamed as she fell in, but it wasn't out of fear. When she came up from under the water, she gasped.

"Joey! I can't believe you actually did that!"

"You of all people should know I'm not one to bluff."

"I also know you love me enough to get me out of this water."

"Ah, you do know me," he said, crouching down so he could help her out of the water. They laughed together as he hoisted his sister over his shoulder and walked along the dock back to shore.

"Now, in all fairness, you helped Jessica get her moment—well, until Jason got her in the end. God knows it won't happen again."

"Yeah. Actually, after all the years of torment we

put her through, she deserved the glory," Kelly said, and Joey placed Kelly back on her feet when they'd reached the end of the dock. She looked up at him, hair wet and dripping, waiting for his smart remark.

"You're already planning a payback, aren't you, Joey?"

"Of course!"

The Johnson table was full of laughter as Joey led the jokes about their high jinks. Mrs. Johnson wasn't so happy to see the front of the cottage marked with the water-downed paint, but the siblings worked together to get it scrubbed off. It needed to be back to normal before dinner, and with that many hands it wasn't hard.

"Mom's face when she first saw the house . . ." Joey began.

"Priceless," Jason finished.

"Jason's face when I totally creamed him," Jessica laughed.

"Even better," Kelly joined in in her sister's amusement. Jason just looked annoyed.

"It may be funny now, but I wasn't laughing earlier," Mrs. Johnson said.

"That's the best part, when you can look back and laugh. Maybe you should think of that other times when you get angry," Joey teased. "Like me forgetting to bring the video camera. Sure it's a big deal now, but next year we'll laugh at it."

"We reminded you five times the morning we left," Mr. Johnson said wearily.

"I can see it now. Remember, we reminded Joey so many times and he still forgot: cue laughter and all's good," Joey said, smiling sheepishly.

"It's a little too soon," Mrs. Johnson said. "Now when you are all too busy and grown up and we put together the collage of all the years, we will miss this one. You won't see the look on my face when I came home and saw that house."

"Yeah, that is something to miss," Mike spoke up.

"It would've been good," Joey had to agree.

"If you want I can drive into town tomorrow to get one," Melanie suggested.

"That is so sweet of you, Melanie." Mrs. Johnson looked at her daughter-in-law with joy. "Joey, I don't know how you got such a wonderful wife."

"Yeah, it's not like our meeting wasn't set up," Joey said, letting out a mocking laugh. Only Kelly and her parents understood what he meant. "But no, I don't know either. I certainly don't deserve her." The two stared each other in the eyes and smiled.

"Lay off the mushiness. I am trying to eat," Jason said.

"Mommy, can I go color?" Lisa piped up.

"Finish your food first," Mrs. Johnson answered.

"I have. If I eat anymore I will explode." Lisa and Mrs. Johnson continued their conversation, while the other sibling started their own. The table was full of the sweet sounds Kelly had missed. Overlapping conversations, laughter. This night was perfect.

"Hey, Dad," Zach spoke up. "Are we going to continue our Aponlean discussion tonight?"

"No, no, no, no," Joey got agitated. Kelly couldn't understand why it was such a touchy subject for him. "This is a vacation. Remember the good ol' days when we just ignored the fact that we hold onto meaningless traditions?"

"A lot has changed since you left, Joey," Zach remarked. "Turns out there's a lot of meaning behind them, and it's quite fascinating."

"Dad, can we please avoid that sort of talk," Joey half whined.

"Honey, what's the problem?" Melanie asked.

"It's torture," Joey responded.

"Basically, he doesn't want to take the responsibility of being the oldest son," Mike accused, unexpectedly.

"I haven't seen you volunteering, Mike," Kelly defended her oldest brother.

"This is not the time for arguing," Mrs. Johnson said firmly.

Joey ignored his mother's comment as he shot back at his brother. "Mike, why are you calling me out like that?"

Before Mike could respond, Kelly said fervently, "Because if you refuse it, he's next, and he's a cop-out too!"

"Kelly!" Mrs. Johnson raised her voice a little. Mr. Johnson echoed, looking at his daughter.

"What? It's true!" Kelly didn't waver in her emotion. The whole thing frustrated her.

"Kelly, watch your tone with your mother and I," Mr. Johnson said.

"I am calling you out, because Mom and Dad won't," Mike finally said. "You joke around all the time as a way of distracting people from all the things you weasel out of. You're not a man just because you got married. Dad wanted to count on you for things, but you backed out of everything he wanted of you."

"Maybe I got tired of everything in my life being planned out and preset," Joey yelled. "When you don't know the whole story, maybe you should shut the hell up!"

"I've seen enough of your irresponsibility. I've been left to clean up all of your mess," Mike shot back.

"Boys, that's enough!" Mr. Johnson was finally able to interject.

"See, this is what happens when you invite Aponlea in your home," Joey started again. "That's why the name of it won't even be mentioned in mine. It preaches unity but brings division. Time and time again. You've seen it enough in your life, Dad."

Kelly could see Melanie was getting uncomfortable. She didn't seem to agree with Joey on the topic.

"That's enough from you too, Joey," Mr. Johnson said. "This isn't your home right now, and you are the one bringing division and disgrace to this family."

"Well, I am sorry if I failed you again!" Joey stood up from the table and left. Melanie quickly got up and followed. What just happened? Kelly wondered. Her family never fought like this.

"Walking away certainly proves you're a man," Mike called out to him as he exited the room. "When are you going to face things?"

"Shut up, Mike!" Kelly couldn't help but shout. "You have no room to talk." She also couldn't help glaring at him, angrily.

"Kelly, go to your room," Mr. Johnson said.

"Gladly," Kelly responded, tears starting to well in her eyes. She stormed off to her room. She grabbed her pillow and screamed in it. She was still unsure of what just happened. She had never seen Joey and Mike fight like that; they always seemed fine with each other. She tried to picture past episodes. She realized they never were buddies. They didn't do things together, except with the rest of the family. Maybe they just tolerated each other and were holding back their true feelings. Maybe they fought all the time, just not in front of their siblings. She didn't know what to think anymore.

Her door was opened abruptly and her dad entered.

"Kelly, what got into you out there?" Mr. Johnson asked.

"A lot of stuff," Kelly responded in a heated tone. She tried to show respect, but with all her frustration, her voice just wouldn't stay even. "You've suppressed Aponlean stuff for so long and everything has been so secretive and now all of a sudden you expect us all to accept it."

"If you remember, you asked that first night," Mr. Johnson said. "Joey's been taught this stuff from the beginning. There are a lot of expectations set on his shoulders, and it's understandable how he feels all this pressure all of a sudden."

"Why didn't you tell any of us, besides him and Mike?"

"Because it wasn't important for you to know everything. Joey is the one who is supposed to carry on the Johnson name; once you marry another descendant, you'll take on his name and his family line."

"And if I don't marry a descendant?" Kelly asked, still burning with anger, but also curious.

"You would bring disgrace to this family. There are expectations for each of you to uphold the traditions and values of our ancestors."

"Then why not teach us their values?" Kelly shouted. "It's always been 'keep this tradition—do this, do that, it's the Aponlean way.' We don't know why, so why should we care?"

"Look," Mr. Johnson said, his tone softening as he went over to Kelly. He put his arm around her and led her to the bed where they sat down. "There's a lot of pressure on me also. I constantly have to make decisions knowing that the consequences of my actions are far greater than others'. There is a whole nation that I help keep in order, keep focused. If it weren't for the Council, there would be so much chaos. If it weren't for the traditions set in place, Aponlea would be lost. It would soon be forgotten, and our identity would fall by the wayside."

"Why does it need to be remembered?"

"Because true Aponlea is true unity. It is true peace. If we can get back to that paradise, it will be like nothing else. All the lives lost for it will be redeemed." Mr. Johnson paused briefly. "Mike is right in a way. Joey knows a lot more than any of you. He knows what is right and what he needs to do, and right now he is rebelling against it. Now, I believe he will come around. He is young, but when the time is right, he will take full responsibility."

"Why does it have to be him? Why not Mike or even Jason?"

"Traditionally it's been the oldest son," Mr. Johnson began. "That was broken only once in the whole line of Johnson heritage, and that was by my grandfather, who in spite of the Council chose my mom."

"Grandma Thalia?" Kelly's gasped.

"Correct. She never played by the rules; the Council thought of her as a loose cannon. Why she was selected is a story for another time, but since her selection was out of the norm, she opened her selection up to any one of us. Only the two oldest sons were interested though."

"Dad," Kelly said, before he could continue. "I want you to consider me. I know I am young now and am not ready yet, but I will grow older and I will take full responsibility, and I want it, Dad. It wouldn't be so farfetched, since just a generation ago, Grandma Thalia was selected."

"Kelly." Kelly looked at her father. He looked as though he was looking for a gentle way to put it.

"You don't have to decide now," Kelly said, again before he could continue. "Give it time. I will prove to you I can do it. Just wait till I am older and you'll see."

"Kelly, you are truly a beautiful young lady, and I am proud of you in many ways. I will consider you, but I want you to know it isn't very likely that you will be selected." Kelly's heart sank as those words left his mouth. But those emotions dwindled as a thought came into her head. She could prove to her father she could do it. Somehow. He would see that she was the one born for this, because that was the one thing that made sense to her. Even after he left, Kelly continued to meditate on this thought and how she would make it come to be.

She didn't understand, if Joey and Mike wouldn't step up to the plate and she was willing to, why was it such a foreign thought to her dad. The Aponlean people needed hope and she could bring it to them. Even if she wasn't the one to usher in the ingathering, she would set it up as much as possible for the next person. This was the answer she was looking for. She finally understood her longings. It was a greater substance calling her to step up, rise to the occasion and save her people.

It had been too long that they had wandered in a land not their own, assimilating into a culture not belonging to them. How they had managed to keep the idea of Aponlea alive was beyond her, but they had, and that meant it was important. It was important for someone to complete what many had been searching and fighting for. She would have a lot of work ahead of her to prove to her father that this was her job, a thought she was convinced of.

She knew the hardest thing to do would be letting go of Dane. She tried avoiding that fact in her mind, but was confronted with it. If she was to be chosen for her family's sole lineage, she couldn't marry a descendant of Morr. She would have to marry whomever the Council selected for her. She would need to play by most of their rules until it was her turn to call the shots.

Kelly collapsed backward into her bed, feeling the burn of the salty tears falling from her eyes. Letting go of Dane would be hard. She was beginning to think she loved him and he loved her. He had been so kind to her, so open with her; he was perfect for her. Everything important in life has its sacrifices, and this was hers. She just didn't want to break his heart. He had no friends that she knew of, and if she abandoned him, maybe he would revert back to his old self. "I will always love you, Dane," Kelly said in an attempt at a conscious goodbye.

* * *

Dane was fuming over his last exchange with his brother. What did he want with Kelly? Was it all just to provoke him, or was there more? His brother was so unpredictable and had always had plans of his own. The fact that he hadn't told his father about the Samorik was just proof he was in this on his own. Similar to the great Morr, his brother Moore was only focused on the end goal. Nothing and no one meant anything to him. So why all the attention on Kelly?

Dane's pacing ended when he heard Moore's car drive off the compound. He went straight to his domain. He saw notes upon notes scattered all over his desk. The rest of his room was spotless and in pristine order.

The writings on the desk were partly in Aponlean, partly in legible English, and partly in chicken scratch untranslatable to anyone beyond the originator. It was clear he didn't want anyone finding out what was on them. Dane tried his bookshelf next, pulling his black leather-bound journal off the shelf. It looked newer than his others. It must've been his latest. Dane flipped through the pages, scanning what was written. This was entirely in Aponlean and very legible. Dane used his knowledge of the language to decipher its meaning.

It seemed to be mostly prayers to Radehveh. One caught his eye immediately, as it started with "I am the Great Morr." The rest of it was in ancient Aponlean, with slightly altered symbols and a different grammatical structure. He still managed to read it slowly, with determination. In his disgust he dropped the notebook, not wanting to hold such foul writing in his hands anymore. He was also shocked by its contents, which sounded as if it were written by the great Morr, but it didn't ring a bell from anything Dane had read before. His brother's mind was demented. He picked the journal up and placed it back on the shelf.

He scanned the room some more before seeing the statue in his closet. It was of Radehveh. He walked over to it and scoffed. The mote still had evidence of his brother's dedication. It was crusted with spots of blood. For what? Dane questioned. It was all pointless; Radehveh couldn't save him. Dane knew this now. Anger flooded over him at the sight of it. He thought back to his conversation with Beauty and the pain he saw in his mother's eyes. For what? He asked again, this time kicking the image of the family's god. Dane was surprised to see that the idol was made of two separate pieces, the mote and the god himself. Between the two was a small compartment, where Moore had placed the Samorik. He recognized it from one of the books in the library.

182

Dane crouched down to lift the device up. It fit in the palm of his hand. It was pure silver, the shape of a three-dimensional teardrop. It was completely smooth. Dane examined it. How had Moore found this? So many people had searched for this device, but to no avail. His brother's obsession must've exceeded any former descendant's. Dane stood back up, with the Samorik still in his hand. He walked back over to the notes and scanned over them.

"He shouldn't have this," Dane said aloud. It was too much power for such a wicked person. He didn't know Moore's ultimate goal, but it couldn't be good, and Dane could help him along with some setbacks. Dane placed the device on the ground and went back over to the statue. He picked up the top half and turned it upside down, Radehveh's head toward the ground. He crouched down again, lifting his arms above his head and slamming them back down on the device. It slid out from underneath it unfazed. Dane put it back in place and attempted again, this time with even more force. The device split in two down the middle. He picked up the two pieces and put them in the compartment and placed the body of the god back on its base. "I guess it wasn't in Radehveh's will for you to have it," Dane said, arising and departing from the room.

He surprised himself with his lack of fear of the repercussions of his act. A few weeks ago and he wouldn't have had the guts to even enter Moore's room uninvited. Now he felt no fear in that regard. He did question his own motives, though. Was it out of anger over his brother's interest in Kelly, or did he really believe he was helping mankind?

Dane's confidence stayed with him as he made his way downstairs. He walked around the stairwell to get to the game room. Before he could make it there, his mother caught his eye. She was seated at the dining-room table. Dane walked over to her and sat down across from her.

"Are you alright?" he asked. She raised her head

from her hands.

"Just tired," she responded, her voice monotone and void of any real emotion.

"Mom, I have to tell you something," Dane said. He had carried his fearlessness to the table. His mom didn't respond. "I don't believe in Radehveh anymore." This finally caught his mother's attention as she made eye contact with him.

"Shh," she said, lowering her voice to a whisper. "What do you mean?"

Dane didn't follow in her lower tone. He maintained an average level. "I follow the God of the Bible and His Son. I think that you would be happier following Him also."

"I once did," she responded, still on edge. She looked around.

"Mom, don't be afraid. You can come back to Him."

"I was raised Catholic, but abandoned the faith when I fell in love with your father. I can't go back now, and you need to keep this to yourself, Dane. I don't want to lose any more children."

"There's nothing to fear with Him. I don't anymore."

"You'll have plenty of time for that sort of thing when you move out. If your father finds out, it's not just you who will deal with it. It'll just make everything worse. Son, I know it's hard. Things are bad here, but keep this to yourself. Let that be your strength to make it through a few more years and then leave. Walk away from all of this and never look back."

"Mom, I can't . . ."

"Dane, things are going to change soon. A house built on this much turmoil can't stand forever." Mrs. Morris arose. "Listen to me, I don't want you to talk about this anymore." She left Dane in his seat to meditate on her words. He didn't understand how things could get much worse than they were, couldn't she see that? He wanted to help her. He wanted to be there for her. Why were Beauty and his mother so crushed by wickedness but so appalled at his care and concern?

184

Had they become that callous?

Dane felt the mood of the room changing. That fear he had dodged before hit him full on. It sunk in. Moore would know exactly how the Samorik broke, and he would find out sooner or later about his new faith. Either one made Dane a walking dead man.

Chapter Seventeen

The rest of the trip was very different from all the others. Joey and Mike apologized to each other and the family, but everyone could see resentment still lingered on both ends. They hardly talked to each other at all. Kelly was now alert to their behaviors and saw it. She had been so blind before. This wasn't an-all-of-a-sudden thing. It had been going on for years. Despite the tension, laughter and fun filled the rest of the days. That night wasn't brought up, nor Aponlea, the rest of the trip.

Kelly remained mostly silent throughout the trip, to divert attention from her behavior that night. That was the first part of her plan, and when she reemerged she would be the most responsible person her dad had known. But as for the rest of the trip, she needed a little time out of his limelight, allowing him time to forget her transgression.

When it was over, Kelly found herself back in her room at home with a suitcase to unpack and a mysterious silver cube hidden away. She felt exhausted. There were so many things she didn't know or understand. There was way too much stuff to process, and she wished she had another week off from school to do so.

She went to the cube, holding it, examining it. It was seamless like the disc Zach had, but it had Aponlean inscriptions on it. She went to the book her dad had given her. She had tried to read it in the first week after she received it but had given up. Aponlean was hard to learn. Maybe if she stuck to it, she could read the inscriptions and find the on switch. What did this cube even do?

She thought about taking it to Zach but was wary about that with her new plan. She didn't want her dad finding out; that would be the worst thing that could happen.

She sat at the desk with the cube and the book, flipping through a few pages. Who was she fooling? She couldn't just figure it out that easily. She dropped the book, just holding the cube. She tried imagining where the switch would be and twirled her index finger in a few different spots. She sighed heavily, tossing the cube over her shoulder in frustration.

She stalked over to her bed and collapsed on it, exhausted. It wasn't long before she dozed off.

"So Peter survived and recovered another Schernol. This good fortune continued until they had an equal amount of Schernols. Hope began to sprout among the hearts of all who counted on these men for their future:. the ten men — Yo'nan, Qisvet, Mika'el, Miveloy, Toma, Akmalo, A'qo, Malra'on, Hem, and So'on — those are who the Aponlean forefathers were. Of course, we know them by the names they received once exiled. John, Peter, Michael, Wilhelm, Thom, Carmelo, Jacob, Munroe, Henry, and Carson, respectively."

"Ours was John, wasn't he? The best of them all!" It was a young, tiny, familiar voice who'd shouted it excitedly. Kelly's voice. A chuckle from a man followed, his deep voice resounded through Kelly's small frame.

"He was the leader, yes, but you know what? You are special. Not only is your dad from the direct line of John, but your mother is from the direct line of Jacob, one of the king's sons."

An amazed inhale from Kelly and a squeal later, "I'm a princess!"

"Well, not exactly, but you do have royal blood. Now, are you going to let me finish, miss?"

"Oh yes! But, I know the good guys are gonna' win . . . they win right?" There was a longer pause than she'd expected. The man sucked his teeth and a low groan emerged

from deep within his throat.

"I wouldn't say that, Kelly. The good guys don't always win the initial battle, though they do in the end. This one's sort of a . . . disappointing ending. Power corrupts, sometimes even the most innocent of people. Some of the men found their power, but they were never satisfied with the amount, and they craved more and more of it. One by one, they began fighting for their own victory in hopes of obtaining all the Schernols for themselves."

"But those people – they weren't John or Peter, right?"

"No. If anything, those two remained the most loyal till the end. They battled against the swayed good men and Morr's army. That's why you'll hear your dad say, 'may we be like John and Peter and rise to the occasion, stand for good while others fall for darkness around us and remain untouched by the greed of this world.' They were the only two who didn't fall into the greed that the power of the Schernols brought them. Every other person felt the extra power and wanted more."

John and Peter found themselves surrounded by their own men and Morr's, pitted at the center of the palace Morr had built for himself. It looked to be the end. Even if they did win, they'd have done so through the blood of their comrades.

Morr gave them a chance to surrender their Schernols, but at this point there was no reason to trust his word. He would kill them in an instant, and chances are he would move onto their fellow soldiers next. John calculated and weighed his options. What seemed like hours in his head, took place in split seconds. He had to decide quickly.

Kelly could have sworn she screamed, because when she bolted upright from her bed, the remains of its high pitch still rang in her ears. Her hand was outstretched, still wanting to grab John from Morr's grasp. As she forced herself to calm down, touching her chest as her heart drummed against her ribcage, she reeled from what her mind had just conjured as a dream.

Her hands were shaking, her stomach clenching. Were they really what took place in the past, these scenes she'd just seen? Things like this did not go ignored. This was the second time she'd dreamt something that felt so real. She needed to know where these were coming from.

She looked over at the clock. It was five minutes till eight o' clock. She sighed tiredly, sinking her body back into the warmth of the bed. Suddenly, she had an urge to check on the cube, a feeling that rushed through her body in the form of fear.

She jumped out of bed and slipped as her feet stumbled over strange marbles. She nearly fell on her head. She maneuvered her feet trying to find an empty spot on the floor. What was she stepping on? She rubbed her eyes and looked down. What was going on? There were silver spheres all over the floor. She needed to wake up. This must still be the dream! She panicked: how could she find out if she was awake? She carefully stepped to the door and opened it without the spheres getting out. She left her room and headed down the hall. She knocked on Jason's door. He didn't answer, so she burst in.

"Jason!" she gasped loudly. He didn't budge. She ran over to his bed and nudged him. "Jason."

"What?" He flinched, a scowl forming across his lips.

"Are you really awake or is this my dream?"

"I'm awake now, jeez. What's the deal, Kelly?" He groaned.

"What day is it?"

"It's Sunday. Go away!" He pulled a pillow over his head. It all seemed real enough. Kelly went back to her room and opened the door. The spheres were still there. This was not a dream.

Kelly fumbled over the spheres and sat on her bed, placing her head in her hands. She had to think of something. What was she going to do, barricade her room so no one could ever get in? That wasn't going to work. She stared at the cube in the corner. She should have never taken it. She could've placed it on a bookshelf in the library. She could have given it to Dane when he was comforting her. He would've understood.

She knew when she left his house that day exactly what she was doing. She wanted it. She wanted it to give her a sense of hope. Maybe this was the greed the ancestors fell for. Even though the cube wasn't a Schernol and didn't give her any sort of powers, it held her captive. She thought back to her dream; she didn't want to end up like the other men. She was taught to be like John and Peter. But John and Peter were never in her situation.

How would she explain this to her dad? This could ruin her chances of him considering her as the honored child.

There was too much to weigh, but she needed to do something. She had an idea. She pushed spheres aside with her foot, making a pathway, and made it back to her bedroom door. She quietly went downstairs and turned the corner. She lightly knocked on the door of the bedroom under the stairway.

Her younger brother answered. Kelly knew he had been awake for hours, taking apart something new or reading some book.

"Yes, Kelly?" Zach asked, with a questioning look on his face.

"I need your help."

"With?"

"If you promise not to tell anyone, I will show you a device you have never seen in your life. You can forget about your microwave with what I've found."

"You have my word," he cracked a smile. "I won't tell a soul."

"Follow me," Kelly said, still in a hushed voice. She didn't want to wake Lisa, who shared a room with Zach. Kelly headed back upstairs, and Zach followed closely behind. They entered the room. Once Zach was fully in, Kelly shut the door behind them and locked it. She watched briefly as her brother looked around at the silver marbles.

190

"What's with the marbles?" He finally asked.

"I will show you," Kelly said, letting out a yawn. The excitement of her startling awakening was wearing off. She went to the corner and picked up the cube, bringing it back to her younger brother. She handed it to him. He examined it.

"What's this?"

"That thing you are holding in your hand is an ancient Aponlean device that somehow, overnight produced all of these silver marbles." Kelly said. Zach's eyes widened. He was showing more emotion than she had ever seen him display. He picked up a marble, examining it.

"Are these actual silver?" Zach asked.

"I have no clue!" Kelly said. Zach sat down at Kelly's desk, examining the cube further. "Did you see it actually disperse these spheres?"

"No," Kelly responded. "I woke up and they were all over my floor."

"This definitely tops the microwave."

"The cube itself was dispersed from a shield that I did see."

"Where's the shield?"

"I don't have it."

"Well, where is it?"

"Somewhere inaccessible."

"Kelly, I need you to tell me everything. I give you my word I won't tell anyone."

"It is in possession of the Morrises. It is one of the very shields used in the Aponlean battle that got our ancestors exiled. I was over at their house and saw the shield, held it. I accidentally dropped it and it started rearranging its shape and spewed the cube out before taking its shield form again, as if it never held the cube. Then I didn't know how to put it back in, so I took it. I've had it for a few weeks now and all of a sudden it freaks out and decides to release all these silver marbles everywhere. Please don't tell our parents!" Zach didn't respond but just looked more intently at the cube. Kelly watched and waited for an assessment.

"This is incredible," Zach said, expressionless, but Kelly could tell his mind was racing with excitement at a new discovery. "I'm going to have to examine it more. Can I work on it in my room?"

"Um," Kelly pictured Lisa getting into it or maybe taking it to her dad.

"I'll take good care of it."

"I guess, but what about these spheres?"

"Yeah, I'll take a few of them also."

"No, I mean, what am I going to do with all these spheres?"

"Hmm. That is a good question." He looked around at them, thinking. "If they are actual silver, you could sell them."

"I want them gone, Zach," Kelly said frantically. There was no way of explaining these to her parents.

"Okay, I have an idea, but we'll probably need Mike's help."

"Out of the question, he is too close with Dad."

"We make up a story. You're good at that, aren't you?" Kelly looked at him, feeling insulted. She wondered how observant he actually was, what he actually knew about each of the siblings. "Come on, I didn't mean it that way. Well, maybe I did. But you have always been creative in that area."

"How about this: you have been hosting underground marbles tournaments every week, and these are the ones you accumulated."

"And why are they in your room?"

"You asked me to stash them here, so Lisa wouldn't get a hold of them."

"All over your floor?"

"In a suitcase, of course, but I poured them out when I had to pack for the trip."

"Then why would we need to get rid of them?"

"That's a good point. Hm. You decided marbles are too childish for you and I am sick of storing them in my room"

"You would leave stuff all over your floor for this

amount of time."

"I am starting to appreciate your silence more."

"Hm. Now you see why . . ."

"Forget I said that. Sorry. As a representative of the views and opinions of your siblings, we want to hear more from you."

"Okay, well, let me help you with a better story, then," Zach said.

Once both parents were either out or distracted, Kelly was able to get Mike's assistance. Zach had rigged a chute from Kelly's balcony that led down to a wheelbarrow. She was able to scoop spheres up in a bucket and drop them down into the wheelbarrow that would make it easy to transport them elsewhere.

Kelly remembered a giant hole near Dane's tree house where construction on a sewer system had begun but was never finished. She and her brother were able to haul all the spheres to the hole, minus a few that Zach took to examine. It took them two trips, which wouldn't have been so bad if the tree house weren't so far away and the forest ground weren't so bumpy and they didn't have to maneuver through the trees.

As Mike unloaded the second load into the hole, Kelly dumped the ones she had picked up from the ground as they fell out of the barrow.

"I won't ask you the truth about what's going on if you hear me out about something," Mike said as he picked up one of the shovels they had brought with the first trip and started dispersing dirt over the spheres. Kelly followed his lead. Kelly knew he was too smart to believe her story or any story she could have come up with. Mike had a way of reading people.

"What's that?" She asked.

"I just wanted to set some things straight about that night at dinner during the trip," Mike began, still shoveling dirt.

"Oh, well, I am sorry for how I reacted." She hadn't officially apologized to him yet.

"It's alright. I understand. You and Joey are very close, so I know you were just defending him, but I want to set a few things straight, because I am not sure how much you believe some of the things you said about me that night."

"Mike . . ."

"Let me finish," Mike interjected and then sighed. "It's just Dad juggles a lot. He works with the Council, is CEO of a company, is a father and a husband, and constantly bails out Joey's restaurant. When I started interning for him, I got to see a lot of what he goes through firsthand. He was very open with me about a lot of things, and though he acts tough and like everything is together, I could see the pressure he feels." Kelly tried to focus on shoveling as she listened, but her arms were getting tired. She perched the shovel in the ground and leaned against it as Mike continued. "Joey and I have talked before. He was going to take over Dad's corporation, but opted out when he was eighteen. Then we made an agreement: I would step up to the position so he could devote his time to Aponlean matters. He was already slated for it, but we felt a split from the two responsibilities was important, given the stress it has been on Dad. Dad has been talking with both of us about the Council and our Aponlean responsibilities since we were little."

"Then Joey decides he wants no part of it. He's out. I love Joey, I do, but this has been our entire lives. He decides a task is too hard and quits, leaving me to pick up the pieces for someone else. Dad had to hire someone to do his job at the restaurant, because a lot of Joey's responsibility was falling on Dad's shoulders. Sure, Joey does well with creative ideas, designs, advertisement, keeping his workers happy, but he needs to stop taking on things he can't finish." Mike stopped talking and shoveling a moment to look at Kelly. He was waiting for some sort of acknowledgment from her of understanding.

"I see where you're coming from, Mike, but maybe you should try looking at the things Joey does do right. He's helped keep this family together for years. He is one of the main reason we are all so close, because he's always made an effort for us to do things together, have fun, and share memories. He motivates us and has always put family first. Anyone of us can go to him, and he listens, he cares, and he will help. Maybe you establish security, but he keeps us functioning."

"I do see that, Kelly," Mike started shoveling some more. "But carrying on the family responsibilities, taking care of the Aponlean people is so important, especially to Dad. Of all the things Joey has backed out of, this is the one thing Dad cares the most about."

"But dad shouldn't put that on Joey. Joey should have a choice in the matter."

"Sometimes things are bigger than us, Kelly. Some circumstances demand action. This is a time when Joey needs to rise to the occasion."

"What if you need to?"

"It's not my place. He's the oldest."

"Maybe circumstances call for you to take action, to rise to the occasion."

"It is definitely looking that way, and I will if I have to, but I don't think I should."

"I will," Kelly said looking Mike straight in the eyes, as serious as ever. "I will live up to John's name, and if Dad won't give it to me, I will live up to my own name. I will give my life for our people, for Aponlea." Kelly wasn't sure where these words were coming from; they just flew out of her mouth from the inner parts of her heart. They were fervent and unwavering. Mike had stopped again.

"Kelly, I admire your patriotism, but I don't think that's your place."

"Why? Grandma Thalia took that place. She wasn't the oldest, nor a son."

"You don't want to hear my reasons why," Mike turned to face the hole; the spheres were covered well enough. He put the shovel in the wheelbarrow and turned it around to head back. Kelly's blood boiled. Was he just going to leave it at that? His clarifying of things had only made her opinion of him worse. She loved her brother but was livid with him. Why was the idea of her taking the line so far-fetched? She ran up beside him, bringing her shovel along.

"I'm sorry Kelly, there's just a lot you don't know yet. Maybe if you did know, you wouldn't want that responsibility after all."

Kelly didn't respond. She was still too heated to not say anything disdainful.

As they continued to walk through the woods in silence, Kelly managed to say in an even voice, "Thank you for helping me, Mike." It still sounded kind of angry.

"Anytime, Kelly. We may not agree on everything, but you are my sister and I love you and would do anything to protect and help you." Kelly's heart softened a little.

"Thanks," she said and meant it this time. The rest of the trip back was in silence.

"Hey, what's going on?" Dane asked once he was in his room with the cordless.

"Dane, I sliced my hand accidentally on some glass today," Beauty said from the other side of the line. "That was the latest thing that happened to me. I sprained my foot just last week."

"Okay?" Dane questioned.

"It's Radehveh. He's angry about what you've done. I've already repented and have cleansed my house, but since you haven't and won't, I am bearing the consequences of keeping your secret."

"Those are just accidents that happened, Beauty."

"No, Dane, it's more. I can feel it. You need to tell Dad so he can decide what needs to be done, or you need to repent."

"I can't do that Beauty."

"Then I will need to," Beauty responded.

"Beauty," Dane was about to plead with her, but then he started hearing her tear up on the other end. "Are you okay?"

"I'm not gonna' tell, Dane," she said with a shaking voice. "It's not you. I brought this upon myself. I sinned against him and it's time I owned up to it."

"What do you mean?"

"I mean I've been playing victim, but I knew the relationship was wrong. I was defying Radehveh, and now I am trying to blame my consequences on you. You said you found freedom, I believe you. Mine will come one day too."

"It can come today."

"Dane, no, this pain. This pain is my punishment. I just have to live with it."

"No—" Dane could hear the dial tone. She had hung up. Her ears were so closed. How could anyone accept pain as normality? It didn't have to be that way. He had to prove it to her. Maybe she just wasn't ready to hear, but one day she would be, and Dane would be there for her. He would have to be the bridge between his family and kindness. His family and peace. His family and the joy he had uncovered.

Chapter Eighteen

"Peter, are you still with me?" John asked, as the two men used all their power and the power of the Schernols to prevent the pending attack.

"Death will be our only separation," Peter vowed through his gritted teeth, sweat streaming down his face. His body ached from the force he was letting out.

"Then not today," John said. "Give me your Schernol, and with two I will be able to overpower them. Teleport to safety and let me win this one."

"They could just give Morr two of theirs and he'll again have the upper hand."

"But they won't."

"How can you be so sure?"

"I can see the possession on their faces. They're slaves to their power." Peter looked around, the men trying to move forward, but the force John and Peter's Schernols were giving off prevented them from getting too close. All their swords were hovering above the two men's heads, controlled by the minds of the greed-filled men, aching to pierce their flesh.

In a flash, the gold Schernol was under John's control and Peter gone, the swords dispersed and headed toward each of their owners ready to take whatever life was left in them. Yet they didn't break the flesh of one of them, as John gave them one more chance to turn around. John fell to his knees and cried out to heaven, he couldn't do it. He knew it wasn't the men but the corruption of the power of the Schernols and therefore couldn't shed innocent blood.

"Radehveh! Don't let it be so! Have mercy!" He shouted out releasing the swords and both his Schernols, as well as

all power. The men immediately charged, but found them-
selves outside of the palace and outside of Aponlea, in a
foreign land. A rural area of an ancient Europe. Radehveh
had stepped in and delivered them from their destruction
to save whatever sanctity of the land of Aponlea he could.
Once in this new land, they and the shields were power-
less. The men who fought alongside John and Peter were
back to their liberated selves.

"Radehveh had a promise through all of this: one day
the doors of Aponlea would be opened once again to the
descendants of the exiled men. And the one to open those
doors would be a descendant of John." A low voice that
rumbled smoothly passed the ears. A man with knowledge
beyond present time. A familiar man.

"What happens next?" Kelly's soft voice. A girl in-
trigued by a story, and a chilling yet exhilarating idea of
its possible truths.

"John, seeing the potential of this war continuing,
dispersed the Schernols throughout the earth. The eight
good men who had been corrupted for a time were convicted
of their ways, and each settled here, including John and
Peter. The ten evil men had already begun to search for the
Schernols, but the work was tedious and required sacrifice.
One man gave up on the search and settled down, Perez.
He turned good once on earth; he was the youngest of the
men, the son of Stan. Eventually, all of the bad men had
given up on searching until only Morr and Stan were left.
It is believed that Morr was so dedicated to finding the
Schernols that he died in search of them. And before he
died — though he never settled down — it is also believed
that he once loved a young woman, probably around six-
teen years old when they were married. Together, they had
Keira, his only heir. His wife died soon after her birth,
and when Morr continued his search for Schernols, his
daughter followed.

"In the present day, there are people like us and the
Morrises." A blurry image of a man holding a thick book
became visible. Seemingly large hands with long fingers
closed the book shut. The story was finished.

"So that's really what happened?"

"It's what the Sceptra says, but the Sceptra is just a parallel to what the truth is. Kelly, the thing to remember is that there is truth within the mysticism. Our forefathers wrote this to guide us to the truth, not to teach us what really happened. They wanted us to search, to find out what really happened in order to secure the future."

"But what does that mean?"

"It means that they believe we will return to Aponlea one day."

"Will we?"

"That I don't know, Kelly."

"I thought you knew everything, Uncle Richard." A voice that tried to sound light and humorous, but clearly held disappointment. Deep laughter followed the rich tone of the man still obscured from clear vision.

"No, sweetheart, not everything. It's impossible for someone to know that much, but I can say I'm getting pretty close to finding what I'm looking for. And when I do, I'll let you know."

"Do you promise?"

That's annoying – what is . . . The heaviness of Kelly's awakening thoughts surfaced to somewhat coherent reality when her ears registered that the loud screeching beeps were coming from her alarm clock. Utterly frustrated that it had woken her up at such a high point of her dream, she slammed her hand on the snooze button so hard the clock skidded off her bedside table, its plastic insides rattling when it hit the floor.

She raked her hands through her now shoulder-length brown hair and closed her eyes. Still drowsy, she hoped her dream would pick up where it left off, but sleep didn't return. She sighed heavily and pressed her warm hands against her face.

Uncle Richard, she thought. Had he been the one telling her the whole story? He used to tell her stories when she was about five years old. He used to visit weekly then. It wasn't until now that these memories were coming back to her.

She opened her eyes, pushing herself up from bed;

200

the rush of air from the ceiling fan hit her skin as a sudden revelation arose in her head. Uncle Richard was her ticket. He would provide the answers she had longed for. But he'd be hard to reach, she knew. She hadn't spoken to him in years, hadn't seen him for longer. Where would she even start? She remembered asking her mother about him, but she would only give answers that obviously showed the family hadn't been keeping in touch with him.

Her thoughts had her up and active now that she felt the need to start the day early. And since it was early, she would be able to catch her dad before he left for work. She jumped from her bed, threw on her robe, and headed downstairs. He would be eating breakfast by now.

To her dismay her mother was at the table also and Lisa.

"Good morning, Kelly!" Her precious little sister greeted her and ran up to give her a hug. Kelly picked her up and twirled her around. She had a feeling she was more excited to leave her plate of food than to see her older sister. Kelly carried her back to the table near the end her parents were at.

"Morning Mom, morning Dad."

Kelly rushed to get the appropriate greetings out so that she wouldn't be scolded by her mother. Her parents responded with good mornings as well.

"Hey, Dad," Kelly chimed. "I wanted to ask you a few things."

"Make it quick, I was just about to head out," he commented.

"Okay, well—hmm, how do I begin—Dad, do you still keep in contact with Uncle Richard?"

"Hmm . . . Uncle Richard—I'm afraid I lost his number." Kelly's heart dropped.

"Who's Uncle Richard, Daddy?" Lisa asked. Kelly realized neither she nor Zach had ever met him.

Mr. Johnson stood. "He's my little brother."

"Oh, like Uncle Jimmy?"

"Lisa, I'll tell you about Uncle Richard later."

Kelly hushed her little sister, putting her on the ground. Her mom gestured for her to sit back down to eat her food and she walked over with a pout.

"Dad, is there any way I can reach him? I've really been wanting to speak to him."

"I'm sorry, honey, there isn't much I can do about it. Come to think of it, I haven't talked to him in a while."

"Dad," Kelly said abruptly. "I know what kind of business he's in, and I know he keeps his contact information confidential, but I think that he would trust you enough to give you something. He was always closest to you, wasn't he?"

"Sadly, we haven't been so close, Kelly. He and I had a falling out a few years back. Even if I were able to call him now, he'd refuse to talk to me. Besides, your mother wouldn't want you getting filled with any ideas from him," said Mr. Johnson. "Well, honey." Mr. Johnson gave his wife a kiss and then kissed Lisa's forehead. He walked over to Kelly and gave her a hug and a kiss on her head also. "You can ask me your burning questions. I know a thing or two that Richard doesn't."

"It would be nice to see him again, though."

"It would be," Mr. Johnson agreed before heading out of the dining room. Kelly sighed. She needed answers or she would explode.

Chapter Nineteen

There were only a few weeks of school left, but that was enough time for it to be hard for Kelly to ignore Dane. Sharing fifth period with him and not talking to him would be excruciating. She would try to explain, but he wouldn't understand. She had to be harsh about it and stick to her decision. And she would need to get to class earlier to get a different seat.

"Good afternoon," Dane greeted her. His smile and that look in his eyes made it even harder. She couldn't do this — what was she thinking? This was all too much, the trip, the spheres, Uncle Richard, and now this, all in a little over a week. She could put it off to the end of summer and make excuses of why she couldn't hang out outside of school.

"Is everything alright?"

She forgot he was very good at reading her, not to mention that her face was probably expressing her internal conflict. "Yes, Dane." The bell rang. "I can't talk with you anymore or hang out with you." She couldn't look at him as she said it. She watched Mrs. Farr as she instructed the students to answer the questions she had written on the chalkboard. After the instructions the teacher took her seat. Kelly took out her notebook and her textbook and began to work.

"Why?" She heard the whisper coming from her left.

"Because, you're a descendant of Morr and I am from John. It is not permitted."

"What happened, Kelly?" Kelly could see his eyes from the corner of her own. Here came the hard part.

"I have to start putting the people of Aponlea first, and I have a responsibility being born into the family I was, to act a certain way, follow certain traditions, and not develop feelings for a Morr." She tried hard not to let tears form but could feel them coming. Still she managed to keep them suppressed.

"Kelly, that's ridiculous. I am an Aponlean, just as much as you are. Just because my ancestor was a bad person doesn't make me one. I'm sure you heard of Neil Johnson, right?" Kelly had heard of him. John had two sons, and one of them, Neil, turned corrupt and worked with Morr; she was from the other son's line, though.

"Yes, it isn't right, I know." She finally faced him but couldn't look him in the eyes with her words, so she looked back at her paper. "Maybe one day I can change that, but for now things are a certain way, and I've got to play by the rules for a time to get to the place where I can change things like that. I am sorry, Dane. I do care about you, but if you care about me you will respect my wishes and leave me alone."

"I can't do that." His voice was firm. Kelly was glad he wasn't backing down so easily; it showed he did really like her, but it also made it harder for her to stay just as firm.

"Kelly and Dane," Mrs. Farr began. "There is life outside my class for you two to socialize, but now is not the time."

"Sorry," Dane said. Kelly's apology followed. Kelly tried working on the questions but found that even more difficult than convincing Dane. She could feel him watching her, thinking of things to say. She couldn't ignore it, but she had to press on.

As soon as the bell rang, Kelly nearly jumped out of her seat, having her things packed a few minutes before she knew the bell would sound off. Dane was close behind her. He managed to grab her arm in the hall and turn her around.

"Kelly," she had no choice but to look at him now. "You can't do this."

"It's not that I want to, Dane. A lot has happened since spring break."

"Like what?"

"We have to get to our next classes."

"We have to talk about this."

"I had a wake-up call, Dane." Now it was Kelly's turn to be firm. "I've been finding answers to everything I have been trying to find out since we first started hanging out, randomly, but now I know why. Aponlea needs someone to step up and finally bring about a change, so we can see the ingathering in our lifetime. My dad expected that person to be one of my brothers, but so far neither have stepped up, so I must, and that means making sacrifices. I will bring dishonor to my family if I continue to hang out with you, and that is something I do not want to do. Please understand this and let me be."

"But Kelly, Aponlea's dead and gone. There is no Aponlea; there are only memories of a dismantled nation."

"You're wrong, Dane!" Kelly shouted, but caught herself, "Aponlea is out there and the reason it is not fully forgotten is because it is begging to be found. That's our home, not here."

"I'm sorry, Kelly," Kelly was taken aback by his sudden softening of tone. "I don't want to fight with you. I just know that you and I share something special. We understand each other, and that's what's real to me."

Kelly couldn't respond; she knew his words were true. They were how she felt. She wished she could show him why she was doing this; maybe he still wouldn't understand, but she had to decide which was more important. In her heart Dane was; in her mind Aponlea's future was. "I've got to go to class." Kelly turned to leave. The bell sounded for the sixth period, and Kelly began to sprint, not looking back. She couldn't look back.

The feeling she felt now was far worse than her burning desire for answers, but it would only be a matter of time. Things were always hardest at first but eased with time. Time healed all wounds, or so she was told.

That night when Kelly got home, she distracted herself with tiding any and everything. She looked around for whatever needed attention and proceeded to keep herself busy. This was a good distraction but also her way of showing responsibility. She needed to do whatever it would take and kept her ears wide open for opportunities.

She found herself helping her mother with dinner preparations, doing most the work and quickly.

"This is nice, Kelly," Mrs. Johnson began. "Thank you."

"You're welcome, Mom. You work hard enough for us and you deserve more of a break. If you ever need it, I can cook dinner all by myself."

"Okay, now what do you want?" Mrs. Johnson looked at her daughter warily.

"To be a better daughter and person. I want to be the best Aponlean I can be."

"You know, Kelly. As nice as that sounds, there's usually a catch when you do things like this."

"Things have changed since the family trip. I truly am sorry for all I did, and I'm sorry for the hard times I've caused you throughout my life." Kelly really did mean it, despite her agenda. She was different now, and she would prove it. It had to be a lifelong commitment for the responsibility she was asking for.

"Well, if you're being sincere, I do appreciate that." Her mother pulled her into a tight squeeze. "I always have been and always will be very proud of you, Kelly."

Kelly's heart jumped; she had never heard those words from her mother. She knew her mother loved her without a doubt, but she was never good at encouraging words, mostly corrective words.

Kelly was very happy with how the rest of the evening went. She could see it in her dad's eyes, a look of delight. He saw her change, but she would have to keep it up. It would be so hard, but she was determined to make it happen. She dreaded day two of her week back to school.

More confrontation with Dane — she didn't know what to expect with him. She had rushed from fourth period to fifth, even carrying her fifth-period books with her to fourth period to avoid a locker stop. She needed to get there before the seats were full.

In her haste she had bumped into another student, causing the books and notes she was holding to fall all over the ground. She quickly picked them up with the help of the other person. Finishing as fast as she could, Kelly stood to go to class. However, she was called back by the other student when he discovered they'd switched a book. This was incredulous. She ran back and switched books before moving on. When she arrived at the classroom it was too late; the only seat available was her usual spot next to Dane.

To her surprise there was a wrapped present sitting on it. It looked like a book. She knew who it was from. She walked to her desk at a normal pace and moved the gift onto Dane's desk and sat down, without making eye contact. She felt awful, after all they had been through and his kindness to her. From the corner of her eye she saw him moving it back over to her desk, "It's for you."

"I can't accept it," Kelly said, eyes up front. She held it out to him, looking at him now. She didn't know how she was managing to lock eyes with him without completely breaking down. This was practice. She needed to be tough but wasn't sure this was the right kind of tough. He didn't take it from her. "Please take it."

"It's yours," he said searching her eyes. He needed to stop; he was killing her. "Call it a goodbye gift if you want." Kelly sighed and put the book in the middle of her desk. She gave her attention to the front, to the lecture of the day. Her eyes drifted to the object on her desk. She had to see what it was — there was no question about it. She quietly slipped her finger through the overlapping wrapping paper, having to rip it slightly. When she had completely unmasked it, she flipped it over to its front side.

It was a book, a very old one. It must've been from their library. Its title was The Theory of Aponlea: The Fight for a Lost Civilization, by Ambros Wilhelm. She opened its cover; it was from 1888. She flipped through a few pages, trying to figure out what it was about. She skimmed through the introduction. It was by a descendent of Wilhelm and explained his exploration of the different theories about what Aponlea actually was. It seemed to dissect each theory in an unbiased manner to present the evidence for each based on the author's studies. He had worked on it for over twelve years.

Kelly couldn't help but smile. She whipped her head to Dane. "Thank you so much!"

"You're welcome" was all he said, and he faced the teacher again. Kelly looked at him a little longer before turning back to the book and then to the lecture. Her mind raced with all sorts of thoughts. She was excited to read the book and felt touched that Dane would give her something so thoughtful, and she remembered again how hard it would be to let him go.

When the class ended, Kelly put the gift on top of her other books and held it against her chest. She watched as Dane made his way out of the classroom without a word to her, and her heart hurt. When was time going to do its healing? She had to remind herself this was only day two. She walked slowly to her locker.

When she arrived at her locker, she saw a cold bottle of lemonade, hanging from her lock by a ribbon — another gift from Dane. He needed to stop. This was torture to her. She slid her books inside her locker, all but the one she had just received, and grabbed the lemonade. She knew how determined Dane was himself; she remembered their former feud. He was persistent and dedicated, and she feared that same persistence and dedication would now play in trying

208

to get her back.

◆————◆————◆

Kelly followed her brother through the front door, dragging behind him. She managed to get up the first step of the stairs before her mother called her from the kitchen. She dropped her backpack by the stairwell and walked over to the dining room. She tried to not look so sad.

As she approached, she noticed a giant arrangement of red roses in a vase on the corner of the dining room table. She wondered why it wasn't in the center.

"Yes, Mom?" Her mom smiled at her.

"Jake Peterson sent you some flowers," her mother said, almost giddy. She knew her mother condoned her relationship with Jake and hoped it would carry on. She didn't know the reason it had ended. A redheaded beauty had gotten in the way, and instead of ending things, he tried to play both girls. She would never like Jake Peterson again, despite how close she was with his sister. She knew those flowers were not from Jake at all. Dane had struck again.

"Oh, nice," she said, not able to muster up enthusiasm.

"Young lady, this is just so sweet of him. I am shocked you are not displaying more excitement. Are you two back together?"

"Well, we're off and on," she lied. "These are his latest attempt at an apology, but I am not sure if I forgive him yet."

"Let me tell you something, Kelly. The fights we get into when we are young and in love, they don't hold a lot of weight. I can look back at all of mine and find they were so pointless. Over nothing really."

"Yeah, I'll get over it, but do I have to keep those?" Kelly asked.

"Yes. If you don't take them up to your room, I can always use them as our centerpiece. They are so beautiful." Kelly rolled her eyes internally. If her mother knew who they were really from then they wouldn't be so beautiful to her anymore.

"I'll take them up to my room," Kelly said. It was better than staring at them surrounded by her family. They represented her old self. Why was Dane allowed to become a new person and not her?

She carried the bulky arrangement up to her room, managing to swing her backpack on one shoulder before making her trip upstairs. Jessica was heading downstairs as Kelly reached her door.

"Ooh, who are those from?" she asked excitedly.

"Jake Peterson," Kelly said without sharing her excitement. She knew her sister was full of questions and gushing remarks, but she didn't want any of it. She kicked her door shut quickly behind her, avoiding further probing. She dropped her backpack on the ground and went to the balcony, opening its door. She placed the flowers on the ground against the outer wall of her room. She let out a sigh, looking at them a moment.

Kelly went to the edge of the balcony, leaning against its railing and staring off at the Morris estate. It suddenly didn't seem so magical anymore. She didn't care to catch a glimpse of Moore; she wished her room were on the opposite end of the house now. This couldn't be right. It certainly wasn't fair. Why should she have to give up Dane? Why couldn't both of her desires be fulfilled? Was it worth it? Couldn't she go back to a hidden life and still show responsibility to her father? There had to be a way, right?

Maybe Dane could prove to her parents that he was different, convince the Council of it. These were impossible thoughts. She could imagine the Council seeing the plea of a Morr, claiming to be good, as a ploy to sabotage their efforts

She remembered the book she had received and rushed into her room. Maybe if she understood Aponlea more she would come up with a better solution, one that didn't cause her so much pain. She walked over to her backpack and pulled the book out. She backed into her disc chair and began to read.

Kelly woke up exhausted. She had finished reading the first theory, the one supported by the Sceptra and what Dane had told her that one day, the one that proposed that the Aponleans were like gods and had powers. That theory supported the marrying of other descendants to maintain pure blood. The purer the blood, the more power you'd have when the doors of Aponlea were open.

As much as Kelly wanted that one to be true, she didn't believe it. She was never taught that one by her parents, and her uncle had doubts of it. She had it set in her mind that Uncle Richard would have all the answers.

Kelly looked at her clock. She needed to get going. After attending to her usual preparations for school, she headed downstairs. Mike, Jessica, and Jason were finishing up their breakfast, eggs Benedict. Kelly didn't care much for eggs; she opted for one of the muffins.

"Good morning, Kelly!" Jessica was in another one of her cheerful moods.

"Morning," Kelly said, sliding into her chair, taking a bite of her muffin.

"Guys, be ready in five," Mike said, picking up his and Jessica's plates and heading into the kitchen. Jason rapidly stuffed the rest of his food into his mouth before standing and taking his own plate. Kelly just grabbed a napkin and put her muffin in it. She could eat it on the road.

"Kelly, you haven't talked much since the trip," Jessica called back from the front seat of Mike's car. Mike's summer had already begun, so he was available to take them to school the rest of the year, as well as pick them up.

"I'd say that's a good thing," Jason commented.

"Jason, do you always have to say something mean? I mean, really?" Jessica asked.

"Whatever," he turned his head toward the window, folding his arms.

"I just have a lot on my mind lately," Kelly said.

"Care to share?" Jessica probed.

"Just Aponlea stuff," Kelly said, hoping that would deflate her sister's interest.

"Oh." It had worked. "Well, aren't you excited for summer?"

"More than ever," Kelly said, knowing it would make things a little easier to get over Dane. "Mike, do you think Dad would let me intern this summer?"

"Oh, uh, probably," Mike answered. "Why don't you ask him?"

"I just started thinking about it recently."

"You're going to sacrifice your summer for work, Kelly?" Jessica asked.

"I hope to," Kelly answered.

"Don't you think you'd enjoy getting a job at Gilby's instead?" Mike asked.

Kelly sighed. She would love to work at Gilby's and be around Joey more, but she needed more opportunities to show her dad her capability. "It's not about enjoyment, I just want to be around Dad more and learn what he does."

"It's not like you'd get to really hang out with him. He is constantly managing different things," Mike said.

"I know that, Mike. It would be a growing experience. I have to grow up sooner or later. Maybe it'll be sort of my rite of passage or transition."

"Oh, if only everyone would realize there's a time to grow up," Jessica said, looking back at Jason.

"And I am the one saying mean things?" Jason shot back.

"Well you're taking long enough to grow up," Jessica said.

"What about you? You don't even have your permit yet, while Kelly and I do."

"Guys," Mike interjected. He rolled up to the drop-off loop and Jessica and Jason relented, grabbing their backpacks and getting out of the car. Kelly jumped out too. "Kelly," Mike called from his rolled-

212

down window.

"Yes?" She ran back to where he was sitting.

"I think you'd do well working with Dad. It's a good idea," Mike said with a smile. "I didn't mean to sound so negative before."

"Oh, it's okay. Thanks," she responded before running off.

Kelly loaded her books from third period into her locker, debating whether or not she should bring both her fourth- and fifth-period books with her. She could attempt again to get to class early enough to switch seats, but then Dane could always be there early enough to sit next her regardless. "Oh well," she said opting to not carry an extra load.

"Kelly." Kelly shut her locker to see Dane standing right there.

"Dane, please." She turned away from him, beginning to walk away. He grabbed her arm.

"Hold on," he said once had her attention again. "I have something for you."

"Stop giving me things," Kelly said harshly.

"Listen, I had to risk my life to get this to you today," his voice sounded playful, but it wouldn't be abnormal for that to be true. Either way, he had her attention. He pulled out a leather book from his backpack. It was black and looked like a journal. "This was Moore's journal when he was a kid. You asked me what he was like, and this should probably answer your questions."

"I can't take that," Kelly said, the opposite of what she was thinking. She most definitely wanted to devour its contents, but it wouldn't be right. "That's his personal property."

"He was like eight or something; he probably talks about robots and toy cars."

"Still, it's kind of creepy," Kelly said, wishing she could grab it from him already. She held back.

"Well, I can always put it back or we can read through it and laugh." Dane looked at her with a smirk. He was just too cute. She couldn't be mad at that face.

"We?"

"Yeah, why not?" Dane asked. He was incredulous, not heeding one word she had been saying to him over the past few days. Kelly sighed and rolled her eyes.

"Just put it back," she said, and pushed away from him. She walked away not looking back. She didn't know how much longer she could do this. This was just getting harder. The more she was away and distant from Dane, the more she longed for his company. She walked very slowly, not wanting to walk at all. Her heart was begging her to just turn around.

Her feelings had to count for something, didn't they? Sure, emotions come and go and are as fickle as the wind, but even the wind has its purpose.

She looked back, he was walking at a slower pace than her to avoid walking next to her. Both their classes were in the same direction. He didn't look up at her but kept his head down. In an instant, she was by his side, and linked her arm through his.

"So, what did his little self think back then?" she asked with a smile. He brightened up and held the book out in front of them as they walked.

"Oh, this is good. I actually read part of it earlier and was cracking up. He had quite the imagination," Dane said before he read from one of the pages. The two laughed hysterically as they walked. Kelly felt relief. She couldn't pretend to be someone she wasn't anymore.

Chapter Twenty

"Oh my gosh, slow down, slow down!" Kelly screamed out from the twirling merry-go-round. She had originally taken a walk to the park alone, and Dane had apparently decided the same. Kelly hadn't been more happy to see him, and it was freeing when she could admit it to herself.

Dane stood with his hands in his pockets. While he watched Kelly spin, he was smiling. She loved his smile. The evening out of Dane Morris' eyebrows. The soft crinkle at the ends of Dane Morris' eyes. And that wide, open smile. The whites of his teeth were merging with her surroundings, illuminated among everything else. It was so rare to associate Dane Morris with a light. It was probably unheard of.

"What's that? Faster, you say?" Dane teased, pushing all the more.

"Seriously Dane, I'm going to throw up and you know where it'll land," Kelly warned.

"Alright," he conceded and began slowing it down. Kelly could barely stand straight, wobbling her way to the edge. Dane grabbed hold of Kelly's waist, helping her down.

"You alright, there?" Dane asked with amusement.

"I am now, no thanks to you." Kelly playfully glared and sat down in front of him at the edge of the merry-go-round. Dane sat a bar over.

"Did I not stop it for you?"

Kelly just rolled her eyes. "Are we still going to find the Samorik?"

"Oh, yeah," Dane said unenthusiastically, with a

look Kelly didn't recognize. "That's going to be a no."

"You look like there's a little more to add to that," Kelly grilled him.

"It's nothing, just family business."

"Tell me your secrets and I'll tell you mine," Kelly said playfully.

"Didn't your family teach you not to trust a Morris?" Dane played back.

"Oh come on, you don't have an ounce of the great Morr's blood in you."

"On the contrary, I'm in a direct line, the purest it gets."

"Oh really? So, you've given up your act. You're true colors are showing, huh?"

Dane laughed. "I am just messing with you."

"Just flirting with me," Kelly corrected with a smile.

"And if I were?" Dane asked.

Kelly looked at him, wanting that more than ever. "It would never work."

"Why?"

"Because we're supposed to be enemies."

"We've been down that road. It didn't work out."

"Yeah, because you suffered a near-death experience and saw the light."

"Maybe that's what it took to wake me up to the truth."

"The truth being?"

"That we can bring peace between our families," Dane said softly, eyes locked with Kelly's, his hand gently brushing her hair back from her face.

"Dane," Kelly pushed his hand away, not wanting to, but feeling this wasn't right. She shouldn't have been playing with those emotions, but it wasn't ever something she had planned. Things like that just happen. Kelly stood up distancing herself from the merry-go-round and from Dane. He came up behind her and slid his hand in hers.

"Let's go for a walk," he said softly. Kelly didn't protest this time. Her heart pounded with emotion and fear. On one hand she was enjoying this moment, and on the other she couldn't stop imagining someone from her family appearing at any moment. The idea wasn't so far-fetched, since the park was just around the corner from their neighborhood. She and Dane began to circle the pavement around the playground.

"Now, what's this about secrets?" Dane asked.

"That day Moore and your dad came home with the Schernol, I took something. I . . . I don't know what it is, it just came out of the Schernol and I didn't have time to put it back, so I took it." Kelly felt completely vulnerable. She trusted Dane more than anyone now. She had no more doubts about him; she was very possibly in love with him. It frightened her that this might have been a possibility. She didn't want to, but didn't care anymore. She knew what she felt now, and that made it all okay to her.

"It must not have been that important," Dane said as they continued. "They haven't said anything about it."

"Yeah, maybe it's just something the Schernol produces. Perhaps it is capable of making other objects."

"Oh well," Dane said.

"What about yours?" Kelly asked.

"Moore's had the Samorik all this time, and I broke it," Dane said. "Which could mean I am a walking dead man. That's why I don't care anymore."

Kelly couldn't help but laugh. She stopped walking a moment. Dane did also, looking at her strangely. "What?"

"I don't know," Kelly said, continuing to laugh. She wasn't sure why it was so funny. "We're both so clumsy." Dane started to laugh too.

"I guess we are," he smiled, looking at her. He was looking right into her very core, causing a sensation to flood her body. She looked into his eyes as well, and the more she did, the more their surroundings melted away. Dane cupped her face in his hands and starred at her more intently, as if admiring each of the features in her face. He inched his head closer, slowly;

217

Kelly closed her eyes waiting to feel the warmth of his lips on hers, her body burning with exhilaration.

"Kelly!" Kelly's eyes flew, open and her head whipped to the direction of the voice that interrupted her yearning. It was Jason, on his bike. Dane let go of Kelly's face and faced her fuming brother. Jason dropped his bike and marched over to the two of them. Kelly quickly moved in front of Dane. Jason's fists were clenched and his eyes full of fury.

"Jason," Kelly warned.

"It's over, Kelly," Jason shot back. "You're dead, Dane."

"Calm down!" Kelly shouted. "Why can't you just mind your own business?"

"I would if you wouldn't act so stupid!" Jason shot back. Kelly was pushing her brother back. He moved to either side, trying to get to Dane.

"Jason," Dane said calmly. "It's not worth it." Jason swung Kelly out of the way, causing her to hit the ground hard. He threw a fist at Dane, but Dane dodged it. Dane backed up, but Jason was intent on causing him harm. Kelly quickly got back up, despite still hurting from her fall. Dane was in defense mode, but showed not initiative to fight Jason. Before Kelly could get to her brother, he had lunged his fist in Dane's stomach, causing him to hunch over in pain. "I don't want to fight you," Dane managed to get out with little breath. Jason swung another punch at Dane, this time at his face, knocking him to the ground.

Kelly grabbed Jason's arms from behind. "Jason, stop it! He's not even fighting back," Kelly shouted. Kelly held on to Jason's arms with all her might as he tried hard to wiggle out of her hold. He tried kicking, but Dane had scooted back, able to lift himself off the ground.

"It's over, Kelly," Jason warned. "Mom and Dad are finding out today." Jason turned Kelly in the opposite direction as he turned around back to his bike. Kelly let go of him and he grabbed her arm, forcing her toward the exit of the park. "You're going home now. And you . . ." He turned back to Dane. "You're never going to so much as look at my sister again!" Dane didn't respond, he looked at Kelly; Kelly's eyes watered as she looked back. She was so upset. She knew what this meant. She didn't know when she would ever get to talk to him again. "Go home!" Jason shouted, Kelly finally turned away from Dane and made her way to the house. She started bawling. Life had gone from perfect to disastrous within a matter of minutes.

Kelly entered her house, still in tears. Jason was behind her. He walked his bike home beside his sister, not letting her out of his sight. She had given up on everything, knowing all was hopeless now. Jason led her to the kitchen, where their mother was preparing dinner. Jessica must've been in her room, working on something.

Mrs. Johnson turned to her children waiting for an explanation. "What's going on?" She asked.

"Kelly," Jason said, urging her to tell their mother. Kelly couldn't speak. She was too distraught.

"Tell me what happened," Mrs. Johnson demanded, sounding concerned. "Kelly, look at me." Kelly couldn't. She was a coward; she couldn't face her mother. "Jason?" Mrs. Johnson was sounding more urgent.

"Kelly has been spending a lot of time with Dane Morris. I went for a bike ride and found them at the park." He didn't mention how he saw what they were about to do. "She's been going to his house a lot."

"Only three times," Kelly managed to say. That detail didn't seem to help, as Kelly finally looked up at her mother, her face had dropped. She was speechless. This was the first time Kelly had ever seen her mother speechless. Instead of her mom displaying anger, it was disappointment and hurt. Kelly's tears started coming again. She hated this.

Her mom's voice was deflated — soft and calm. "Kelly, go wait in the living room until your father gets home. I will have him talk to you." Mrs. Johnson turned to finish preparing dinner. Kelly wished her mom would scold her. She felt so ashamed. She didn't realize this would affect her mother in such a way. She never wanted to hurt her. "Jason, go to your room until he gets here."

"Mom, I'm sor—,"Kelly tried to say, but her mother spoke over her. "Kelly, go to the living room. Both of you, go." Kelly walked out, head hung down, and slid into the sofa. This was the first time she thought of the consequences of her actions.

Mr. Johnson arrived thirty minutes later. When he entered the house, he saw Kelly sitting there. She could see him approaching, but didn't lift her head. She was too ashamed. Mrs. Johnson came out from the kitchen and greeted him.

"What's going on, Kelly?" Mr. Johnson asked as his wife greeted him.

"She has been hanging out with Dane Morris, going to his house. It's Joey all over again. Now will you consider moving?" Mrs. Johnson asked. "I don't know how much more of this I can handle." Mr. Johnson comforted his wife a moment and then turned to Kelly.

"Kelly, come to my office," he said and headed there himself without waiting for her. Kelly quickly got up and went over. It was better to get this over with as quickly as possible.

"Sit down, please," her father said, standing behind his desk. Kelly quickly seated herself. Mr. Johnson grabbed a folder from his filing cabinet and plopped it on his desk. "I want you to look at those photos."

Kelly grabbed the file and opened it. After seeing the first image, she couldn't look at the rest. She quickly shut the folder.

"Go on, look at the rest," Mr. Johnson said.

"I can't, Dad," Kelly said.

"Xavier Morris is involved with some very dangerous people. He is a dangerous person himself. He is in a group, an alliance with the Normans and the Stanforces, that does that kind of stuff to people who get in their way. There are plenty more photos like the ones in that folder."

"Why do you even have that, Dad?"

"I had to have a similar conversation with someone before, and I found those more persuasive than any words I could muster up." Mr. Johnson said. "I want you to understand that we haven't prevented you from interaction with our neighbors because of some long, dated family rivalry. They are a real threat."

"Mr. Morris and Moore may be, but Dane isn't," Kelly said boldly.

"No one from that family can be trusted."

"Dane . . ."

"No one, Kelly," Mr. Johnson said again firmly. He didn't know Dane. She knew he wouldn't understand. "Family comes first over there and if it came to choosing between you and his family, he would choose his family."

"I don't think he knows what his family does."

"You are young and naïve," Mr. Johnson disagreed. "You grew up with people you can trust, so it's hard for you to see the people you can't. You haven't seen the things I have seen. They killed your aunt. Richard's wife."

Kelly couldn't respond to that. She didn't know how to.

"I stopped going over there, Dad. I realized the danger of it, but Dane isn't a part of that. He doesn't believe in the things his family does. He doesn't even serve Radehveh anymore."

"You are to cut all ties with him immediately. Period," Mr. Johnson said firmly.

"But we go to the same school," Kelly said.

"Then you will be homeschooled the rest of the year."

"There are only a few weeks left."

"I don't care. It is my job to protect you, and I will do what it takes to do so. You aren't going out anywhere without being chaperoned by me or your mother, or possibly Mike."

"What about Joey?"

"I don't know about Joey."

"Dad, that's ridiculous."

"Obviously, it's necessary. You want to talk to my brother? Maybe that's a good idea. Maybe he can talk some sense into you." Kelly didn't say anything. There was no convincing him, and he was starting to convince her. She was so confused right now, so angry.

"You're consideration of being the honored child is over."

"But Dad!" Kelly shot her head up quickly. "I am sorry. It won't happen again. I will do anything to prove that to you," she pleaded desperately.

"Go apologize to your mother," Mr. Johnson ordered, turning away from her. "Prove that to her." Kelly waited a moment longer, before heading out to her mom. She couldn't help but weep uncontrollably. What had she done?

Dinner was the most agonizing thing ever. Everyone but Lisa knew what had happened and so silence was abundant. Silverware clanking the porcelain plates was the only sound at the table that night. Kelly's eyes were swollen and red. Tears were falling every now and then as she sat there. She was so embarrassed and upset. She didn't make eye contact with any of her siblings. She just sat there, barely touching her food. She couldn't even find pleasure in drinking from her glass of lemonade.

She felt like a failure, a complete disappointment to her parents. She didn't know how she would recover from this. She wished she had never known Dane. She wished she had never even been born into an Aponlean family at all. She could finally understand Joey's disdain for it all. She wanted to march up to her room and throw the silver cube as far from herself as possible.

As each person finished eating, they silently took their plate to the sink and went to their room. Kelly was the last one to leave. She picked up her plate and cup and carried it to the kitchen, dumping almost a full plate of food into the garbage. She started on the dishes. She would be doing them for a while now and most of the chores. Her punishment seemed unending.

She was glad to be alone, washing in the kitchen; it was better than being around her parents. She didn't know when she would feel worthy to be around them. Suddenly, she felt someone beside her, taking the dish from her hand and drying it, before putting it on the counter.

"Hey," Jessica's soothing voice came from beside her.

"Hey," Kelly managed to say.

"It'll be alright," her sister comforted. "They'll get over it eventually."

"Thank you," Kelly said. It meant a lot to her. "Thank you for helping me with the dishes."

"Of course. I love you, Kelly." Jessica put the towel down a moment and hugged her. Kelly's spirit lifted a little. She heard the swinging doors open and turned to see Mike enter.

"You alright, Kelly?" he asked.

"I will be," she answered.

"Here, let me help you guys." Mike approached them. "I can put the dishes away."

"Thank you," Kelly smiled. Joy pierced her heart. She loved her family.

"Did I ever tell you that Dad once caught Joey and me sneaking over to Morris Manor?" he asked. "We got in so much trouble."

"Was that the one time you ever rebelled?" Kelly asked, teasingly. Tears were still moist on her cheeks.

"Uh, yeah," Mike laughed. "I guess so. What about you, Jessica?"

"Oh, I'm sorry. I can't relate, I'm perfect, remember?" she joked. Mike and Kelly laughed.

"There has to be a time," Kelly said.

"I really can't think of anything," Jessica said.

"I can think of a few," Mike spoke up.

"Were they before I was ten?" Jessica asked.

Mike thought a moment. "Yeah, I guess the age

of ten was when you became perfect."

"Or when she learned to tattle on everyone else to prevent Mom from seeing her mistakes."

"Shh, Kelly. Don't give away my secrets." Jessica laughed. The three siblings all broke into laughter. Kelly forgot her troubles for that moment of bonding. It was so nice to have siblings like hers. Life didn't seem so hopeless anymore. Her parents would eventually get over it, and she knew they still loved her.

Chapter Twenty-One

The next few weeks felt awful for Dane. He missed Kelly. Dane managed to get Michelle to tell him what happened, since Kelly was taken out of school. He had no idea that time in the park would be the last time he was able to speak to her.

He was upset at his circumstances. It wasn't his fault he was born into that family. He had changed, but he knew there would be no way of convincing her parents of that. That would not stop him from trying. A week after the incident he found himself waiting at his gate for Mr. Johnson to arrive home. As soon as he saw the car pull in the driveway he marched over.

"Mr. Johnson!" Dane called out as he made his way to the driver's side. Mr. Johnson got out of the car.

"You have some gall to come over here?" Mr. Johnson said with anger burning in his eyes.

"Mr. Johnson, please hear me out," Dane pleaded.

"Dane, there is nothing you can say that would make me change my stance."

"So that's it? Just because I come from the bloodline of a wicked man who died hundreds of years ago, my character is sealed in your mind?" Dane asked fervently.

"No," Mr. Johnson stated back at him with the same fervor in his voice. "I don't condemn a person because of his bloodline. But I know your family. They are wicked and cannot be trusted."

"I am not like them. What can I do to prove that to you?"

"Nothing," Mr. Johnson stated firmly. "And if I

find out you so much as make eye contact with my daughter, I will take actions far worse than your father ever has."

Dane stood there, hopelessly. He searched his mind for words to say. How could he show him?

"Mr. Johnson . . ."

"Get off my property!"

Dane looked at his eyes. With the anger in them, there was nothing he could say to persuade him. Any effort was useless at this time. He would have to wait till things cooled down more, if they ever would. Dane turned to leave, longing to turn around and say more.

His heart cried out to God. He loved her, he always would. He couldn't give up. He would prove himself to them, he just had to figure out how. He prayed for wisdom.

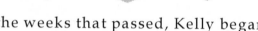

With the weeks that passed, Kelly began to feel a little better. The dinner table was back to normal, and her confinement was becoming more bearable. Her parents were starting to allow more and more freedom. She was able to go out to eat with Joey, her first time out without her parents, and she was loving it.

Kelly sat across the table from Joey. They were at their favorite sushi restaurant.

Kelly and Joey had gotten a sushi boat, packed with a variety of sea creatures. Kelly was focusing on the eel rolls, her favorite. She had one after another, not giving any mind to which ones Joey would want.

"I see things haven't changed much," Joey started, trying hard to sound mildly upset. "Still hogging all the unagi rolls."

"You don't like them, remember?" Kelly replied, keeping an innocent look as she said it.

"No, one day I didn't feel like them and since then you have assumed that I don't like them." Joey said.

"Oh was that it?" Kelly kept up with the oblivious act.

"Yes, we've gone over this every time since, but

somehow you just don't seem to register it in your mind."

"Fine, if you're going to make such a fuss, I am making a mental note for you," Kelly said for appeasement, slyly inching her chopsticks to the last roll.

"Right, you haven't used that one before," Joey said seeing her sneaky tactics.

"By the way, thanks for getting me out of the house," Kelly said.

"Of course. I know how tough it must be. Now you can see why I choose to distance myself from that stuff."

"It's not Aponlea."

"Oh, really? Then what would you say it is?"

"I don't know. Dad."

"He does it for a reason."

"I'm sick of hearing that. I know Dane far better than he does. Dad won't even try to get to know him."

"Do you remember when I told you not to date a Morris, that it doesn't end well?"

"Vaguely."

"I know exactly what you are going through. I dated Beauty Morris. I felt the exact same way about her. Mom and Dad didn't even try to get to know her. To this day I believe she was my first love. And I will never forget the day Dad found out and cut it off."

"What?" Kelly was in shock. This was something she had never heard before. Why hadn't Joey told her about this sooner? Maybe it was too painful for him to recount, even now that he was with Melanie. Beauty was still hurting after all.

"It was pretty bad. I didn't talk to him for weeks. In fact, he shipped me off to boot camp. Do you remember that?"

"Oh, yeah. I always wondered why."

"It was one of the hardest things I've gone through. Sure, I knew what I was doing was wrong, going behind their backs and all. Part of me did it for that reason, but I didn't realize how much I would actually hurt from it ending that way. It bothered me for quite some time, I just stopped being vocal about it after boot camp. I held it in and built up so much resentment. At first it was resentment for Mom and Dad, but then I realized it wasn't them. It was the whole system, the way of life of being a descendant of Aponlea, and so I decided I wanted nothing to do with it."

"But, Joey . . ."

"Kelly, because I am the oldest son, I've come to find out most of my life has been planned out, predetermined. What school I'd go to, what friends I would have, everything. I want to make my own decisions. I want to control my own life. I'm done with it all. If I reject the inheritance, then it doesn't matter what I do. I can make mistakes and they won't be made monumental." Joey paused a moment. Kelly looked at him with sympathetic eyes. "Do your best to forget about him or forget about Aponlea. Aponlea doesn't care about exceptions. It cares about the rules. You will have to choose between them."

"No, that can change. I can change that."

"No, no you can't. This stuff has been around for centuries. But the good thing is there is a life apart from it. I am living proof of that. Melanie and I are so happy, Kelly. I wouldn't trade anything in the world for the love I share with her. She is my passion. If you love Dane as much as you say you do, pursue that, be with him. The rest, Aponlea, it really isn't worth it."

"Everyone has a different purpose, Joey. Melanie's yours, and I am happy for you. But Aponlea is calling me. This is what I am passionate about. If I were to quit now, knowing what I know, feeling what I've felt—I just couldn't do it. I don't know how I'd live, Joey. If I can get to a certain point, find what it is I am looking for, then I can pave the way for Dane and I and for all Aponleans to put aside their differences and live in harmony. It can be done, and I will live to see it."

"Oh Kelly, don't lose that hopefulness. It is refreshing," Joey said more softly. Kelly knew how much he hated division or rifts between relationships, and he often avoided confrontation with humor. He just had so much resentment from his past experiences, and now Kelly could understand why. Kelly knew this would be one of the few topics she and Joey wouldn't agree on. That was okay with her, because she was sure of this.

After brief silence between the two of them, Joey tried to change the subject. "So, Kelly," Joey said with a smirk. She couldn't help but smile; he had something exciting to share with her. "Are you ready to change a lot of diapers?"

Kelly squealed. "Oh my gosh, Joey!" Kelly squealed again before clobbering Joey with a hug.

"Congrats!"

"Thank you. You're the first person I've told. We're about twelve weeks in."

"I am so excited for you! I'm going to be an auntie!"

"Yes, yes, be excited now, 'cause, like I said, you're gonna' have a lot of diapers to change."

"Is that because you'll want my amazing babysitting skills often?"

"Well, that and I figure I shouldn't make Melanie do all the dirty work. I gotta' lend a hand sometime."

"When you say lend a hand, you're referring to mine, right?" Kelly pried.

"Exactly, I don't know what other hand to use. There aren't many hands that I trust in the first place, especially these," he held up his own.

"Oh, Joey. This is probably the best news I have ever heard!"

"I figured it would be, I mean who better to reproduce than . . ."

"Okay, too far," Kelly interrupted.

"Yeah, sounded better in my head."

"So, you going to eat that last unagi, 'cause there's plenty of the crab left," Kelly asked holding out the one she had picked up with her chopsticks but hadn't put in her mouth due to a pang of conscience.

"Oh, wow. You're actually asking me? This is

bizarre. Are you feeling okay, Kelly?" Joey felt her forehead, checking for a fever.

"Is that a no? ' Cause it sure sounds like it," Kelly smiled.

"Go for it. I don't care," Joey shrugged.

"Really?"

"Yeah, I'm actually not feeling like them today."

"Then what was all that fuss earlier?" Kelly asked in mock confusion.

"I just wanted to prove a point, but next time if I feel like them I'm going to have to put up a fight, I'm sure," he said rolling his eyes.

"Whatever. Or we could get separate orders," Kelly suggested.

"And take the fun out of it? I don't think so."

She couldn't help but laugh at his response.

Chapter Twenty-Two

Dane had been focusing a lot on prayer lately. He didn't have a lot else he could do. He didn't understand his life or the circumstances he was born into. He had been talking with Jordan a lot, learning more about God through him, though he felt he had a lot more to learn. He was not sure of his purpose anymore. He had originally believed he was supposed to share with his family the truth he had uncovered, but his efforts had been shot down. He believed he could play a part in the unification of Aponlea, but his connection with Kelly had been cut off. He felt trapped.

Dane's eyes were fixated on the wall, zoned out from the meeting his father and brother were having. He couldn't focus anymore.

"Three months," he finally heard his father saying through barely opened lips. "They still haven't been able to locate him," he added, his teeth grinding together. He was referring to Richard. Dane couldn't understand why he was hung up on him. Dane could see his dad's obsession was an annoyance to Moore also.

"Do you boys even know why this is so important?"

"To be completely honest, no, sir," Moore spoke up first. Dane gestured his agreement.

"The Council members walk around like gods. No one can touch them or their families. We have an unwritten law: we stay out of their business and they stay out of ours. Then Richard comes around and takes the Sceptra, dabbles in our findings, and we can't

231

fight back. He's a mockery to our establishment and our pride. As long as he is alive, our privacy and our power is a joke to the other bloodlines. With him dead we show everyone we too are strong."

"I understand that, father, but as long as we put up such an effort to find him, we are showing ourselves as weak. We need to prove that we are independent of him and are flourishing despite his efforts," Moore said with passion. "We have the first Schernol; all we need are the remaining nineteen, and the Council won't even matter."

"We need the Sceptra for that."

"We need the Samorik."

"Then find the Samorik."

"I have it," Moore said.

"How long?" Mr. Morris asked. Dane watched his expression looking for surprise, but his father kept his emotions locked tight.

"I just recovered it last night," Moore said.

"Go get it, then," Mr. Morris said. Moore left the room with a juvenile type of excitement. Dane thought about some excuse to leave. He could make a run for it, and hide out somewhere — anywhere. He didn't want to wait for Moore to return.

"You've been very quiet Dane,"

Dane's thoughts turned to his father. "I've been observing," Dane said.

"Take more initiative, son. Don't let your brother dominate the conversations. I'm sure you've uncovered some answers in your personal quest," Dane's father winked at him, leaving Dane feeling unsettled. What did he mean by that?

"Yes, sir."

"We'll discuss that when Moore returns," he said. Dane waited eagerly for Moore to appear again. He needed to know what his father meant.

Moore returned stiffly with a split device clanking loudly on the marble table in front of him, his father's heightened spirits were very much short-lived. His eyes fell on the questionable piece.

232

"Is it supposed to work as two pieces?" Mr. Morris asked, even as he knew the answer. Moore was fuming; he turned to Dane, who refused to make eye contact.

"You know who did this, father. You know who did this, right?" Moore said, speaking furiously through his teeth. Dane didn't look up, which he knew made him look guilty. He wasn't planning on denying the accusation. He would face the consequences of his actions.

"No, actually, I do not," Mr. Morris replied, eyes blank. He blinked. Moore pressed his lips together.

"Who else could even come close to screwing up so badly?" Moore said, quickly, as if he were in a rush to get the words out. Dane could feel the tension. He knew his brother was seconds away from lashing out at him. Mr. Morris closed his eyes, hinting disappointment. "Who else could destroy our biggest lead without a care? Father, who else have I been saying is a disgrace to our family, to the name of Morr?"

"You mean to say between last night and this morning, Dane snuck into your room while you slept and broke it?" Mr. Morris asked. Dane could see now his father wasn't surprised. Mr. Morris stood up. "How long have you had it, son?"

"Months," Moore responded, fervor shifting to fear.

"Then, I'd say you were to blame. You could have told me sooner and we could have placed it in a more secure place."

Both sons were silent, waiting for their father's next move. "You two think I haven't been around the block before. I have been in this business a long time, and it is my job to know things. I knew the night you retrieved this, Moore, and I figured you had a reason for hiding it from me. What was that reason?"

Moore didn't respond. Dane had never seen him speechless before. He couldn't even look up. "Blood is everything here. We trust each other," Mr. Morris said firmly. "It is fine to work on separate projects, so long as the goal is always mutual."

"Dane, did you have anything to do with this being broken?" Mr. Morris asked.

"Yes, sir. I broke it on purpose. I'm sorry, Dad. I will do whatever I can to fix it."

"You will, the both of you will. You should have time, now that Nick's halted your plans with his daughter. This may help the two of you recognize the importance of family." Dane wanted to scoff at those words. What did his father know about the importance of family? And how long had he known about Kelly?

Chapter Twenty-Three

Kelly found herself risking a lot going out without a chaperone, but the attention given to her had waned quite a bit over the course of a month. She had been extra careful with what she did and had become overly cautious. Her parents were beginning to trust her again. It was summer break. The days were agonizing without school to distract her and the now limited time with friends. She missed Dane. She missed the excitement she had grown accustom to.

There didn't seem to be any danger in her life, and so everything that was thrilling before about the Morris home had become boring. She was able to get Michelle to give Dane a note at school, apologizing and telling him how much she missed him. She told him that times would change and they would be reunited, she just didn't know when. She told him that she loved him. He was the only person besides Joey she could completely be herself around. She hoped that the feelings were returned.

Now it was summer break, and she hadn't received a response from him. Instead she found a note left on her bed in unfamiliar handwriting. She was told to meet the person who wrote it in the Morris tree house.

She hoped it would be Dane. Kelly would start back at square one with her parents regarding him if she was right. But she doubted that theory. How would he have gotten the note in her room? How would anyone have?

She finally arrived at the tree house. The fear of being there, alone with a person she may not even know, caught up to her. What was she doing?

The Beginning

"Come on up." A low and much older voice called from the other side of the fort. This made Kelly pause where she was. Had she made the wrong choice? Though there was something familiar about this person's voice, the fright of the unknown seized her. She could make a run for it while she still had the chance. "I'm on the other side, Kelly."

Alarmed that the man even knew her name had her conflicted. She risked it, taking a few breaths and making gradual steps to the source of the sound. A tall, middle-aged man sat at the edge of the fort where a few bars of railing were missing. His legs were dangling carelessly at its edge. He had some worn-out jeans on, an old T-shirt, and a ball cap over a head of thick brown hair. Sunglasses hid his eyes. With his back facing Kelly, he looked like he meant to enjoy time to himself, but he patted the open space next to him. "Come park it here, sport."

He had a welcoming tone, which eased Kelly's tension slightly. She was still wary about the unknown.

She sat at a distance away from the man and warily glanced at him. "I heard you wanted to talk with me," the man began in a slightly amused voice. But then Kelly caught the seriousness of his tone and wracked her brain to think of who it might be. "I'm sorry it took me so long. I had to take the appropriate precautions."

"What's with all the secret talk?" Kelly asked in a hushed tone. The man smiled.

"I thought you'd enjoy it. Besides, I'm not too keen on being out in the open like this," he said. That would explain his inconspicuous attire, and Kelly just began to notice his tense shoulders, even as the rest of his body read relaxed. He was the image of a person always on the move.

"I can't say I enjoyed it much at all. You scared me more than anything," Kelly said, but she indeed

236

felt some adrenaline coursing through her. She felt cool talking to someone in a fairly hidden place, led by a written note, while still managing to be safe.

"But you liked that sense of danger, didn't you," the man replied knowingly. Kelly's eyebrows scrunched together.

"A little, maybe," she admitted in a small voice. She looked down at her hands. The conversation was getting awkward. Kelly didn't know where it was going. The man seemed to know her, but she could not recognize him.

"Kelly," the man said, in a tone of voice that made Kelly turn to look at him. He took off his glasses and his cap and smiled wide. Kelly's eyes widened as a flood of memories washed over her.

"Uncle Richard!" She breathed, her voice caught in her throat. Her uncle scooted closer to her and opened his arms. Kelly hugged him tightly and closed her eyes. He smelled earthy; he had definitely been out and about. For how long, Kelly would never know.

"It's been ages," he murmured, laughing a little. Kelly pulled back to get a good look at him. He'd aged quite significantly since she'd last seen him, but that had been nearly ten years ago.

"Your stories have been flooding my dreams," Kelly let out with exasperation.

"Wow, after all these years? Keep that memory, kid. It'll do you real good."

"Uncle Richard, I'm hardly a kid anymore," Kelly protested. She had to sound as capable as possible. If her father couldn't see her potential, then maybe her uncle could.

"Sorry. It's just the last time I saw you," he said as he proceeded to chuckle. Kelly picked up that this might be a nervous habit of his. They returned to their seats on the wood planks of the fort, shoulder to shoulder. "But you are right. You are quite grown up now. About the age of Evan."

"How is Evan?" Kelly asked. She could barely remember any details about her cousin.

237

"He's been better, but he's safe, and that's what's important."

"Why are you in hiding? What did you do?"

"I, uh, took something, from some, uh, people." Kelly didn't have time for him to be coy. She needed answers. She had a good sense to believe the "uh, people" had something to do with the Morrises. Once she had that thought, a connection was made in her head.

"You stole the Sceptra?" She gasped. Her surprise mirrored her uncle's.

"Yeah. Did your dad tell you? Kelly, listen, he wanted me to warn you . . ."

"He didn't tell me. Dane did," Kelly interrupted. Maybe if she was completely open with him than he would be with her.

"Now, Kelly, why would Dane tell you about me and the Sceptra? See—this is why your dad wanted . . ."

Richard's hesitant speech made it far too easy for Kelly to interject. "Uncle Richard, can we just not beat around the bush? I'm going to be frank with you, and I expect the same in return. I know your time is precious, and I think if we recognize what we have going on here we can avoid a lot of pointless chatter." Kelly stopped for any comments her uncle wanted to make. It wasn't the most polite way to get that out, but she had been waiting far too long for this opportunity. And now it appeared like her uncle wasn't taking her seriously, as a smile cracked on the side of his face. "I think we need each other, Uncle Richard. I believe we have a similar calling, and that is from Aponlea. The land, whatever it is, is begging us to rise to the occasion." Kelly started to get annoyed when her uncle let out a small laugh. "What?" She finally asked. "I am not trying to be amusing here."

"I know, I'm sorry. You're just reminding me of myself when I was your age and even your father."

"Dad was once eager?"

"Oh, yes, he gave me a run for my money. He, uh, he wasn't always perfect," Uncle Richard winked at Kelly.

"What happened?"

"Well, let's just say he decided it was most beneficial to play by the system at hand and I, uh, decided it was more beneficial not to, so we parted ways. He got the family name, and here we are today," Uncle Richard sighed.

"Where are we today?" Kelly asked. "What do we need, Uncle Richard?" He didn't answer, choosing to stare off into the forest. "Uncle Richard?"

"You mentioned a calling earlier, Kelly. I know far too well about that calling, but it's not an easy route. It comes with heartache and setbacks. After some you get back on your feet and others you take a while to recover from, or just stay down. I've been down a while, Kelly."

"Why?"

"They took my wife. And when that happened, I started to wonder what was more important. What if they took Evan next, or what if I lost everyone who was important to me? But if I located Aponlea, would I look back and think it was worth it?" Uncle Richard fidgeted a little, trying to find a more comfortable seat on the wood. "I decided it wasn't, so I've been protecting Evan."

"Do you miss it?" Kelly asked. She noticed her uncle moving some more. "You know, the tree house is fully furnished inside. A lot more comfortable."

"Okay, that'll be fine." He stood up, and the two of them went inside. "Hm." Her uncle admired the inside before choosing the large chair Dane normally sat in. Kelly opted for the couch. "Where were we?"

"Do you miss it?"

"It's impossible not to. I got back in the game three years ago. I let the Morrises find me and created a code that made them believe Aponlean had a deeper meaning and that this deeper meaning revealed the location of the Schernols."

"Wow, that was all staged?" Kelly was thrilled at this. She was hearing the other end of what she had witnessed. "You really had them fooled, especially when they brought back the silver Schernol." Richard sat up abruptly, giving Kelly a curious look that seemed to hold some reservations. She realized she had said too much.

"That's why I'm here. See, Kelly, you . . . you shouldn't know that. How . . . how do you know this? What have you gotten yourself into?"

"A friendship with Dane," she said calmly. She was trying to choose her words carefully, but it was hard. She didn't know what her uncle would want to hear. "He trusts me."

"Do you trust him?"

"Yes," she said without hesitation.

"That is a problem—a big problem, Kelly. You don't get too close with anyone from that family, you just don't. They . . ."

"Are bad people, I know this. My dad showed me the folder, but I can tell you that is not Dane Morris. He is different."

"How do you know this?"

"He's been open with me about you, about the Sceptra, the Schernol, everything. He's held nothing back."

"And you, do you hold anything back?"

"I haven't felt the need to, but if you need me to, I am in this, Uncle Richard."

"Tell me, did you see this Schernol?" Her uncle was still on edge, but reclined a little more in his posture. Kelly thought about what answer would be most beneficial to her in this situation.

"Yes, I held it. That was the moment Aponlea called me. I moved my hand on the shield to open its hidden compartment and it dispersed a cube."

"So, you know about the decoy casing?" Uncle Richard asked. Kelly maintained her poker face. She had no idea what he meant, but she would have to go along with it.

"Yeah, I took the cube and put the shield back in its place. They didn't notice."

"Do you have the Schernol now?" Uncle Richard asked.

"No, just the cube," Kelly responded.

"It's okay to admit when you don't know something. That is why I'm here. Well, I guess, that is, now that we are working together."

"We are?" Kelly asked, sounding a little too childish in her enthusiasm. Her uncle smiled, amusedly.

"The cube is the Schernol, Kelly. The shield is the decoy."

"But how?"

"John and Peter went through great measures to prevent what happened in Aponlea from happening in the outer world. They wrote the Sceptra for that reason. Sure, it's a history book, and each thing that happens in it is a metaphor for the truth. There were never powers, never any of that mystical stuff, but they wanted the dark bloodlines to believe it. They knew that future generations would believe that was the truth, and as long as they believed the lie, they would fight for that lie and be that much further from reality. You can't fight what's real when you live in a fantasy world."

"But I have a book, and that's just one theory."

"Are you ready to listen to me, Kelly? I'm going to tell you what you need to know."

"Okay." She shouldn't try to teach her uncle anything. He had been in this game a long time.

"The truth, instead, was passed down orally to the honored child from generation to generation. The things your dad knows would quench every bit of thirst you could have for knowledge on our waiting kingdom. He told me some of it, and some I had to find out for myself. I still don't know half of what he knows, but it's enough to do what needs to be done. See, in case an honored child didn't have any children or died before passing it along to the next in line, John, Peter, and a few other patriarchs set up a system. A group of men whose purpose was the preservation of our nation and the protection of its key members.

241

They are known as the shadow men. The shadow men are not seen but often present. Some are assigned to protect important families." Richard could see Kelly's wheels churning. "Yes, you have some guardian angels. You've got them working overtime with your involvement with the Morrises."

It was a hard thing for Kelly to accept. Where would they be, how could she never see them?

"Some of them protect the Schernols. Each Schernol has its own group assigned to it, and no one group knows more than one location. Everything is oral, no paper trails. They switch them out every few years to prevent the idea of greed. And then there's the Recruiter, he is given the Samorik, or one of them at least. The Samorik is the map to each Schernol. He is selected based on his zeal for Radehveh and future for Aponlea. His selection is most important for many reasons."

"I'm sorry to interrupt you, Uncle Richard," Kelly began. She couldn't wait for him to continue, but had a burning question. "All this is done to prevent one person from gaining the Schernols, but if that is the case, how will Aponlea ever be a nation again?"

"Okay, the Recruiter is a zealot, and so are the shadow men, not to the same degree, you see. They know that Aponlea needs to become a nation again, and that is also why there are two Samoriks. The second one is for whomever Radehveh chooses to locate the Schernols and bring about the ingathering. The ingathering of Aponleans all over the world to return to their homeland. They are waiting for certain prophecies. They are constantly watching, and when Prostasia is alive, they will take action to awaken the people."

"What if Radehveh chooses a Morr?"

"Impossible. It has to be a descendant of John, and to prevent possible contention, maybe a descendent from Jacob as well. A perfect breed."

"Like me?" Kelly asked.

"You said it," her uncle smiled.

242

"Why does the Jacob thing matter?"

"Because Jacob was the king's biological son, even though John was selected as heir. If the person is both, than it's more of a win-win situation."

"Are you a zealot, Uncle Richard?"

"That's why I am telling you all this. Kelly, it's all making sense now. I don't believe in coincidences."

"So, we're going to do this? We're going to find the Schernols?"

"Well, let's start with the Samorik and move from there."

"I can get it," Kelly said quickly.

"Alright, I've done enough talking. Tell me what you know. I see the eagerness all over your face."

"Moore has it, but Dane broke it. I believe Zach can fix it. If Mom and Dad can be distracted, I can go over there and retrieve it."

"Hold up, um, you see, my limit lies with the Alliance. You start messing with the Morrises or Stanforces or Normans, and it's bad news, especially if you take something from them."

"But I have guardian angels, right?"

"No, no, no, no. I did not tell you this for you to get some sort of death wish. There are some boundaries. Fear is a gift to keep our hands from the lion's mouth."

"Fine, but I can get Dane to just hand it over. Give it to me as a gift."

"I feel like I'm not getting my message across strongly enough. Xavier, Moore, bad people."

"What about a replica?"

Uncle Richard didn't have an immediate response to that one. He answered slowly, "I have a replica."

"No coincidences, right?" Kelly asked.

"Right," Uncle Richard said scratching his head. He was already mapping out the plan. Kelly could tell.

Chapter Twenty-Four

The moment Dane walked in the front door of his house after his bike ride, he could feel that something wasn't right. The tension churned deep in his stomach as he closed the heavy door behind him and swallowed hard.

He heard an eerie ringing in his ears as he took to the stairwell, where Moore suddenly appeared. They almost bumped into each other as Dane rushed to get upstairs. Dane braved a glance at his brother's eyes, those dark masses that appeared to see through everything. Dane had gotten as tall as his elder brother, and it probably infuriated Moore all the same. But he wasn't showing it. Dane thought he couldn't handle the raw fury that was clearly in Moore's glare, but now he would take that over the weird "friendly" facade his brother wore every day.

"Welcome home, brother."

That smooth voice sometimes spellbound Dane. Moore put his arm around him, pulled him into a hug more intimate than his father had ever even given him. He wouldn't dare push him away, but it felt so absurd of Moore. Dane was more terrified than he felt he'd ever been since that fateful night.

Moore pulled back, looked Dane square in the eyes. "How was your day?" When he realized Moore was actually waiting for an answer, he quickly cleared his throat, not trusting his voice.

"Um — uh, it went well. Y-yours?"

"It was excellent," Moore said, smiling and showing all those perfect white teeth. He was doing an exceptional act; Dane couldn't find a crack in his mask yet, which had intensified his terror. Moore started up the stairs with his hands folded behind his back. Dane followed behind like an apprentice. "I've been thinking about what Dad said and realized I need to change. We are family, after all. We share the same blood. And I haven't been treating you much like a brother, have I?" he said, and his tone turned mocking.

"I — I suppose," Dane stuttered. They were up the stairs now, standing in the hall nearest Moore's bedroom. He cocked his head to the side, drinking Dane's fear, feigning sympathy.

"It's okay, Dane. Don't be frightened," Moore was saying, laughing even, as if he weren't even capable of any harm. "I just wanted to have some, you know, brother bonding time with you."

"Okay," Dane said. He figured if he was obedient enough, Moore would let him be on his way. But in the back of his mind, he didn't think it was going to end well. His elder brother escorted him to his room. Dane looked around, and never had he felt so uncomfortable and foreign anywhere in his life. It was ironic; this was his home.

"When was the last time I've let you in here?" Moore asked.

"I don't think you ever have."

Moore tsked a few times. "What a shame. I've really been horrible to you, now haven't I?" he said. Dane wanted to tell him to quit the games. He didn't like it one bit.

"I don't know if that's the right word," Dane replied, trailing off. He was gaining a bit of himself back. The fear was waning just a little. Moore clapped his hands together, and his voice took on a startling increase in volume.

"Well, good thing there's always room for improvement, huh? Go ahead, look over my notes, or maybe the artifacts I've collected. It's about time I include you on my discoveries," he said, his voice dark, laced with menace. Was Dane hearing right?

He was hesitant, but he braved a quick look around, picked up some artifacts. He could care less about their significance right now, though. He was waiting for Moore to explode on him. "We need to get this thing fixed sooner or later, right?"

Dane's stomach started churning. He didn't like this one bit. "Yeah, of course."

"But before we start, we should probably ask Radehveh for his guidance in fixing it."

The eeriness was always there, but now it was unmanageable. Dane couldn't carry on with this. Moore walked over to the corner, where the idol was, and lifted it to move it to the center of the room. He got down on his knees before it and inclined his head to Dane, who was still standing stiffly by the computer desk.

"You coming?" he asked. Dane knew he couldn't possibly bow to this false deity, but he also knew he'd have to if he didn't want to get hurt or worse, die. When Dane didn't move, Moore's facade quickly deteriorated. He spoke in a firmer voice, more to the familiarity Dane still feared but was more relieved to hear. He felt strengthened by it even as his brother began to act like he was reading from something. "Thou shalt have no other gods before me. Thou shalt not make unto thee any graven image — or any likeness of any thing that is in heaven above, or that is in the earth beneath, or that is in the water under the earth; Thou shalt not bow down thyself to them, nor serve them," he quoted under his breathe.

"I can't," Dane said asserting himself for once.

"Really? Why is that?" Moore demanded. The silence buzzed between them as Moore waited for the answer. Dane could swear his brother would be in his face the next second. The hardness of everything in Moore's face seemed to prove it.

"I don't serve Radehveh," Dane said, toughing it out with his eyes closed again. Still some silence.

"Uh-huh, and who is it that you serve?" Moore continued. Dane couldn't believe this. Moore sounded like he knew Dane had other beliefs already. This news wasn't surprising his brother? Then again, had anything ever surprised him?

"The God of Abraham, Isaac, and Jacob."

Moore promptly stood up. As Dane had been expecting, Moore was in his face like a wild, untamed dog. "Is this the God you wrote about on this paper?" He pulled the paper out of his pants pocket, one he found while scavenging through Dane's bedroom. This was when it hit Dane. This was why Moore had been acting this way.

"Yes, it is," Dane said evenly. If he was going to leave this earth today, he was going to do it right. "The God I love and pray to. He's the only God I'll bow down to, the true and living Elohim."

"Shut up!" Moore screamed, furious at his brother's sudden boldness. But Dane kept on. His fear was somehow melting away. Emotion welled in his heart. "And His Messiah, Yeshua, my Master and Savior," he said, finding strength in his words. He would say it aloud now—he didn't care. He was saying it for himself, anyway. Only his God could save him, after all.

⸻ ◆ ⸻

Kelly entered through the back gate of the Morris estate, the one they had gone through to the tree house, only she was going toward the house now. She didn't feel much fright as she went through the yard, not so much as when she snuck around back after pretending to go to Michelle's earlier. She had hung out in the tree house a while to pass time.

She had a little concern. She knew if she got caught by Dane or Moore, she would be alright; it was Mr. or Mrs. Morris she had to worry about. Kelly walked across the lawn with purpose. She knew the Samorik was broken but hoped Zach would be able to fix it.

Kelly arrived at the back door; it was always unlocked. For being such a secretive family, the Morrises were very bold. Their reputation was their security. Now was the time for her to be careful. She needed to take the Samorik without Dane knowing, although she wasn't entirely sure how she would do that.

She cracked the back door and peaked in through the kitchen. She made her way in, listening intently for any sounds. She was on edge, nerves piqued with adrenaline. It only thrilled her. She was beginning to like the dangerous aspect of what she had been doing. She had missed it in her time of house arrest. She walked quietly through the kitchen and to the main hall. She eyed the stairwell behind a column. No one seemed to be around. She made a dash to the stairs, ducking beneath them. It was safe for her to go. She walked carefully up the stairs and down the hall. It would be in Moore's room, but she could hear sounds from there. It sounded like rage. She inched closer against the wall, making it to the cracked door, and listened in. She was to the ground, peaking through the crack of the door near the floor.

Moore swiped Dane across the face. Dane continued praying aloud when Moore's hand engulfed his forehead, pushed him backward, and slammed him into the nearest wall. Dane started sputtering, the back of his head searing in pain, black dots clouding his vision. Before he could see straight he was bent to his knees from the number of times Moore had sunk his fists into his unguarded stomach. With the wind knocked out of him, Dane choked for air to fill his lungs. Moore forced him to stand straight, pulling him up by his hair, bringing his arms behind his back. Dane's eyes were screwed shut from the pain, the throbbing in his midsection, his head. He gagged as he tried to breathe in more air. Moore wrenched Dane's head in his direction, his eyes wild and bloodthirsty.

"Look. At. Me," he growled. It was as if something feral and dreadfully evil had possessed Moore, turning him into something even more horrible than he already was. Dane forced himself to open his eyes. "Repent before Radehveh!" Moore ordered, but Dane looked him in the eye and managed to speak.

"All praise be to the God of Israel."

Moore threw Dane to the hard floor and began kicking him mercilessly. Moore's new shiny leather shoes dug into his brother in every direction, intensifying with Dane's gradually withering praises. All the while Moore demanded him to repent before Radehveh. Dane was throbbing from the pain. He was coiled into a ball to protect himself, but with no success. Why hadn't he blacked out yet? When was this going to end? It was like déjà vu. This was happening all over again.

<hr />

Kelly backed against the wall. She couldn't watch any further. She wanted to scream, to stop it, but was afraid now, very afraid. This was the side of Moore Dane had warned her about. Sure, he was nice to her when he was calm, but who knew how Moore would react with the rage that had possessed him?

Kelly's eyes began to water — she had to do something. She couldn't watch Dane go through this. It wasn't right; it was so wicked. Kelly closed her eyes, wanting to ignore it. She couldn't — this wasn't right.

At one point, Moore even stepped on Dane's fingers. Dane made a bloodcurdling cry, screaming, howling, Moore demanded the words he wanted to hear again. Dane was cradling his hand, rocking himself on the floor, ignoring his brother completely. "Make haste, O God, to deliver me!" He croaked under his breath between strangled cries, his face wet with streams of tears. "Haste to help me, O Lord!" He was scared now; who in their right mind wouldn't? "Let them be ashamed and confounded Who seek my life; Let them be turned back and confused Who desire my hurt, in the name of Yeshua ha Mashiyach." Moore was kicking him again, finally stopping Dane from speaking any further.

Now was Kelly's time, or Moore was sure to kill him with any further blows. She jumped up and swung the door open. "Stop it!" She shouted.

Moore's head whipped toward her, his eyes vacant or possessed by some wicked animal. He barely looked human. Any attraction she had to him previously vanished with his present appearance.

Moore stepped away from his battered brother, scraping his hands through his hair, tugging at it in the leftover rage. Kelly looked at him in shock. He was like some sort of creature. She ran over to Dane. Liquid rose from Dane's throat. He coughed crimson onto the floor. Kelly began to comfort him, kneeling at his side, holding him on her lap.

She looked back up at Moore, with fury in her eyes, "What's wrong with you?" she managed to get out with the burning lump welling in her throat.

"I . . . I don't know." Moore began to return to his old self again and looked confused. He got up and left the room without another word.

"It's okay now, Dane," Kelly said, holding him. He began to push himself up. "If it hurts too much, don't move."

"I . . . I'm fine," Dane managed to say. He certainly didn't look fine. He tried again to get up and finally was able to sit with his legs out across the floor. "Thank you, Kelly." Kelly began to cry, she wanted to stay there and just take care of him, but was reminded of the time constraint. She would need to get back eventually — who knew if her family had already called the Petersons for her to return for the surprise visit from her uncle? "What are you doing here?" Dane asked.

"I had to see you," Kelly said, knowing it was partially true.

"God sent you," he said. "He used you to save me."

"Yeah, I guess so." Kelly had to agree with him, as he was in such a state. "Now, when you go to the hospital, don't go changing back on me."

Dane laughed as much as he was able to. "I don't need to go to the hospital. Just a few battle wounds."

he winced, trying to play it off. "I'll heal." Dane leaned against Kelly. She put her arm around his shoulder. The two of them just sat there, saying nothing. They were both taking in what had happened, processing. Her eyes scanned the room, when she saw the Samorik. She had something that looked just like it in her pocket. It was split down the middle. She had broken the replica at the tree house, the only way it was able to break, down the middle.

She no longer had a desire to get it in this moment, as her focus was on nurturing Dane, but she knew her uncle was expecting her to complete her mission.

"How much time do we have?" Dane asked.

"Not much, I have to get back pretty soon."

"Sorry I didn't respond to your letter. I didn't want to go behind your parents' backs. I want to gain their acceptance the right way."

"Good luck with that."

"I am determined. Almost as stubborn as you." Kelly chuckled. "Can you help me up?" Dane asked.

"Are you sure you're ready?"

"Yes, I want to get out of this room."

"Good point." Kelly stood and carefully helped Dane get up. Her mind was scheming how she would get the Samorik. Dane, now fully up, took a moment to regain composure. Kelly inched her way backward toward the desk.

"Well, let me take a look at you," she said now leaning against the desk. Her heart was pounding, not from fear, but from the feeling that she was betraying Dane. She put her hands against the desk. "I'd say, you look alright," Kelly smiled.

"Yeah," Dane looked around, bending down to pick up a paper from the ground. Now was Kelly's chance. She quickly made the exchange, grabbing the two pieces and shoving them in her pocket, placing both her hands in her pockets as if it were her normal stance. Dane stood back up.

"What's that?" she asked.

"It's a verse," he answered. "Come on, let's get

out of here."

Dane led the way to his bedroom, a few doors down. They went inside and Dane turned to Kelly, with an unfamiliar look on his face. "What are you doing?" he asked, and she questioned him with her eyes. "The Samorik?"

Kelly didn't know how to respond. "I need it Dane," she finally said, shame lacing her voice.

"So, you'd just take it? That's why you came here?" He looked so disappointed. Kelly couldn't seem to win.

"Yes," she answered, eyes apologetic.

"Why didn't you just ask me for it?"

"I. . . I don't know. I'm sorry, Dane." Her face pleaded for forgiveness. The last thing she wanted was for him to think she had been using him this whole time.

"Well, you got it. Maybe you should go now." Kelly stood there. She couldn't leave on this note, not when she didn't know when she'd be able to see him again.

"I can't. Not until I know you forgive me," Kelly said, staring at the battered young man she loved so dearly. Dane didn't respond. He just stood there, looking down. She knew she deserved it — she'd betrayed his trust. He trusted her with a secret, and she took full advantage of it, but she had no choice, did she? This was her destiny. She didn't want to have to choose between Dane and Aponlea. She couldn't. She wanted both — couldn't she have both?

She went toward him; she was never one to give up. She placed her palm on his cheek. "Dane." He didn't look up.

"Kelly," Dane eventually responded, but paused again. He looked up at her. "I forgive you." He moved her hand down from his face, distancing himself from her. "I'll cover for you if Moore realizes it's a fake. Take it, you need it more than I do."

Kelly could still feel the disappointment. She again approached him. "Dane."

"What more do you want from me, Kelly?" Dane asked, looking at her again. Maybe Kelly couldn't do this. Dane was part of the reason she wanted so badly to accomplish this, but was hurting him in the process worth it?

Kelly's determination battled the guilt she was feeling now. The concern began to well in her heart. Dane had always been selfless to her, and what had she ever done for him? She couldn't answer that in this moment, but she could change it. She took the pieces from her pocket and held them in front of her clenched in her fist. She loosened her hand and tossed the pieces forward, allowing them to skid across the floor, her eyes not leaving Dane's for a moment.

"I wanted it for us anyway, but it's not worth causing you this pain. I don't believe I came here fully on my own. God needed me here in this moment for you, and He used the Samorik to bring me here. I don't know what Moore would have done to you if . . ." Kelly choked. Dane remained silent, still staring at her. His face relaxed a little.

Kelly looked at Dane, badly beaten, mistreated by his own family, and yet he claimed freedom. She would feel like a prisoner if she were in his shoes. The romance of the palace had worn off — she now saw the asylum it really was. It was cold and dark and lacked the comfort she had grown up with. Dane had such a pitiful life, but he now had a joy and peace she couldn't fathom.

She always wanted more. Sometimes she would recognize her blessings, but often she battled discontent. She admired everything about Dane in that moment. She wanted what he had. Maybe she would have that when she found Aponlea.

"What do you think, Kelly? I don't think we were brought together in vain. I believe God has a purpose for us, for this occasion. Are you ready to rise to the occasion?" Dane asked.

"What did you say?" Kelly quickly asked, eyeing Dane warily.

"Are you ready to rise to the occasion? Help me bring about the peace of our people."

"Yes," she didn't believe in coincidences anymore. The way Dane had phrased that was not by mistake. Kelly continued boldly, "and I think I know how now."

"How?"

"If the both of us become the honored descendants, you'd head the Alliance and I the Council and we can make peace."

To Kelly's surprise, Dane shook his head. "I can't take that from Moore."

"Did your wounds heal that quickly, Dane? Your brother is a monster, put him in charge and he will cause the second civil war."

"I think that'll happen either way, and it will probably be worse if I take that from my brother. Besides, I can't convince my dad of that."

"You can try, just like I will try. It's worth it. We can start working together."

"Not as long as you dad is against me . . . Kelly, I'll try to gain his approval. I have more of a shot at that than with my own father."

"In what universe, Dane?"

Dane sighed and walked to the side of his bed and bent down to pick up the pieces of the Samorik. He walked up to her, locking his eyes with her again. A smile cracked through his lips. He wasn't disappointed with her. He loved her regardless. Dane slid his hands beneath Kelly's, the Samorik between his right and her left, but the opposite sides were joined. He moved his left hand over to her right.

"You should take this, Kelly." Dane said.

"Are you sure?" Kelly asked.

"You'll use it for better purposes than Moore. That's why I broke it in the first place."

"I will use it for us," she said.

"You do what you feel called to, Kelly, and I will do the same. We have to say goodbye for now, but I promise you we will be reunited, in the open, again one day. We'll be the Light to our people. You, once you submit your desires to Him," Dane pointed upward. "He'll fill that drive, that gap in your heart and you'll find fulfillment in Him alone." Kelly didn't understand Dane's words. They were foreign to her. Maybe he was talking about Aponlea, but in a metaphoric way. That would be the only fulfillment.

"Okay," was all Kelly could say, embracing Dane. He held her close to him and she sunk into his arms. She let him hold her, knowing her embrace might stir the aches in his bruised body. She knew his holding her might be just as bad, but she also knew he didn't care. He loved her. She didn't know when she would get to be this close to him again after this moment. She believed in them, that they would be reunited, but she was unsure of how long it would take.

She had the Schernols to find, Aponlea to save, and a standing tradition to overthrow. He had her parents to convince, which might be as difficult as her tasks. She hadn't gotten her stubbornness from nowhere. In that moment she wished she could fast-forward time to a moment when they didn't have to let go. That moment would come; she had more faith in that than in Aponlea.

But still, prophecies were coming to a conclusion—advances occurring that were never breached before. Centuries of battles were leading to an approaching day. Her parents were chosen for each other for a reason. The Council knew this, the Alliance felt it approaching, as did the shadow men, Uncle Richard, and now Kelly. Kelly could almost feel the rumble of Aponlea beneath her feet, as if it were alive. As if it would erupt at any moment, but not yet. It had a designated time, it had designated circumstances, and it had a designated activator.

Kelly finally understood. She was the activator.

MARIA MCKESSEY began the craft of storytelling at a very young age. Entertaining her siblings with engaging stories became second nature to her. Once she learned how to write in grade school she found the joy of capturing her stories on page. This developed the dream of becoming a writer "when she grew up". Ever since then she has not stopped writing. Maria has had the pleasure of writing four plays for her church's drama ministry, and has published a few poems. *Dismantled Aponlea* is her first novel.

RAEVEN BROWN is a lover of all fiction. Before she could read or write, she daydreamed. After, she wrote stories. Now she does both! Although writing never became a serious pursuit or career for her, writing has always been a passion and a pleasure. Having published work remained a goal she wanted to accomplish. Now, as an author of *Dismantled Aponlea*, Raeven hopes to build a literary portfolio for herself and refine her writing style.

Made in the USA
San Bernardino, CA
10 November 2016